"Comedically dazzling." —*Vulture*

"This absurdist genre-mash romp of a story collection dials its modern subjects . . . up to 11, and then blows up the amp."
—*Vanity Fair*

"[Jen] Spyra goes beyond the parody as she cleverly takes on topics from Hollywood and woke culture to white women, the wedding industrial complex and influencer culture."
—*The Hollywood Reporter*

"Jen Spyra's book *Big Time* is a dose of Jack Handey–approved absurdity." —*Vice*

"Brilliant and bawdy, let *Big Time* be your proper introduction to Jen Spyra: Creator Of Worlds." —*AV Club*

"Weird, wonderful, and sometimes wacky tales. With stories that focus on a time-traveling actress and the anti–Frosty the Snowman, *Big Time* serves as the perfect introduction to Spyra's work outside the realm of TV." —*Bustle*

"An irreverent collection of tales about motherhood, marriage, work and more." —*Good Morning America*

"These stories are absolutely hilarious. For those who want to laugh, and I mean full-on, put-it-down-and-slump-over-on-the-couch guffaws, this is the book for you."
—*Pittsburgh Post Gazette*

Big Time

Big Time

Stories

Jen Spyra

FOREWORD BY STEPHEN COLBERT

RANDOM HOUSE

NEW YORK

2022 Random House Trade Paperback Edition

Published in the United States by Random House, an imprint and division of Penguin Random House LLC, New York.

RANDOM HOUSE and the HOUSE colophon are registered trademarks of Penguin Random House LLC.

Originally published in hardcover in the United States by Random House, an imprint and division of Penguin Random House LLC, in 2021.

Grateful acknowledgment is made to DM Records, Inc., for permission to reprint an excerpt from "Space Jam," copyright © 1996 by Quadrasound BMI. Reprinted by permission of DM Records, Inc.

LIBRARY OF CONGRESS CATALOGING-IN-PUBLICATION DATA
Names: Spyra, Jen, author.
Title: Big time: stories/Jen Spyra; foreword by Stephen Colbert.
New York: Random House, 2021.
Identifiers: LCCN 2020034376 (print) | LCCN 2020034377 (ebook) |
ISBN 9781984855282 (paperback) | ISBN 9781984855275 (ebook)
Subjects: GSAFD: Humorous fiction.
Classification: LCC PS3619.P97 B55 2021 (print) |
LCC PS3619.P97 (ebook) | DDC 813/.6—dc23
LC record available at https://lccn.loc.gov/2020034376
LC ebook record available at https://lccn.loc.gov/2020034377

Printed in the United States of America on acid-free paper

randomhousebooks.com

1st Printing

Book design by Caroline Cunningham

For Thomas

Contents

FOREWORD BY STEPHEN COLBERT   ix

Bridal Body   3

The First Influencer   13

The Snowman   22

Dinner at Eight   32

Birthday Girl   41

My Dearest Caroline   78

The Adventure of the Mistaken Right Swipe   86

Monster Goo   100

One Thousand and One Nights   127

First Kid, Second Kid   140

The Boyfriend Identity   146

The Secret Meeting of the Women's Club   172

The Tale of Mr. Mittlebury, Millennial Pig   186

Big Time   200

ACKNOWLEDGMENTS   299

Foreword

STEPHEN COLBERT

Containment Level 7
Vivos Bunker 212
Stovepipe Wells, CA

To Whom It May Concern:

I write you today to recommend Ms. Jennifer Spyra's book, *Big Time,* an artifact of the Great Realignment. If the blast shield of my bunker has been breached by your marauding Spicetribe (I say *if* because the bunker is not without certain countermeasures to discourage the Ravening from seizing our gold, potable water, and fertile women—*you were warned*), it may be that you hold my actual copy of *Big Time* in your trembling bloodstained hands. Look inside the cover. If it says "To Stephen. This book made me laugh out loud. I hope you love it as much as I do. Barack," then it's mine. I used to forge his name on a lot of things. (Pretty easy, actually, once you get that big O down.)

What will you do with this book now that you possess it, Ravener? Jennifer Spyra's work cannot be held to blame for the Downfall! Yes, her words drove the sane to madness and the mad to mayhem, but that's exactly why we used to have a First Amendment—to protect collections of short stories that provided no societal benefit but were really funny. And show me not your Code of Pain, etched in agony on the backs of the Disobeying. I know what your Spice Lord decrees! Destruction of this book and the Long Death to those who would defend its author. If that be His will, then let this Free Dweller declare in the sight of all assembled at the edge of the Pit of Judgment: I did not know her well.

Don't get me wrong—Jen was a very funny writer on *The Late Show* for years, and delightful company—sharp as a tack, eager to help, quick to laugh, punctual, and diligent—she would be a solid addition to any team, but we were more work friends, ya know? Like "Hi" in the hall or "Hey, girl, loving the bangs!," but not super close. I think her husband's name is . . . Mike? Tom? Your guess is as good as mine. It *is* Tom? I promise you, that was a total stab in the dark. I seriously thought it was Mike! We never did anything socially outside the Christmas party—sorry, *holiday* party (don't get me started). She was very pleasant and all, but between you and me and the Punishment Post, something about her was *off*. You know? Like, I know she's a writer, and I think we can all agree that writers are generally a bunch of odd ducks, but the fact that she seemed totally normal at first blush just made the little glimpses behind the mask that much more unnerving. Her Twitter feed should have tipped me off.

For that matter, many of these stories feel warm and familiar, almost comfort food, but inside the burrito of this book there is a small dusting of broken glass—sparkling prettily but stinging. I think that's why I like *Big Time*. It reminds me of Jen Spyra—funny and strange and strangely honest.

She's in the next bunker. You hide, I'll draw her out.

Big Time

Bridal Body

I wanted to look and feel my best at my wedding. What bride doesn't? So three months before the big day, I stripped naked, stepped in front of a mirror, and took stock of my goals.

I had work to do, no doubt about it. My hips have always been my biggest problem area. I definitely needed to do something about them. Same with my stomach. And of course, my neck tattoo, which says PROPERTY OF CHAIN-SAW. I traced my fingers over the faded script, sighing in disgust. I don't care how good of a kisser your ninth-grade boyfriend is; never get a tattoo of his name outside the bikini area.

These problem areas weren't going to magically fix themselves, so I decided to join a gym and booked a session with a personal trainer named Diego.

After we'd introduced ourselves, Diego asked me about my fitness goals. I told him that my wedding was in three months, and I wanted toned arms, a flat stomach, and sculpted legs. He told me he'd like a nine-inch cock that prints money.

I thought that was harsh, but I had to respect his tough-love approach. And I realized it might be just the ticket.

Diego walked me over to the machines and instructed me to jog on a treadmill while he tracked my time by playing *Grand Theft Auto IV* on his phone. I logged thirty minutes, and then we set up a schedule where we'd meet twice a week. He also suggested I clean up my diet by drinking more water and prioritizing lean protein. I recognized that I had a long road ahead, but I left the gym feeling pretty good about my plan.

As I was walking down the street toward 7-Eleven, mentally listing the reasons why a Monterey Jack taquito and Sour Patch Kids counted as lean protein, an unfamiliar voice called out to me. I turned and saw a fit forty-something woman with spiky hair leaning against a brick wall.

"Hey. Are you serious about getting that bridal body?"

Hell yes I was. But how did this lady know my deal? She answered me before I could even ask.

"I saw you talking with Diego," she said, eyeing me up and down. "They give him . . . cases like yours."

"Hipcentric?"

"Five-alarm shitfires."

I nodded. She was plainspoken, like Diego, but I liked her candor. I gestured to my body. "What should I do?"

She took out a scrap of paper and scribbled something on it.

"Meet me at the docks at one A.M. And bring this in cash."

I looked down at the paper. "This is a receipt from Pick A Bagel."

"On the back."

The mysterious stranger had written down a huge sum of money. Enough money to straight-up buy a new life. And almost as much as what I'd been quoted to have a scientist graft my face onto a really hot person's body.

I pocketed the paper and told the spiky-haired lady I'd have to think it over.

And that night, as my fiancé, Matt, slept peacefully beside me, I did.

I thought back to our first date, in Central Park. It was a sunny afternoon in early autumn, and we lost track of time walking around the reservoir, talking and laughing. As I cast my mind back to that golden day, I reached out and touched his hair, overcome with love for him. I just completely lucked out with Matt. He was sweet and funny, and what's more, he made me feel sexy as hell. But our chemistry went so much further than our physical connection; we electrified and nourished each other on a deep soul level. I'm not a religious person, but in Matt I had found a kind of cosmic completion, a reason to exist. A reason for anything to exist.

So at the end of the day, I had to admit that he deserved a bridal body that was hot as freaking hell. I slipped out of bed, made a few calls, emptied our savings account, and kissed Matt goodbye as he slept.

When I got to the docks, the spiky-haired woman seemed startled to see me. "I wasn't sure you had it in you," she said.

"You're damn right it's in me," I said, tossing over the bag of money with a swagger.

Spiky Hair checked to make sure it was all there, then rose and knocked me out with a single quick punch.

When I came to, I was blindfolded in the back of a truck, my head throbbing and my hands tied behind my back. I could hear low, guttural voices, but I didn't recognize their language. My mouth felt like it hadn't touched water for days. Finally the truck came to a stop, and my captors dragged me out. Spiky Hair ripped the blindfold from around my eyes. The light was blinding, and all I could smell was mud. "March," she commanded, and I did. Later, when my eyes adjusted, I saw that we were trekking through a barren gorge. Two grueling hours later, we reached the opening of a cave.

By this point I had had just about enough. I was starving, sunburned, and wheezing from the repeated blows meted out by Spiky. To be honest with you, I was also waffling over whether I had made the right decision. I realized that I needed a snack and a breather, just to check in with myself and kind of see where I was at. So I stopped and asked Spiky if she had a healthful treat, such as a Clif Bar in the Carrot Cake flavor.

She turned back and looked at me like I was nuts.

"I know," I said. "It's no White Chocolate Macadamia Nut, but you have to save those bullets for when you really need them, right?"

Spiky grabbed me by the front of my fleece and flung me down into the mouth of the cave. My head bounced off the hard-packed dirt floor. As I lay there, spitting up dirt and a shard of a bloody tooth, she kicked me in the ribs. Hard. It was at that moment that I mentally disinvited her from my bridal shower.

Staggering into the cave, I squinted my eyes and struggled to make out the dark shapes that loomed before me. Slowly, my vision began to focus.

There were about forty women training in a cement studio. Rock-hard abs, chiseled triceps, and hollowed-out clavicles for miles. A bare fluorescent light bulb hung from the dripping ceiling.

Spiky strode past me and blew a whistle. The women froze.

"Brides, we have a new recruit." She dragged me forward and pushed me toward the group. I felt the daggers of forty pairs of eyes on my broken body. Spiky continued. "You're here because you have the desire to succeed. But do you have the will to endure?" She swept her hand around the room. "Look around you. Only half will survive."

I looked to the woman on my left. She was cute and blond, with adorable freckles and pearl studs in her ears. I guessed she was in her midtwenties. She was wearing a tank top that said THE MRS. in glitter, and her ankles were wrapped snugly in pink one-pound weights. I was just about to ask where she'd found her adorable fitness accessories when she snapped her head forward, knocking her skull into my forehead with a sickening *thwack*.

My journey had begun.

I was assigned a straw mat on the floor of a long tunnel, and I kept to myself. My only possessions were my Fitbit, my slop pail, and my picture of Matt. I drew it from memory on a scrap of bat wing. Every night, after Zumba and our vicious nude wrestling matches, I would kiss it.

Two weeks after I'd started the program, I looked better than I'd ever dared to dream. I had lost five pounds and I could actually see some definition in my arms! I went to my room, packed my bags, and thanked my trainer for all her help.

When I awoke from the beating she gave me, my trainer informed me that I wasn't even 5 percent of the way through the program. For starters, I needed to drop my BMI by 40 percent, add eleven pounds of muscle and six pounds of tittyfat. And even if I did achieve those stats, I wouldn't decide I was done; I would be told.

I couldn't believe it. I was going to look so amazing on my wedding day.

Later that night, as I rubbed a numbing poultice into my wounds, a troubling thought crept into my mind. When I was through with the program, I was going to be really hot. In fact, I would probably be so hot that I didn't really know if Matt and I would make sense anymore. I mentally scrolled through the men who would be left in my league, and all I came up with was Tom Hiddleston, nineties-era Denzel, and Shang from *Mulan*. I sat for a moment and pondered the absurdity of my situation: training for a wedding that would be rendered obsolete by my very training. But I decided I had to see where this journey would take me. So I blew out my lantern, lay down on my mat, and went to sleep.

Seven winters passed.

One morning, I almost lost it all. I was doing my daily training of rolling boulders up and down the ravine on an

empty stomach. By now my arms were hard brown py-
thons, and I got giddy when I thought of how perfect
they'd look in the Chantilly sleeves of the lace bolero I
planned to wear when I eloped with Emmanuel Macron.
My trainer, Ashleigh, monitored my progress from the
watchtower, shouting death threats to keep me motivated.

Every time you rolled the boulder down into the ravine,
you had about a four-second window at the bottom where
you were completely out of sight of the tower. That day,
with my body crying out from fatigue and hunger, I decided to roll the dice. I had hidden a meal pellet inside
myself for exactly this type of opportunity. Flattening my
body against the limestone, I devoured it, luxuriating in
its foody crunchiness. Then I grabbed the boulder and
hurried back up the side of the ravine.

Ashleigh was waiting for me there.

"What were you doing in the ravine?"

My thoughts raced wildly, searching for any excuse. The
punishment for disobedience was death. "I was doing
extra calf raises."

She smirked at me. "Let's see what Leader thinks of
that."

Ashleigh turned and started back for the compound. I
knew I had no choice. It was her or me. I lunged for her
legs. At that close range, their definition made my eyes
mist with respect.

She was quick, and grabbed for her dagger. We wrestled
on the frozen ground, grunting and growling as we tore at
each other like wolves.

Finally, I grabbed a nearby boulder and slammed it into
her skull.

When I looked up, my face dripping with blood and

brains, I realized we were surrounded. Leader and the other brides began to clap.

"You are ready," Leader said. "You have completed the program."

There is no satisfaction like revealing your bridal body to your groom after seven years of hard training. Even though I was going to start my new life with an AI hybrid of Timothée Chalamet and The Rock, I figured Matt at least deserved a look at my bridal body. So I decided to pay him a visit.

When I got to his house, I was surprised to see that Matt wore contacts now. And his hair was a little thinner. And he had a wife and two sons.

"I thought you were dead!" he screamed.

I was prepared for this moment. The program taught me that reactions to my bridal body would be extreme.

"Where have you *been*?" his voice cracked. "You *disappeared*! You fucking disappeared *three months before our wedding!*"

Matt's face was splotchy, the way it got when he was really upset. A cute kid who looked to be around four peeked out from behind his thigh. He looked just like a mini-Matt, with the same sleepy blue eyes and wavy hair. He stuck his fingers in his mouth and looked up at me as he sucked. I had to admit—it being almost a full day since my last food pellet—they looked pretty tasty.

Matt ran his fingers through his hair, the way he always did when he was overwhelmed. "We had a celebration of life ceremony for you last year. I unveiled the headstone. You're legally dead!"

A blond woman walked up beside him. She had kind eyes and underdeveloped delts.

"Oh my god," she murmured, staring. "It's her."

She squeezed Matt's hand, pulling him in close. It was at that point that I noticed she was wearing an old apron I'd bought Matt as a joke in Key West. It said MAY I SUGGEST THE SAUSAGE, with a cartoon hand pointing downward. As annoyed as I was to see that Matt had chosen a blond woman for his wife, it was actually pretty funny for a lady to wear it. Maybe this blond chick was cool. I was actually starting to feel a connection with her, and I was thinking about asking if she'd ever want to get together some time, roll boulders up a ravine or something, when Matt doubled over and started to retch.

The blond woman wrapped her shitty arms around him, cooing into his hair as he sobbed. "Get out of here," Matt said, not looking at me.

The truth is, I was anxious to leave anyway. Bridal bodies only have twelve hours before they begin to atrophy, and I still had to find and wed Dwaynothée "The Chalamet" Johnson. By piecing together visual clues from Timothée's Instagram, I was able to locate his apartment. But as I was shimmying up a storm drain to greet him, I heard the growing wail of police sirens.

Later, at the precinct, the cop who arrested me said I could make one call. I couldn't believe it had come to this. I had worked so hard for this day, and here I was, locked away in a cell, watching it all fall apart before my eyes.

There was only one person I could turn to. I winced as I dialed the number, doubting that it would still work. And even if it did—why would he pick up, after everything I'd put him through? I did a series of lunge jumps as I waited, now a nervous tic from my years of training.

To my relief, he took the call. He even sounded worried, and said he'd be there as soon as he could.

As I walked back to my cell, I caught a glimpse of myself in the window and gasped. My body had sagged fully back into its prebridal form. The average arms, the mediocre abs. I hung my head in shame.

Twenty minutes later, the guard announced that I had a visitor. I looked up as Chainsaw walked through the door.

He had put on weight since I'd last seen him, and he was shorter than I remembered. But he was still wearing his leather jacket. The one he (hilariously) stole from a homeless woman on our first date.

"You look fucking hot," he said, grabbing me and lifting me up in his arms. I wrapped my legs around him and looked at his face, taking it all in—the familiar scars, the new wrinkles, the controversial eyelid piercing that, twenty years later, did not appear to have healed correctly. "I'm busting your ass out of here. Then how about we scarf some dumpster pizza and puke off an overpass? You still get into that?"

I smiled and, looking into his eyes, in the presence of God, the police chief, and the hooker sharing my cell, I took his hand to my lips and kissed it. "I do."

The First Influencer

The men were out on a hunt.

Grooga and Crooga were washing their loincloths in the river one cold, sunny morning when Oola walked by collecting medicinal flowers.

"Hey, guys," Oola said, waving as she strolled. "Morning."

"Morning," Crooga said, and she and Grooga watched as Oola walked farther up the riverbank, pausing by a tree stump to groom herself. After straightening up, Oola continued on her way, plucking coneflower and feverfew and yarrow leaves—good for toothaches—and slipping them into her sack.

Grooga and Crooga continued scrubbing their thongs against the river rocks in silence. Then Crooga put down her work. "Did you see how gracefully Oola pulled those burrs out of her ass hair?"

"Yeah," Grooga said. "Her ass hair wasn't even matted with shit or anything."

Crooga laughed, mystified. "I know. How do you not have shit on your ass?"

Grooga shrugged. "Beats me."

The two friends wrung out their loincloths and trudged back to the cave in thoughtful silence.

The next day, on their way to the clump of juniper bushes where they planned to collect berries for the men's posthunt pie, Grooga and Crooga found Oola sipping tea by the Big Rock.

The women were familiar with many kinds of tea. Tea for sleep, for energy, for easing the pain of childbirth. But the aroma wafting over to Grooga and Crooga was new, and Crooga was so curious she couldn't help but ask Oola what it was. Perhaps it was that special ceremonial brew, used to conjure the spirits of the Ones Who Now Live In The Sky.

"It's flat-belly tea," Oola said, blowing on it softly. "With dandelion root to reduce bloating, and caraway for drawing out toxins."

Crooga stole a quick glance at Oola's stomach and, sure enough, it was as flat as could be. It even looked hard. Crooga looked down at her own paunch and poked at it stupidly. It was soft, and the hair was patchy in places. Stupid, fat slut.

Oola stretched her steaming cup toward them. "Wanna try some?"

Crooga was about to say sure, but Grooga grunted.

"We're good," Grooga said and nodded for Crooga to follow her out to the juniper bushes.

On their way to the berries, the women noticed a huge

new painting on the side of the Big Cave. It was done in crushed ochre seed, and it depicted Oola, in a skimpy loincloth, sipping tea. In the corner of the painting were four antelopes, a sparrow, three arrows, and a knife, which translated loosely to "hashtag flat-belly tea hashtag ad."

That night, Crooga and Grooga groomed their children by the fire as they watched idly for predators. "How much flint do you think she pulls in from the cave ads?" Grooga asked.

"Wait a second—she gets flint for that?" Crooga said, picking a gnat egg out of her daughter's back hair.

"Wake up. She gets *something* out of it. She's not doing the ad for free." Grooga finished wiping down her son's neck and moved on to his chest hair.

"Huh," Crooga said, unable to hide her admiration for a person who could turn the simple act of drinking tea into a business venture.

"By the way, you looked like a moron standing there poking yourself in front of Oola today. I was actually embarrassed for you."

Tell me how you really feel, Crooga thought, rolling her eyes as she rubbed her daughter's back over the sleeping pelt. Once the kids were all tucked in, the women crawled in beside them. Grooga turned her back to her friend, but Crooga could tell she wasn't sleeping, and Crooga herself had a hard time drifting off. So the women lay with their backs to each other, staring at the fire's shadow as it flickered on the cave walls, until they eventually fell asleep.

The next morning, Grooga's side of the hearth was neatly made, and she was gone.

Yikes, Crooga thought. But as she was puttering around getting breakfast ready, Grooga ducked back into the cave and made her way over to Crooga. Sheepishly, Grooga handed her friend the flat-belly tea that she'd gone out and bought from the medicine woman earlier that morning, along with a bunch of buttercups—Crooga's favorite. Crooga took the offerings, and the women shared a smile.

Both agreed the tea didn't taste great, but Crooga still made herself a cup every morning for the next week—while Grooga made a big thing of throwing her remaining tea in the creek.

"Didn't work for shit," Grooga said.

Crooga looked at her reflection in the shimmering water. "Really? I swear I've lost two inches from my waist."

Grooga snorted. "Please. This is just a flattering creek. Everybody looks good in this creek."

Crooga looked at Grooga's lumpy reflection and didn't say anything. Instead, she cut her friend some slack. Grooga was obviously just jealous of Oola, and jealousy brought out the worst in people.

Grooga grabbed a handful of sweet creek grass and tossed it back. "Don't feel bad, Croogs. You're either born like that or you're not, end of story."

Crooga knew she should change the subject, but she couldn't help bringing up one more thing. "Did you see Oola this morning? She was wearing a bone in her hair. It's, like, a fox femur or something."

Grooga swallowed her grass. "That's insane. Why?"

"I don't know. She had it tied up in a little ponytail with the femur as, like, decoration."

Grooga shook her head, taking it in. "That girl's nuts."

"I don't know." Crooga laughed nervously. "I think it's kind of cool."

"Yeah, okay. But I bet if a predator comes and she has to run, that stupid bone's gonna fall out of her hair and trip her. Then we'll see who's cool."

Crooga hated confrontation, but she couldn't help saying it. "You know, Grooga, you can be really negative."

A mosquito settled on Grooga's arm and she slapped it away violently. Crooga could see she'd hit a nerve. "So why hang out with me? Why not hang out with Little Miss Perfect with her hair bone and her flat-belly tea and her clean fucking ass?"

Crooga stared at her friend. Grooga wasn't usually this hostile. What was going on? Maybe . . . and Crooga craned her neck to see if she was right.

Grooga let out a groan. "Are you seriously looking to see if blood's coming out of my hole?"

Crooga eyed a pair of elders whittling mammoth tusks nearby and now openly staring. "It's not the time when blood comes out of my hole. This is just me feeling my feelings."

Crooga made eye contact with one of the elders, but he just looked down and whittled faster.

In a few minutes they were back at the cave, preparing the men's meal together in awkward silence. When Flurg darted in suddenly and raped Crooga, she was glad for the distraction. Otherwise, Crooga might have said something not very nice.

The next afternoon, Grooga and Crooga were gathering tubers while the men circled up to go over the highs and lows from yesterday's hunt. Grooga had been cold to Crooga all morning, but she'd started to warm up, and now she was downright chatty. Crooga was relieved.

Kron was standing in the middle of the circle, demonstrating the lancing motion he had used to bring down the mastodon.

Crooga watched as Kron flexed his muscles in the sunshine. She plucked a tuber from the earth and banged the dirt off on the side of the basket.

"Man, Kron's sexy," Crooga said. "I mean, look at those arms."

"Please," Grooga said. "It's not sexy when a guy tries that hard. Do you know what Lurmil told me? He said he saw Kron in his cave lifting the same rock over and over again, like a crazy person—and then admiring his shadow on the wall."

Crooga shrugged. "I don't think it's crazy to work toward a goal," she said.

Grooga rolled her eyes and took a sip of her tea. She said it was plain elk bark, but it smelled like something else, something curiously familiar. "Personally, I think Lurmil's pretty cute," Grooga added.

Crooga looked at Lurmil, on the outskirts of the circle, swatting flies away from his butt. It wasn't his fault, Crooga knew that, but Lurmil's narrow shoulders sloped sadly down from his neck, and he was mostly bald, with long wispy hairs that hung down on the sides, and one time—the whole clan knew this, it wasn't bitchy of Crooga to bring it up, it was just common knowledge—he screwed up the hunt because he farted so loudly he scared off a herd of antelope. Everyone farts, of course, but they'd been stalking this herd in silence for hours.

The fact of the matter was Grooga liked Lurmil because Lurmil was the only guy who'd ever raped her. Crooga didn't say it, but she thought it as she twisted the tubers neatly from the soil and tossed them in the big bowl.

"*What,*" Grooga said.

"Didn't say anything," Crooga said primly.

Grooga stared at Crooga under deeply furrowed brows. "You're thinking I just like Lurmil because he's the only guy who's ever raped me."

It felt cruel, but Crooga let a beat of silence pass between them. A beat too long. Grooga's eyes welled up with tears.

"Oh, so now I guess you're not 'cool' unless you get raped by every guy in the cave, and then the guys start fighting over you, and Kron wins because he's the strongest and then you go and invent a fancy word to describe your relationship?"

The word was "exclusive," and Crooga thought it was actually pretty canny of Oola to have thought of it.

Grooga shrieked and ran off toward the creek, tearing at her hair. Crooga let her go. Frankly, she was sick of the drama.

And that was the end of Crooga's friendship with Grooga.

Crooga and Oola sat in companionable silence as Oola wove a fox femur into Crooga's straggly hair, setting the bone at a jaunty angle. They were eating Oola's favorite lunch—a pile of grasses and seeds she called a "gratitude bowl." Before Oola, Crooga just thought of grasses and seeds as food. But labeling it like this was fun. Crooga could still hear Grooga in her head, ripping Oola a new one over giving lunch a fancy name. But why was that a crime? Oola finished styling Crooga's hair just as Kron arrived with a set of paints.

Oola moved away from Crooga and posed for Kron, pursing her lips and holding up two sets of peace fingers. Crooga sidled up next to her and held up some peace fingers and winked at Kron, but then Oola broke her pose and asked Crooga to get out of the frame, explaining sweetly that Crooga wasn't picture ready yet.

"Maybe try hitting that flat-belly tea a little harder," Oola said, playfully swatting Crooga's paunch. Crooga looked down at her round stomach and laughed along with Oola, because, if you thought about it, it really was kind of funny that she was less attractive than her friend.

Later, when Kron had left and Oola was telling Crooga about her idea for a volumizing shampoo made from bear fat, the women heard a rustling in the brush. It could have just been the wind, or an injured fawn wobbling its way back to its mother. It could have been nothing at all.

But it wasn't nothing, and when the saber-toothed tiger lunged for Crooga and Oola, the women sprang up and took flight, their hair femurs clanging against their skulls. Eventually the bones came loose and clattered underfoot, shaving just a few seconds off their escape. When the giant cat clamped down on Oola's torso, squirting blood everywhere, Crooga gasped as her friend flailed in the predator's jaw, the sunlight glinting off her perfectly flat belly. She had to admit, Oola made getting eaten by a jungle cat look like a pretty cool way to go. And it might actually be something she'd be up for trying.

The next day, a woman from another tribe walked by the mess the tiger left behind. The woman was a little slimmer than average, perfectly proportioned, and as she crouched down to examine the scene, the golden afternoon light fell on what can only be described as perfect beach hair.

She could see that the bones were human. The meat was picked clean off, but as she crouched down among the two sets of rib cages and skulls, she noticed what appeared to be the femurs of a small animal. Strange. And there was so much blood—the dirt was still damp with it.

The woman touched the dirt and the blood, her head cocked thoughtfully, and rubbed the mixture between her fingers. Then, slowly, because she had only just been struck with the idea, she lifted her fingers to her face and blended the dirt and the blood into the apples of her cheeks, creating a flushed, rosy glow.

When the woman returned to her cave that night, no one could look away.

The Snowman

I had hoped for snow all winter, but we hadn't seen a flake. Then one morning, as I awoke to the aroma of Mother's pancakes, I looked out my window and beheld the most dazzling snowfall I'd ever seen.

I raced downstairs and threw open the front door, giddy with excitement. I was going to make a snowman! The morning flew by as I rolled out the snowballs and, with a little help from Papa, stacked them up. When I had finally adjusted the carrot nose and stovepipe hat, I stood back to admire my creation.

"Oh, Papa, look! It's the friendliest, loveliest snowman!" I shouted.

The snowman was big and jolly, with bright coal eyes and a cheerful smile I'd drawn in with my own finger. I patted his belly and shook his twig hand. "Ever so pleased to meet you, Mr. Snowman!"

Later, after a cup of Papa's hot cocoa, it was off to bed,

but I could not catch a wink. As our grandfather clock struck midnight, I pulled my covers higher and tried to fall asleep, but still, it was no use. I just *had* to look at my snowman! Taking care not to let the floorboards creak, I tiptoed to my window, peered down at my creation, and gasped. The snowman was glowing!

I rubbed my eyes—sure they were playing tricks on me—but no, it was true. And it was getting brighter!

The brightness grew and grew, until suddenly there was a brilliant, sparkling flash. And then the most extraordinary thing happened: the snowman looked up at me . . . and waved!

I dashed downstairs and out onto the lawn, sure that I was dreaming. But there my friend still stood, holding out a snowy hand as if to invite me on a wonderful adventure! I took it, and—wonder of wonders!—the two of us floated right off the ground and into the air.

Soon we were flying together over the countryside, and what a marvelous sensation it was! As fluffy white clouds whooshed past underneath us, I looked ahead and saw the glittering lights of the city. We flew lower, and I began to make out the shape of roads and buildings below. It looked like we were flying over a highway, and then a strip mall.

Ever so softly, we glided down to the parking lot. I looked around and saw a vape shop and a twenty-four-hour minimart.

"Got any cash on you?" the snowman asked. Goodness gracious, were my ears deceiving me? Had the snowman really spoken? Until now, my frosty friend hadn't said a word! My eyes went wide as saucers, and I clasped my hands in delight.

"Why, Mr. Snowman!"

"Yeah, look, call me Ken. Spot me a twenty? I gotta take care of something real quick."

I was naked underneath my pajamas, and had no pockets. "Sorry, I don't have any money."

As the snowman looked around nervously, I reflected on my luck. What a splendid surprise! My snow friend even had an accent. He sounded like my uncle Marty, whom I'd only met once late at night when he came to say hello to my father. I think he was from New Jersey.

The snowman looked at his reflection in the vape store window, straightening his scarf and adjusting his dapper, though worn, stovepipe hat.

"I see you went all out with the duds."

I giggled. "Thank you!"

The snowman shook his round, jolly head. He walked into the store then and, a few moments later, ran out with a bouquet of flowers and a bottle of whiskey. The snowman grabbed my hand and flew us back into the sky, really quickly.

"Why, they simply gave you the flowers!"

The snowman flew even faster. "Yeah. How 'bout that?"

I waved goodbye to the friendly shopkeeper who'd come outside to see us off. He waved back energetically, indeed. Who wasn't beside themselves to be in the presence of this magical creature?

The snowman took a long swig from the bottle as he flew. Presently, we alighted on the sidewalk next to an apartment building, where he straightened his scarf and rang the buzzer for 4B. This evening was chock-full of surprises!

"Say you're my nephew."

"What?"

He leaned on the buzzer again. "Maggie, lemme up."

A woman's voice crackled through the intercom. "Kenny, get out of here."

"Just two minutes. I promise. Come on."

Nothing happened. Then the snowman pushed the intercom button and muttered, "Please."

I could hardly believe my luck. I was going to meet one of the snowman's friends! A buzzer rang, and we walked up three flights of stairs. I wondered why the snowman didn't simply fly us up—especially since he had to stop a couple times and catch his breath, which had settled into a wheeze that reminded me fondly of the bellows Papa used to stoke our fires.

When we got to the apartment, a woman was standing in the doorway in a robe. Her hair was tousled, and she looked tired. The snowman took a deep breath.

"Maggie, look, I cleaned up." He squeezed my shoulder. "My sister even asked me to watch her kid for the weekend. I love Matty. Turns out I never realized I loved kids."

The snowman tightened his grip on my shoulder. My name is Elijah Honeycutt, but I said nothing. I saw her glance at the snowman's flowers. She fastened her robe and stepped in front of the door, closing it softly behind her.

"Look, Ken. This isn't a good time."

Just then, a man's voice came from inside the apartment. "Babe? Who's there?"

The snowman stepped really close to the lady.

"Who the fuck is that?"

"None of your business."

Just then the door opened again, and a big man stepped out. He was tan and wore khakis without a shirt. He looked at the snowman.

"Who's the dumbass?" the snowman said. Maggie looked upset.

"You talk that way in front of your nephew?"

"Mikey don't give a shit."

"I thought you said his name was Matty."

The snowman didn't say anything to that. Then he took out a pack of cigarettes, lit one, and took a long drag. I had no idea where he'd kept those. As far as I could tell, he was nude. I shivered a little.

"Jesus, Ken, the kid's freezing."

Maggie disappeared inside and then came back with a Steelers sweatshirt. She handed it to me, and I took it gratefully. It smelled like cigarettes, but it was nice and toasty. The big, tan man put his arm around Maggie, and the snowman coughed.

"I'm glad to see you're doing good, Maggie. I guess I'll leave you to your life now."

"Yeah." She smiled at me. "Nice to meet you, honey."

The snowman dropped his voice. "Just let me get one hit."

Maggie groaned. "Kenny! I don't do that shit no more! You shouldn't, either. You saw what happened to your brother!"

"Oh, so now you're America's Sweetheart all of a sudden? Excuse me, Julia Stiles!" Maggie and I exchanged looks. I think we both knew the snowman meant to say Julia Roberts.

The snowman looked past Maggie to the big man. "You give her dick in the mornings? That's when she likes it."

Khaki Man started for the snowman, but Maggie pulled him back and petted his chest and whispered things to him, and he clenched his fists and walked back inside the apartment.

Then Maggie slammed the door in our faces. She screamed something as she did it, too. I couldn't be sure, but I think it was "Fuck off!"

The snowman and I walked back down to the street. "Shit," he said. And he sat down on the curb, which I'd never actually seen someone do. It hurt to see my wondrous new friend so glum.

"Do you really love her?" I asked.

The snowman wiped his carrot nose with his scarf. "No. Maybe. I don't know."

I scooted closer to him and rubbed his back like Mother did for me when I was feeling blue. "It's all right to feel your feelings."

The snowman made a little gurgle in the back of his throat, like he was choking down a sob. "That was just some fuckin' good puss, you know?"

We were silent for a while as I rubbed the snowman's back. I wasn't sure what to say. But there was one thing I did know for sure: when we returned home, I was going to make the snowman a big, yummy cup of cocoa.

Finally, he gestured for me to climb on his back. I held on tight.

We flew silently through the night. I hadn't noticed it before, probably in my excitement, but it was extremely cold. I mean ice-pop-in-a-blizzard cold! My teeth chattered as we broke through the clouds.

Another thing I noticed was that the snowman was drunk. Papa forbade me from ever getting in a car with someone who'd been drinking, but I figured flying through the air wasn't the same thing. The snowman kept leaning dangerously from side to side as he flew, sometimes almost causing me to roll off his back. I hung on as tight as I could, my scarf flapping behind me. We made it a few miles before, suddenly, the snowman nodded off completely! We plummeted through the air. I didn't know what to do, so I smacked the back of his head and yelled, *"Ken!"* as loudly as I could over the whistling wind. He jerked awake, but I lost my balance and fell about eighty feet. Plunging toward the earth, I imagined the snowman and I were tucked side by side, warm as bugs in a rug in my bed back at home. Then, right before my body would have crashed into an overpass, the snowman swooped down and caught me.

A few minutes later we floated back down to my front yard.

"Fuck, that took forever," the snowman said, cracking his neck. "What kind of food you got around here?"

I took the snowman's hand and led him to the kitchen, giving him a tour of the pantry, the refrigerator, and a special cupboard that was out of my reach. "That's the candy cupboard," I said, leaning in for a conspiratorial whisper. "It's where Mother keeps the sweets!" He didn't respond.

I invited him to take whatever goodies caught his fancy while I prepared a pot of Papa's cocoa for us. As trying as our night had been at times, I knew that after we had a little rest and a snack, there were more adventures in store.

The snowman busied himself piling up deli meats and cookies on the counter while I put a pot of hot water on the stove, then went over to the family computer and googled "what to do toes blue can't feel."

The snowman unscrewed the lid from a family-sized jar of mayonnaise and began spreading it on a slice of bread. "Shit," the snowman said. "I really fucked up with Maggie."

I hobbled over to the counter and took a cookie from the jar. As painful as it was to walk, I had to smile as I watched the snowman fix a sandwich in my kitchen. For I was still in awe of my friend! I'd never met anyone so special! I'd also never seen anyone pair mayonnaise with salami.

"Maybe you'll meet someone even better," I said.

"Whatever. Maggie can have her new dick. Bet she misses me." The snowman had no genitals as far as I could tell, but I ate my cookie and said nothing.

He licked his mayonnaise knife clean, put it back in the drawer, and grabbed his sandwich as he strolled over to the credenza in the living room. He picked up a family photo.

"That your mom?"

I joined him at the credenza. He was holding a photo of me, my parents, and my little sister at the beach last Christmas, in Jamaica. My mother was wearing a two-piece bathing suit.

The snowman picked up another picture, this one of my mom and dad horseback riding.

I didn't like something about the way the snowman was staring at the picture, so I took it from him and offered to make him a special treat. He followed me into the kitchen. I figured he might like something cold, so I fixed him my favorite dessert: a banana split with extra cherries. I made it with vanilla ice cream, taking care to pile the whipped cream high and decorate the sundae with lots of sprinkles and cherries, the way I like it. I had just finished placing the last cherry on a peak of whipped cream when I looked up to hand it to him, and he was gone.

A little puddle trailed from the kitchen to the living room. I followed it, but the snowman was nowhere to be found.

I walked over to the window and looked out into the night, where snow was again falling softly. The sparkle from the Christmas tree lights cast a magical glow on the front lawn and the woods beyond. Shivering, I shut the door.

A single tear rolled down my cheek. My friend was gone. It had been a magical evening, one I would never forget—but I missed him already. Wiping my eyes, I started to make my way to bed. As I passed the hallway bathroom, I noticed the door was ajar.

That's when I found the snowman holding a photograph of my family and jerking his twig hand in an up-and-down motion in front of his snow-waist. He stared at the picture with an intense, slack-jawed expression. I gasped, but the snowman just turned away and moved his twig faster. Sensing that this was not an adventure I should accompany my friend on, I ran to my room, jumped in my bed, and hid.

From underneath my covers, I could hear the snowman groan. A few moments passed in silence, and then I heard him pad back over to the kitchen, where he ate the sundae pretty loudly and then left. I flinched as the front door banged shut.

I crept to my window and peeked over the sill, watching

the snowman trudge back to his place on the front lawn. He stopped just where I had found him, looking out over the forest beyond the lawn.

He stood there, silently, completely still.

I don't remember falling asleep. When I got up the next morning, I didn't even bother looking out the window— I simply raced outside. I was hoping against hope that the snowman would be there waiting for me, his arm out-stretched as if to say, "Come along, Mikey, on a wonderful adventure."

But the snow had melted, and now my friend was truly gone. A sad mound of slush was left in his place. The car-rot, the hat, and the scarf were jumbled together in a wet lump. I picked up the carrot and let myself cry.

Had it all been a dream?

My heart beat faster and I ran back to the house and up to my bedroom, where I checked to see if the sweatshirt Maggie gave me was still under my pillow.

It was!

I cherish it to this day. It's the only thing I have to re-member him by. Well, that, and the photo of my family's trip to Jamaica, which he had ejaculated on.

Dinner at Eight

The mansion sat cliffside on a ragged island in the middle of the Baltic Sea. It was a frightful fortress, with spires that slashed the night sky like daggers, and as lightning struck above, black waves crashed against the rocks below. Inside the library, however, the fire crackled agreeably.

I sipped my champagne cocktail and glanced around at the scattered guests, people with whom I had nothing in common but the fact that we'd all been mysteriously summoned by telegram. Devilishly odd, the whole thing. Each of us had received a missive from a Madame Osveta, who claimed to be a long-lost acquaintance. She wired our aeroplane and train reservations, and then we were met at the dock by a swarthy man with the bearing of an ancient sea captain. Spanish, by the look of him. He rowed us one by one from the mainland to the island, and after dressing for dinner, I found myself installed in an armchair, puzzling it all out as I sipped.

Silly me. I should have introduced myself. My name is Montclair Ellison, of the Weybridge Ellisons. Man-about-town, member in good standing at Pratt's and the Turf Club, happy resident of Upper Grosvenor Street, W1K, Mayfair. Pop by some time. Now, the man leaning on the mantel was the Colonel: a stodgy old boy with a bushy mustache and a limp. Not much of a conversationalist, unless you were keen on the minutiae of grouse hunting. Margaret Hadley, the governess, was certainly easy to look at. The Nussbaum fellow chatting her up was obviously a Jew. Besides the name, he had that shifty, money-changer-y quality. I took another sip of my cocktail as I appraised the unctuous Hebrew. Jews. Sticky sort. Then there was Countess Calcott, who appeared to be rather stern, but not Jewish, so, fine by me.

Suddenly, a fearsome voice cut through the chatter. "Silence," it bellowed, seemingly from nowhere. "This is your host. You have been gathered here tonight to play a game. A game of vengeance."

Shock rippled through the library. Aha! Finally: the reason for our little gathering. Everyone was ill at ease. Miss Hadley clutched her breast. The Colonel took an uneasy sip of his sherry, and the thick-lipped money-banker Jew shifted uncomfortably in his seat—as if he suddenly realized he had left a stack of money on the train.

The disembodied voice again broke through the silence: "But before we move ahead with that, I want to address Montclair's inner monologue. Is anyone else finding it extremely problematic?"

There were several audible sighs of relief. The Colonel blustered his assent. Margaret Hadley nodded, and the butler tsk-tsked softly.

"It's quite outrageous," Hadley said.

The Colonel adjusted his monocle. "And apart from its ugliness, it's simply distracting to the storytelling."

"Storytelling? You're giving this thing a lot of credit," I said. "I'm just adding a little flavor."

Countess Calcott piped up. "Well, young man, your 'flavor' sounds a lot like hate."

Miss Hadley raised her glass to Countess Calcott. "Amen. And besides, the dramatic tension of the revenge angle accounts for more than enough *flavor*."

The slippery little Hebrew narrowed his eyes in my direction. He certainly was a Jewish Jew.

He rolled his eyes and gestured to me as he looked around at the group.

"Come on. This guy's ridiculous," Nussbaum said, continuing to gesture to my person.

I mean to say! Who did this bagel eater think he was? The hour had dawned for a swift correction. I impersonated him effortlessly. "Ooh, look at me, I'm Mr. Israel, policing what's okay to say!"

"*I did not just say that!*" the Hebrew shouted. "I just want to let the record show that that was Montclair *thinking* what I would say, which, I'm sure we all agree, was very offensive."

The Colonel rapped on the table. "Quite right, couldn't agree more. And I'm fairly intolerant myself."

"Enough with Montclair's opinions on the Jewish race. We've strayed from the thrust of the story, which is a mysterious vengeance-themed game leading, quite probably, to murder," Countess Calcott pronounced, fingering her cane. "Montclair, could you please agree to refrain from any unflattering characterizations of Mr. Nussbaum?" She fixed me with a chilly gaze, revealing herself to be a wanton Jew lover, and probably a slut.

"Okay, that's it," bellowed the disembodied voice. "I'm making a change. Colonel, you're taking the reins."

"Gladly," the Colonel replied.

THE COLONEL

The assembled strangers sat in the library awaiting another address by the fearsome voice. The Jew-hating playboy, Montclair Ellison, scowled, but the rest of the group seemed to breathe a sigh of relief—especially the radiant Miss Margaret Hadley, whose delicate sensibilities the ruffian had offended.

I should like to add that in addition to being a perfect lady, Miss Hadley was extremely physically attractive. Her face was pleasant, her complexion fair, and her jugs were the big, round kind, the kind that, if one were to make love to her from behind, would probably swing back and forth and even, quite gloriously, slap together in a most delicious fashion.

"So, obviously we're going to have to make another change," interjected the anonymous voice—quite rudely, in my opinion.

Miss Hadley—whom even a gay man would want to have sex with—blushed, her breasts (again: large, round) heaving as she drew in her breath sharply and gestured toward my person.

"I wish I could say I was surprised, but what did you

expect? You asked another old white guy to control the narrative. What the hell did you think was going to happen?"

Montclair piped up from the banquette, where he had been sulking. "Thirty-nine isn't old."

The disembodied voice broke in again. "Let's try Miss Hadley."

"With pleasure," said the mouth of the beautiful boobs.

MISS HADLEY

The all-white group of overprivileged soldiers of the patriarchy reclined by the fire in the sumptuously appointed library—the very picture of casual entitlement. They were all the kind of people who would say they have a Black friend, but if you dug into it a little, it would just turn out to be someone they worked with.

According to our mysterious host, we were all wanted for the crime of murder. But what about our other crimes, such as the microaggressions we commit every day against groups that for too long have been regarded as "other"?

"Is anyone still awake?" said Montclair, the stupid anti-Semitic asshole whom you'll remember was the first narrator.

"I resent that description," this fucking dumbass dickhead continued, stretching his legs out on the ottoman, subjugating the footrest the same way he so casually subjugated Jews, and probably women and minorities. The fact that he still hadn't denied it was proof positive.

The Colonel cleared his throat nervously. "Speaking for myself, I'd just like to say that, while I may be sexist, I am not racist. My mistress is Jamaican, and I think of Black women in general as being somehow *juicier.*"

"See, that right there is racist, though," Mr. Nussbaum said. At least someone here wasn't a typical dumb-as-shit man.

Countess Calcott groaned. "Miss Hadley. I'm with you, but don't you see how you lose ground when you disparage the entire male gender? I'm not saying your anger isn't justified, but we've got to go high; it's the only path to progress."

Just then, there was a knock on the door. We all looked toward the sound. A collective shiver ran down our spines.

"Pizza's here," Montclair said, then fell apart laughing at his retarded fucking joke.

Suddenly, everyone's eyes were upon me.

This time, it was the butler who spoke up. "'Retarded,' miss?" He put down the sherry he'd been pouring, with a *clank.* "My sister has Down syndrome. Is she 'retarded'?"

"I didn't mean it like that," I stammered.

"You didn't mean it like what? Didn't mean it like 'stupid, blathering moron,' because that's what you think of people who are born with disabilities?"

The knock at the door came again, but this time no one even noticed, now that we were engrossed in this uncomfortable but vital conversation about how we speak of the 'differently abled'—the phrase I would have employed if I hadn't been so distracted by that smarmy little shitbag, Montclair.

The Colonel cleared his throat and addressed the butler delicately. "With the greatest respect, sir, perhaps Miss Hadley hadn't realized that the term to which you took offense had become outmoded. I myself have found that these terms change so frequently that it can be difficult keeping up with them—breasts, big, right there. I mean, you all see them, right?"

The butler rolled his eyes, and a moment later we heard another knock at the door.

"Maybe someone should answer that," the disembodied voice announced hesitantly.

I could feel my face flush, the way it does when I'm nervous. "Colonel, I do know better," I said, then turned to face the butler head-on, to continue this dialogue in a respectful, thoughtful manner. "Sir, please—"

THE DISEMBODIED VOICE

No one was answering my knock at the door, and frankly, I was starting to become uneasy. I had placed the captain's dead body—the Spaniard who rowed my guests to the mansion—in the library, behind the velvet curtains in front of the bay window. It had been easy to club him over the head with his oar after he delivered the last guest, and then, using a small dolly I had stowed by the dock, roll his body to the house while everyone was dressing for dinner.

I'd left instructions for the butler to open the curtains at exactly eight o'clock, ostensibly to air out the library. In actuality, this step was designed only to reveal my gruesome handiwork, and provide my guests with their first clue: I had scrawled the letters O-S-V-E-T-A on the captain's forehead in blood. *Osveta* is Croatian for "vengeance"—a word that hammers home the vengeance theme, and (hopefully!) adds to their growing sense of doom.

But, checking my pocket watch, I saw that it was already a quarter after eight. The butler had missed his cue by a long shot, so now I was knocking on the door—and still the servant did not come to answer it! I twirled my mustache anxiously. The bees were to be released in the dining room at precisely twenty-five after. I needed to get this show on the road. So I began to wonder: should I simply open the door myself, stride over to the curtains, and pull them back to reveal the captain's corpse, then say something scary, like "Behold your fate"?

"We can hear all this," Montclair said. "And I'll have you know, I came armed."

Countess Calcott plucked a pistol from her boot. "I'm armed, myself, and a decorated markswoman at that."

Shit, I thought.

Just then, from my vantage point through the keyhole, I saw the chandelier flicker. Everyone looked toward the light as it sputtered off completely, casting the library into blackness. *Now what?* I thought. This wasn't part of the plan!

A great scuffle ensued. I pressed my eye right up to the opening, but all I could make out in the darkness were shadows and muffled clobberings, a piercing shriek, a yell, a moan.

Then the lights blinked back on, and to my horror, I saw everyone—each of my handpicked guests, my pawns, playthings—lying dead on the floor. Montclair's monocle was shattered and bloody; the Countess was crammed at an odd angle against the grandfather clock, her head perpendicular to her body.

As I fumbled in my breast pocket for the keys, the keyhole darkened with an approaching figure. I scrambled back, sliding down the marble hallway—just as the door creaked slowly open and the swarthy captain, bloody but alive, stepped through and made his way toward me with a menacing grin.

THE CAPTAIN

The squirmy little coward gaped up at me, his eyes full of terror as I lifted the candelabra high above his stupid, eccentric millionaire head. "I'm not a Spaniard," I said, bringing the hardware down with a wet *thwack*. "I'm Basque. Learn the fucking difference."

Birthday Girl

The subject heading was "BIRTHDAY O'CLOCK."

I'd been looking forward to the email for weeks, so when it finally popped up on my phone in the elevator, I think I actually licked my lips. I used it as a desk carrot and went through my morning routine with a little spring in my step: filled my Mount Rushmore mug with Lipton, flicked on my desk lamp, powered up my laptop, and then settled in to savor it on the big screen.

Molly's birthdays are the freaking best. This was her thirty-fourth, and I just knew she was going to pull out all the stops. Molly's definitely my most dramatic friend. I guess you could say she's "extra." Fernando says Molly's a "shameless birthday whore," but I think she just has a big personality and likes her birthday. What's so bad about that?

I mean, sure, Molly's birthdays do tend to take over the

weekend. There's usually a dinner party on Friday night followed up by some kind of daytime activity on Saturday and then a blowout all-nighter—but I don't normally have much going on on the weekends, so for me it's a welcome change. Plus, it usually gives me an excuse to make a trip somewhere exotic, like New Orleans, or even one time, Palm Springs. I can't tell you how much I look forward to these trips, especially since I moved back to Allentown to take care of my family. My mom, dad, and brothers were all left paralyzed and handless after a white-water rafting accident. It happened three years ago, almost to the day. Actually, it happened on Molly's birthday, which was the reason I wasn't with them.

My dad had just recovered from prostate cancer and took everyone on a celebratory rafting trip down the Youghiogheny River. Halfway down the rapids, their raft was dragged into a treacherous stretch known as "Dimple Rock." It's a place where a massive chunk of sandstone juts out of the river, squeezing the water into a turbulent passage. The water slams against the side of the rock and falls back in on itself, creating a "pillow" that flips boats and people, trapping them in the churning water and slapping them mercilessly against the stone, and that is precisely what happened to my family. They were pillowed for almost three hours. It's a miracle the park ranger was able to dredge them out alive—battered, bloody, and now raving mad—but alive. That's where the miracle ended, I'm afraid. Because they ended up contracting staph infections while recovering in the hospital, infections that eventually claimed all their hands.

I found out about the accident at Molly's thirty-first birthday (her "Baskin-Robbins" year—at least that's what

I called it!) on a pub-n-pedal trolley in Savannah. I had pretty awful survivor's guilt for a while, but I managed it by reminding myself of a simple point: your dad might recover from prostate cancer several times over the course of his life, but how many times is your best friend going to turn thirty-one?

Back to the email. This year's Evite came from Molly's fiancé, Tim, a marketing exec at United with an underbite and a passion for fitness. Tim seems like a great guy. I've tried chatting with him at Molly's birthdays, but I'm far from being Molly's most exciting friend, so he understandably ignores me. But I know there must be something special about Tim, because Molly chose him!

I clicked on the floral Paperless Post envelope and beheld the invitation:

SHHH . . . It's a surprise! . . . THAT ANYONE AS BEAUTIFUL AS MOLLY EXISTS

I could already imagine how Fernando would feel about this line. Fernando is one of Molly's college besties, and probably the only one who stands up to her. They have this very special bond, which probably goes back to Fernando's dream of being a dancer.

Fernando is beautiful and round and comes from an elite Spanish banking family. Neat, right? It was understood that after college he would return to Madrid and join Banco Santander. Except he didn't want to do that. His dream was to dance for the American Ballet Theater. Now, besides being mildly obese, Fernando has always been uncoordinated, but Molly said he could do it. She believed in him, and that gave him confidence. He auditioned six times and never got a callback, but I think he just felt powerful knowing that he'd given it a shot. Molly does that for you: she makes you feel like big things are possible. Like when I told her I wasn't going to study abroad with her, because my family couldn't afford the extra tuition, and she said—and I remember her very words—"Fuck that." And you know what? She helped me find a second summer job (working as her assistant) so I could join her and study for one glorious semester in Paris! I guess that's why it feels so good to be around her. Suddenly, your life opens up like a big flower.

We were freshman-year roommates, and I can't express how exciting it was meeting someone like her. Sure, she stole every single one of my boyfriends—all two of them! But it's not like I "owned" them. And sure, she could be mean. You might even say downright cruel! But it was always in a funny way. Like that time she took me to Venice for a spring break vacation with her family, and we snuck out of the hotel and she hilariously pushed me into a canal. Or that time she jokingly sold me into sex slavery in Dubai. Interpol managed to find me after only eleven days—and I ended up picking up *shwaya* Arabic along the way, so it was a win-win. No idea why I was the lucky friend she picked to tag along on these trips, but you can bet I wasn't complaining. Being around Molly just makes you feel more alive.

Dear Molly's Nearest and Dearest:
   Who's more special than Molly? No one, that's who!
My gorgeous, multitalented fierce-yancée (she said
yes!!! Still can't believe it!!!) is about to celebrate her
thirty-fourth revolution on earth.

Fernando's been super territorial about Molly ever since she got engaged to Tim. Fernando can't stand Tim. Personally, I think Tim is maybe just a touch too "into" Molly. Fernando says Tim is "so far up Molly's ass his zip code is her colon." Anyway, I'm just happy Molly and Tim seem to be doing well. It's wonderful when your friends find love.

Let's Celebrate the Day Molly Came Into the World!
Please join us for a weekend of birthday delights....
Details below.

Turns out Tim had quite a weekend planned. I appreciated how thoroughly he'd laid everything out. We'd venmo him $75 for the Friday-night dinner, which was going to be prix fixe. Then it was $200 per person for the Airbnb, and $18,000 a head for the private jet. Various other expenses would be "billed later." Once we landed on the island hidden from man, we'd kick things off with a welcome luau. Then we'd trek to a dormant volcano, where we'd dive nude into an enchanted lagoon and the impure would die. Later, in the underwater cavern, we'd be treated to a build-your-own-poké-bowl station and then all lay our hands on Molly's bare skin, willing our life force into her bloodstream until she levitated, dissolved into a mist, and rained back down on us as holy goo.

I took a contemplative sip of my tea. To tell you the truth, I was feeling a little uneasy about this invitation. It wasn't the money for the Airbnb or the plane or anything—that stuff can all go on plastic. Sure, I'm still paying for Molly's last seven birthdays, and those interest rates are no joke, but the memories are worth a few dings on my credit score. I wasn't even super concerned about the fact that nowhere on the invitation did it ask about allergies, since I have a nut one that is (annoying, I know!) life-threatening.

No, the part that worried me was that the island part screamed "bikini." I wouldn't describe myself as "beach-bod ready" at any time of the year, but if I can have about a month's notice, I can generally straighten myself out enough to feel good in a one-piece. But according to some smaller print near the bottom of the invitation, the heli-copter to the private airfield left at midnight, which didn't leave me a heck of a lot of time to pack and scoot over to New York, let alone whip myself into bikini shape.

I glanced at the photo of my family, taken just before the accident. Everyone looked so happy, with their tans, and their hands. I sighed. Arranging care for them would be tricky on such short notice. But this is Molly we're talking about. And Molly's only going to turn thirty-four once. And that build-your-own-poké-bowl station didn't exactly hurt matters, if you know what I mean!

So I made the arrangements, flew to New York, and then cabbed it over to the helipad.

If you've never been on a helicopter before (I hadn't), heads up: they're loud! Like, something's-wrong-we're-all-going-to-die loud. But there's not, and you're not! Luckily, I scored a seat next to Fernando and Missy. Missy is another one of Molly's besties. I really like her. Missy and Molly went to high school together, where they were co-captains of the lacrosse team. From what I've gathered, they worked this good cop/bad cop dynamic, where Molly was the peppy, pretty captain and Missy was the "heavy."

Missy is also a physically heavy person. She's tall and wide. Most of her heft is muscle. I understand that her nickname in high school was Refrigerator, and that she did not love that name. Not sure why, because refrigerators are freaking awesome. They're probably the most popular appliance in the house! Still, I would never call Missy that, because one time—the only time I ever saw her cry—she told me about how she found it demeaning, humiliating, and ultimately traumatizing. So I've never really understood why she laughs every time Molly calls her that. But again, they're old high school friends, and I can't begin to understand the bond they share. So I don't try!

It was just a quick twenty-four-minute ride to the airfield, and I was planning to soak up every second. I was so pumped about the weekend, I felt like I was going to burst. I turned to Fernando.

"HOW FREAKING AWESOME IS THIS?"

"WE'RE ON A ROCKET TO HELL," Fernando yelled. Missy nodded and took a drag from her vape pen. The lime-green tip glowed invitingly as she inhaled. Fernando shook his head. "CAN YOU BELIEVE TIM'S INVITE? I HATE THAT GUY."

"TIM SUCKS," Missy yelled, then took another drag. Fernando ripped open a bag of Popchips, which the pilot had kindly offered us before takeoff.

He tossed a few chips back and chewed them moodily. "WHAT I DESPISE ABOUT TIM, BESIDES HIS PERSONALITY AND HIS STUPID STRESS PUTTY, IS THE WAY HE JUST ROLLS OVER FOR MOLLY EVERY GODDAMN TIME. MOLLY NEEDS SOMEONE TO KEEP HER GROUNDED, NOT FAN THE FLAMES. CASE IN POINT: THIS FUCKING WEEKEND."

Missy shrugged. "HE HAD TO GO ALL OUT, AFTER WHAT HAPPENED LAST YEAR."

Fernando made a dismissive gesture with his chip. "SO JUST BECAUSE HE FUCKED UP LAST YEAR, WE ALL HAVE TO PAY FOR IT??"

I piped up. "WHAT HAPPENED LAST YEAR? LAST YEAR WAS THE ROLLER DISCO PARTY. THAT WAS AWESOME!"

Missy rolled her eyes. "IT'S NOT ABOUT WHAT HAP-PENED AT HER *FRIENDS* CELEBRATION. IT'S ABOUT WHAT HAPPENED AT HER *COUPLE* CELEBRATION, WITH TIM."

"SO, WHAT HAPPENED WITH TIM?"

"ASK TIM," Missy yelled.

"HEY, TIM," I shouted.

Tim looked up from his putty. I was all set to ask him about last year, but because of the aggressive way he was squeezing the putty and the way his eyes were kind of flar-ing with a liquid hate, I chickened out. "WANT SOME POPCHIPS?"

The pilot's voice crackled through his headset. "I un-derstand someone on board is celebrating a birthday."

Fernando leaned toward the cockpit. "THE BIRTHDAY GIRL'S MEETING US AT THE AIRPORT. WE'RE JUST HER FRIENDS."

"I'M HER SOULMATE, STUDENT, TEACHER, AND LOVER," Tim clarified.

That made me think of something. Why the heck wasn't Tim on the plane with Molly? "TIM," I shouted. "WHY AREN'T YOU WITH MOLLY ON THE PLANE? WHY ARE YOU MEETING HER AT THE AIRFIELD?"

Tim ignored me, and the helicopter began its descent.

Below, I could see our jet idling on the runway, the lights of the cabin glowing warmly.

As soon as we'd taken off and the flight attendants were walking serenely down the aisle, tonging out hot towels, Molly plopped down next to me and asked if it was just her, or was Refrigerator being annoying as shit.

". . . Yes?" I ventured, trying lamely to hide my unease. I hadn't noticed Missy being annoying, but Molly often notices things that go right over my head. By the way, Molly is my best friend, but I know I'm not hers, and that's okay. You're just lucky if you know Molly at all, let alone have her count you as one of her "peeps." I'm a happy peep. That's good enough for me!

"She keeps trying to braid my hair," Molly said.

Uh-oh. I quickly dropped my hands into my lap. I had been quietly separating her silky strawberry-blond hair into three neat plaits. "Right, that's not a thing you like anymore," I said slowly.

Molly sighed; I was doing badly. Mercifully, she switched gears. "Thirty-four sounds fucking old, right?"

". . . No."

She leaned closer. "Thirty-four's old, dude. I found a gray pube. Well, a white one. Like, four of them."

My hands flew to Molly's pubis as I sought the offending strands. Bored, she slapped me away. "Fernando took care of it," she said, and my eyes darted to Fernando, who was pasting the dainty, fanned-out hairs into a keepsake book. Farther down the aisle, Tim sat glaring at Fernando.

A stewardess handed us two cones of toro tartare. Molly popped hers in her mouth as I savored mine. "This weekend's going to be epic. I'm glad you could make it, Horn-stroth."

If we're going over everything with a fine-tooth comb, sure, my name is also Molly, and I don't *love* love my last name, Hornstroth, but that's what everyone calls me, because Molly is already Molly, which honestly makes sense and at the end of the day, why let it bother me? Especially in this moment. I was forty-three thousand feet in the air eating raw fish with my best friend. At this rate, the weekend had already delivered. Of course, I only had myself to blame for drinking from that can of Diet Coke before asking if it had nuts. Apparently, in some cities, you can get special Cokes in all different flavors. I guess I've been in Allentown a little too long! Molly had requested this exotic almond-flavored varietal for her guests, and it's not like I can just assume she remembers my situation. My throat started to close and my heart slammed into my chest, but once I'd stabbed my EpiPen into my thigh, I simply sat back and enjoyed the eleven-hour flight.

If you've never been on a private island hidden from man before (I hadn't), heads up: they're awesome! Like, we're-going-to-stay-here-and-live-forever awesome. But you're not, and you're not! Mainly because it costs $400,000 a night to rent and the jet leaves Sunday at daybreak. I've always been a little foggy on how Molly pays for these trips, but if I had to guess, I think it has something to do with the fact that her dad is a billionaire.

It was awesome to see Molly's birthday crew together again. I only see these fine folks (and Molly, come to think of it!) at her birthday, so I really try to make the most of the weekends and squeeze in as much QT as I can.

There were about thirty of us, and we were each assigned our own personal sleeping hammock, strung between palm trees. Mine was pretty far away from the rest of the group, and when I trekked over to it I noted that it was also strung up pretty darn high. I got quite a workout shimmying up there. I also lost a fair amount of leg skin. But once I made it up and stretched out on my back, staring out at that big blue tropical sky, with the sunshine streaming onto my face and the increasingly violent shrieking of monkeys piercing the air, I was one happy camper. The palms swayed lazily above me, a fluffy cloud drifted by overhead, and I sighed. Life was good.

The monkey's vagina slammed down on my eyeball with shocking force. The first few seconds of the attack were a furry, chaotic blur: one minute I'm living out my own personal Jimmy Buffett song, the next a monkey's clamped onto my face, *Alien*-style, and I do not have a game plan. As my hands flew up to pry the monkey off, a whole bunch more of them landed shrieking on my hammock and began their assault.

Here's the thing. Planning an adult-destination birthday celebration is hard. You can't just expect your host to know which palm trees have been claimed by warlike monkey families and which ones haven't. Still, a guest does expect that a certain level of thought has been given to their physical safety. So as I wobbled on the hammock, mustering the balance required for aerial combat, some harsh words passed through my head. Let's just say if there were Yelp reviews for birthday parties, I was pretty sure I'd dock this one a star.

I managed to rip the first monkey off my face, but my troubles were only beginning. I counted at least nine of them, and they were all united in a common goal: making my life hard. They tore at my hair, clawed at my arms, and tried their best to rip my face off my skull. Of course, who knows what was going through their heads, but I got the impression that they wanted me to die. Well, I love and respect animals, but I also have a natural instinct for survival. So I grabbed my Swiss Army knife out of my shoe, flicked out the blade, and started defending my new home.

The monkeys didn't love that. The biggest one of all was an aggressive, dominant female, and she immediately lunged for the knife. As she did, I slashed her across the chest. That got a huge reaction from the smaller monkeys, who started shrieking to beat the band—and I realized that she must be their ringleader. As the ringleader shrunk back and licked her wound, a smaller one shot up at me, wrapping its body around my face, temporarily blinding me. I had the presence of mind to headbutt the tree trunk, slamming this new monkey against it. I heard a crap-ton of little cracks when its back hit the tree, and that was upsetting, but it did the trick, because the monkey loosened its grip and then fell quite a ways down before I saw it catch itself on a branch and swing away. *Phew.* The other monkeys shot up at me in an angry wave, and I pinwheeled my arms, flipping them over and slamming them into the tree in a churning, violent "pillow" technique. After I pillowed a couple, the whole crew sprang away from me, cowering in fear and looking up to check in with the big one, who sat at the other end of the hammock, still as a rock, staring at me.

The big monkey and I just sat there, staring at each

other and catching our breath. It was hard to tell what she was thinking. Maybe she had had enough. Then again, maybe she was about to dive in for the kill. Just as I thought, okay, I should probably jump up and stab her, the monkey held a finger up to me. At first I thought, is she giving me the finger? I couldn't blame her, given what had occurred, although she certainly started it! But then I saw it wasn't the middle one, it was the pointer. What happened next blew my mind: in a low, croaky voice, this huge monkey said, in perfect English, "There can only be one." And then she swung away into the afternoon, followed by her minions.

For a beat I just sat there, processing. Then I heard the party bugle sound, checked my phone, and realized it was time for the welcome luau. So I shimmied back down and made my way to the fire pit.

Hacking my way through the jungle, I did what I call a "personal pan check-in." "How am I liking the trip so far?" I asked myself. Frankly, it was a mixed bag. The plane sushi was incredible, which boded well for the build-your-own-poké-bowl station (I was still holding out hope there'd be crispy shallots!). The monkey episode, however, had been difficult. But I guess if I had to lodge one serious complaint at this point, it was probably that the Wi-Fi was spotty. I kept checking my phone so I could see how my family was doing with the new nurse, but I couldn't get a single bar. I felt silly whining about Wi-Fi, though, because everything else had been so over-the-top glamorous. "Huh," I thought sheepishly, "I guess all this rock star treatment is making me feel like an actual rock star!"

When I got to the pit area, dinner was clearly a ways off. Tim announced that the pork needed another half hour to marinate before grilling, so I decided to take care of some housekeeping. After finally catching a few bars of reception on my phone, I grabbed a fresh coconut and a silly party straw and headed out onto the beach. My plan was to check in on my family, work on Molly's toast, and also, if I'm being honest, squeeze in a little me time.

A rocky jetty stretched out into the sea, and I walked out to the last sunbaked stone, where I took a seat and pulled out my phone to text Donovan, the nurse I'd hired to care for my family over the weekend. "Everything going OK?" I typed, and then I thought, Hmm, that could have been a little friendlier. I followed it up with "Forgot to mention—help yourself to anything in the fridge that catches your fancy. I stocked it with goodies!" I added a tongue-out smiley emoji and pressed Send. Actually, come to think of it, I kind of hoped Donovan *didn't* help himself to the goodies in the fridge. I'd bought some pretty exciting stuff, stuff I don't normally get, like mini carrot cupcakes, and I was counting on having them at home to soften the blow when I returned from this whirlwind weekend. As I waited for his text bubbles to turn into a response, I looked out at the horizon. A fish jumped in the distance, the sun shimmered on the crystal waters, and I thought, "Hornstroth, you better pinch yourself. Because it ain't gonna get better than this!" Then my phone buzzed.

"EVERYTHING IS NOT OK," Donovan texted back. "NO ONE TOLD ME THESE PEOPLE HAVE NO HANDS. I CANNOT DO THIS JOB ALONE. I LEAVE TO GET BACKUP AND THE YOUNG BOY, HE START FIRE. TERRIBLE SUICIDE FIRE. WHEN I COME BACK, FIRE TRUCKS ALREADY THERE. YOUR FAMILY FIGHT OFF FIREMEN TRYING TO SAVE THEM. MOTHER SCREAM,

'THIS IS WHAT WE WANT.' I MYSELF TRY TO HELP AND BURN MY HANDS BADLY, VERY BADLY. IRONY IS I WENT TO GET MORE 'HANDS,' ENDED UP WITH LITERALLY NO HANDS. YOUR FAMILY ARE ALL DEAD NOW. I AM SORRY."

I took in what Donovan had told me. It was a lot.

I scrolled through the emoji menu on my phone for an appropriate response. Nothing felt right, so I selected the Michael-Jordan-crying GIF and pressed Send. Then I tucked the phone away, in my bag. Out of sight.

Gazing over the sun-drenched afternoon, I grappled with my new reality. The word "yikes" came to mind. I thought back to how selfish I was, just moments ago, concerned about the goodies in the fridge when the real "goodies in the fridge"—my family—were taking their last breaths.

Overcome and ashamed, I wept on the beach for what felt like minutes. When I finally wiped my eyes and pulled myself together, I decided I was going to keep this news to myself. Just because my day was completely ruined didn't mean I had to bring down Molly's entire birthday weekend. So I got up, smacked the sand out of my shorts, and made my way to the luau as the sun glinted brightly off the tropical waters on the island hidden from man.

The next morning, when the wake-up bugle roused me in the still-black predawn, I'd like to say it was from a restful slumber. Well, it wasn't. I don't know how everybody else slept—again, they were very, very far away—but I found that the combination of the height, fear of monkey reprisal, sadness over the loss of my family, and phantom hunger for those carrot cupcakes made for a somewhat restless evening. So I was relieved to put the night behind me, inch carefully down from the tree, and start a fresh day.

Day Two began with a Magenta Method class for Molly's guests. I forgot to mention that this is a very active group. Last year, before Molly's roller derby disco dance party, the whole crew met at SoulCycle for a Rihanna-vs.-Beyoncé-themed birthday ride. I probably burned off two thousand calories in that class—but then gained it all back eating fried Oreos at the party!

I had never done a Magenta Method class, so I hung back with the other newbies as Coach, a chiseled man in a tank top, explained how it worked. First, I learned that the workout studio was lit with magenta-colored lights, which soothed the nervous system and encouraged cellular regeneration. Then Coach passed out armband heart monitors and a tube of electrode jelly and told us to smear some on our biceps to help the bands stick. Bruising from the monkey battle made finding a place on my arm difficult, and I had to avoid several cuts that hadn't closed, but eventually I settled on a spot on my lower biceps and slid it on as I watched Coach demonstrate how the WaterRower's foot straps could be adjusted to our comfort. Meanwhile, Tim and Fernando had mounted side-by-side treadmills and began sprinting hell for leather. Tim is a triathlete and didn't seem to break much of a sweat, but after just a few paces, Fernando was drenched. Exercise is not a part of Fernando's routine; he was actually a low-tone baby and had to have early intervention to help him develop any muscles at all—a detail he divulged during a drunken night out when we ended up at a fortune-teller's in the Village. I thought it was really touching how Fernando was "fighting" for Molly on the treadmill, and I silently saluted him as I smooshed my heart monitor into the electrode gel.

I felt a little lost as Coach explained the merits of excess post-exercise oxygen consumption, but I perked up when he got into the Pow Points. Pow Points were easy to understand. You earned a Pow Point by spending one minute in the Magenta Sector, which meant you were working at maximum exertion. You could check on your progress by looking up at a big screen at the front of class that showed your name and your Pow Score. I asked Coach how many Powies we should be shooting for, and he said twelve and that I shouldn't call them that. I apologized and he said I shouldn't apologize to him, I should apologize to the team—so I turned to the group, but everyone was already walking to their assigned treadmill or rower. I figured I should just keep my head down and focus on my Pow Score, and that's exactly what I did.

Coach turned the lights way down and some hardcore rap way up, and we all got to it. As he spat obscenities at us encouragingly, we pushed our bodies to their breaking point, in honor of the birth of our terrifying friend.

And guess what? I earned thirteen Pow Points during class. Yep, you read that right!! One more Pow Point than Coach challenged us to earn! And you can bet I worked my keister off for each one. Now, before you go calling me Wonder Woman, you might want to get a load of this: Molly earned fifty-nine Pow Points (!), Tim earned forty-six, and Missy earned twenty-nine (even while vaping!). Fernando only earned six, which might not sound like a lot, but he fought for them. While everyone spontaneously filed into a line to high-five Molly after class, I noticed Fernando seemed down. Something about the way he was keeping to himself, and how he was crying hysterically. I walked over to comfort him, but when he saw me coming he waved me away. I hated seeing him like that, but I had to respect his privacy. So I let Fernando be and, after high-fiving Molly, went up to Tim to congratulate him on his Pow Score.

Tim was standing by the lockers near the front desk, peeling off his sweat-wicking performance layer.

"Congratulations on those Pows, my man! Up top!"

I offered a high five but he just nodded without looking at me, which I chalked up as a win, since he'd been dating Molly for two years and hadn't yet acknowledged me.

I figured I'd use this QT with Tim to clear up something I'd been wondering about. "So, Tim. Back in the helicopter, you know that whole thing about last year, and how you had to make up for it and everything? What happened last year?"

His eyes darted around, making sure no one was listening. "We do not speak of Last Year," he said, stepping closer to me. His voice was hoarse, urgent.

"Why? What happened? Did you forget Molly's birthday or something?"

"Forget Molly's birthday?" His eyes flashed, and he spit the words out menacingly.

I took another sip from my Smartwater. Luckily, I'd had the sense to ask if it had nuts in it. Turns out mine did—what are the chances?—but I requested a non-nut one and Coach (grumpily, I might add! Ooh—there's that "rock star" coming out to play!) grabbed me one from the back.

"I mean, it sounds like it didn't go well or something?"

Tim smacked the bottle out of my mouth with stunning

dexterity. I had to admire his triathlete training. I brought my hand up to my lip, which was now bleeding slightly.

"Did I say something wrong?"

He pulled my hair back and brought his mouth right up to my ear. "Of course I didn't forget Molly's birthday. We went to her favorite tapas place and then I took her to see Andrew Bird at Hudson Yards."

I wiggled out of his grasp. Yeesh! "So what was the problem?"

He looked at me wearily. I saw then that his eyes didn't match his face: they were old, weathered. "That's not a birthday night. That's a *date* night."

That sounded like a pretty good birthday to me, but by this point I knew to keep that to myself. Plus, I wanted to wrap it up with Tim. I was starting to see things Fernando-style. There was something off about this guy. So I picked up my water bottle, straightened my ponytail, and prepared to make a polite exit.

"Well, people make mistakes, right? Anyhoozle—"

"Sure. And then they pay." He turned his shirtless back to me then, and I saw it clearly in the fluorescent light: the long jagged scar that carved a diagonal line from his shoulder to his waist. Yeesh 2.0!

I gasped. "Molly did that?"

He brought his face close to mine. "I'm a better man for it."

With that, he left me sweating uneasily by the Magenta Method lockers. I grabbed my stuff and left the studio, passing the huge screen in the lobby with everyone's Pow Scores flashing on it. Molly's score and picture were highlighted at the top of the screen, but next to it, instead of her name, the text read "There Can Only Be One." Huh.

Anyhoo. What the heck was I supposed to do with all that Tim stuff? I probably earned another Pow Point just from the way my heart was racing. I needed Missy. She's the kind of blunt, no-bullshit friend who gives it to you straight. I went back to the beach and found her in the party hut, leaning against a palm tree and staring out at the ocean.

"What did you get Molly for a gift?"

She sighed, a little annoyed to be bothered, and I couldn't blame her. She kept her eyes on the horizon as she answered. "Yeezy Moonbeam boots in 'Oil,' a bronze cast of Molly's torso mounted on a polished hunk of maple harvested from her childhood home's backyard, a monogrammed alpaca blanket, a monthly cheese subscription, and an exercise bike."

I was starting to second-guess my decision to go low-key with my gift this year. I had convinced myself that Molly and I had crossed over into the realm where any gift was a mere token of a boundless love, and thus, almost beside the point.

"I got her a candle," I said.

Missy looked at me, confused.

"It's Diptyque," I hurried on. "And it's tuberose. She loves tuberose!"

"Is it a big one?"

A monkey shrieked in the distance as if to say, "Tonight, you die."

I hesitated. "It's more votive sized."

"Did you get her a card?"

I took out my phone. "I sent her this celebratory string of emojis." I showed Missy the rather cleverly selected emojis I had sent Molly the day before. The text read, "Can't wait to celebrate!!!" followed by a party-hat-and-confetti emoji, a birthday cake, three red balloons, a rainbow, a unicorn, champagne, fireworks, two yellow women holding hands, and then a purple heart and three spinning pink hearts.

Looking back at the emoji string, I approved of it all over again: its exultant, festive tone, the whimsy of the unicorn, the happy yellow women holding hands (remind you of anyone? How about me and Molly!). It was a little over-the-top; it was silly; it was loving. I felt like it struck precisely the right note.

Like the water bottle before it, my phone was suddenly smacked from my grasp in a precision strike, the speed and skill of which I had to admire.

Missy withdrew her hand and pulled her vape pen out of her sports bra. She sucked on it and blew the smoke down on me as I bent to retrieve my phone. She shook her head sadly. "This is gonna take a lot of cleanup."

I brushed the sand off my phone and thought about Tim's back. "I'll do anything."

Missy returned her gaze to the horizon. "Poster board. Glitter. Pictures of you and Molly from kindergarten. Forty gallons of acid and a shit-ton of paper towels. When you have a gift this shitty, you offset it with shlock. You're going to make a vision board for her thirty-fourth year on earth."

"What's the acid for?"

"Amanda."

"Why does Amanda need acid?"

Missy rolled on a pair of rubber gloves she'd grabbed

from her back pocket. "Amanda told Molly she'd have to leave early. She got pinned for a Sprint commercial that shoots on Monday."

"Oh my god, that's awesome! *Go, Amanda!* I'm gonna text her right now."

It really is so cool when you hear good news about people you like. It's almost like getting good news yourself! I texted Amanda—an old friend of Molly's from tennis camp—a congrats message with a couple fun emojis thrown in and promptly heard a text message alert *bloop* from what sounded like inside a nearby cooler. Missy snickered, which piqued my interest. I peered inside and then reeled back from the stench.

"You don't bail on a thirty-fourth destination birthday," Missy said. With a hand over my mouth, I looked back into the cooler at Amanda, purple now, her phone balanced on her jaw, glowing with my new text message. My eyes bulged in horror and I turned to Missy slowly.

"Who the hell do we think did this?"

Missy didn't respond but tossed over a pair of elbow-length rubber gloves. "Anyway. I'll help you with the vision board after we take care of this. You have a long road ahead of you, brother man."

As I slid on the gloves, almost retching from the smell now, I couldn't help wondering if Missy was just cracking the whip about this birthday present because she felt like she was on thin ice with Molly, what with the braiding snafu on the plane. And also because you never really know where you stand with Molly, and when you're on her poop list, you feel disconnected from the sparkle of her orbit. Missy grabbed Amanda's top half and I grabbed her legs, and we carried her body to the back of the party hut, where Missy had a plastic tub and several canisters of acid waiting.

That's when my phone beeped with an incoming text. It was Donovan.

"WHAT ARE YOUR PLANS," he wrote. "THE HOSPITAL NEEDS TO KNOW YOUR PLANS."

I had my hands full, so I stuck the phone into the crook of my neck and dictated to Siri while I worked. "Donate whole bodies to the University of Slippery Rock Medical Center period select dissection cadaver period send cremated remains to Acme Innovations PO Box 4322 Saylor City Utah comma thanks."

A few minutes later, I got another text from Donovan. "BEYONCE OR RIHANNA?" This guy has a lot of questions, I thought, before dictating, "Both have their merits."

My phone beeped almost immediately. "THERE CAN ONLY BE ONE."

What the heck, Donovan, I thought, nudging the top off the second bottle of acid with my chin. I put the bottle down for a second to send a response, but before I could write anything, Donovan texted back saying that he was sorry, he meant to text someone else, and that I had his sympathies as I navigated this difficult time.

Who knew what kind of game Donovan was playing? All I knew was that I had to help Missy dissolve Amanda, then wash up and head down to the beach for paddleboard yoga. Apparently you do yoga right there on the water, with tropical fish swimming beneath you. How neat is that?

Missy said the acid would work faster if we cut the body into chunks and let it marinate like a stew. Together, we hoisted Amanda out, and then Missy ran to the party hut to get something. She came back holding a bone saw. I'd wondered why she had that on the plane. "We'll take turns," she said, handing it over to me. "You start."

Ay, caramba, right? I mean, I'd just come to Missy to get some advice about the birthday gift, and now here I was, rowing a blade through the rigor-mortised calf of a very cool friend-of-a-friend. I grunted my way through a particularly tough chunk of muscle and paused to wipe some sweat off my brow. The train to Pleasant Afternoon City had officially departed the station—and I wasn't on it.

We ended up having to work right through the paddle-board yoga class. I did *not* love missing that, but thankfully we made it back in time for the picnic. To my dismay, it was a meat-focused taco spread, with big trays of ground beef and short rib. But after vomiting discreetly in a nearby garbage can, I was able to turn a mental corner and stack my plate high.

After the picnic, Missy and I were walking back to our hammocks for a pre-party nap when I realized I hadn't seen Fernando all afternoon. I asked Missy if she knew where he'd snuck off to, but she just stared straight ahead and took another drag from her vape pen.

Before climbing up to my hammock to recharge for the big night, I left a peace offering on the ground for the monkeys: a plate of short rib tacos I'd "borrowed" from the picnic. I set it down on the ground and arranged some leaves on the plate, to make it clear that it belonged to the jungle.

Once I was cocooned again in my sky bed, it took me a beat to drift off. As exhausted as I was, my brain was still buzzing from the past few days, and those words kept clanging around in my head: There can only be one. There can only be one. There can only be one.

When I climbed down to go to the party, the tacos were gone. In their place, someone had left a banana, thoughtfully half-peeled. I munched it as I made my way to the cavern for the big birthday blowout.

My heart quickened as I reached the top of the volcano and saw the glow of the tiki torches around the lagoon below. How's *that* for a thirty-fourth birthday venue? This was it: the final celebration. I stepped up to the edge, stripped, looked out at the sunset, and then jumped to what was certain to be either a rockin' shindig with my besties or a quick, violent death.

After piercing the lagoon's surface, I let my body's momentum pull me down to the entrance of the cavern, which I swam through. I then paddled upward and emerged, gasping, into a massive domed chamber where everyone was gathered wearing their "Molly's Birthday" T-shirts. The front of the shirt was emblazoned with the wearer's Pow Point total, and the back had side-by-side pictures of Molly as a diapered baby and a beautiful picture of her now, with a caption underneath that read, in bubble font, FROM SQUIRTY TO THIRTY(FOUR)! I was a little thrown by the "squirty." After all, we were about to enjoy an upscale meal. But then I had to chuckle. Who did I think I was, the queen of England? It's not like we were at Buckingham Palace! Then I abruptly stopped laughing as I thought of Tim's follow-up email after the Paperless Post, saying that anyone who diverted attention away from the birthday girl would be shot. A glance at one of the snipers wedged up between the stalactites confirmed this.

The T-shirts were bright pink, which was fun. Pink is Molly's favorite color, and she'll be the first to tell you, "Basic, I know!" Which I really like. Yes, she has a critical eye, but she's just as willing to turn it inward. So, even if she greets you at her party, in front of everyone, by saying something like, oh, I don't know, "Well if it isn't the lard-ass with the three-dick mouth," you know she's just as ready to poke fun at herself with some similarly light-hearted quip.

A waiter made his way down the table with a platter of cocktails. I stuck my hand in my purse to feel around for my EpiPens, reassured myself that I had a couple on me, and then took a sip of Molly's signature birthday cocktail—cotton candy confetti martinis. Yum! Unfortunately, the cotton candy was made from spun macadamia nuts, and Missy ended up having to cut the birthday T-shirt off my torso when I swelled up, but Tim said he had plenty of extras, so, with a new, nut-free vodka cranberry in hand and an extra EpiPen practically burning a hole in my pocket, I was feeling pretty groovy by the time Tim dragged the mic to the center of the cave to get the toasts rolling.

Tim was in a great mood. I'd never seen him this chipper. After setting up the mic stand he flitted around the room, chatting up the guests, clapping them on the back. He even kicked me flirtatiously as he passed my chair.

Tim started with a cute rap he'd written himself. "My name's T-I-M and I'm here to say / Molly enriches my life in a serious way! / She's gorgeous and she's scary and she makes me say hooray / I call her the Dao, because Molly is The Way!"

Missy had changed the words to the Mariah Carey ballad "Always Be My Baby" to "Molly's Baby Always" and gave a stripped-down, emotional performance, which I accompanied softly on the maracas. The rest of the toasters followed one by one as Tim sat at the foot of Molly's throne with a little notebook, grading them on style, originality, and soul.

In between sets, albino eunuchs flocked to either side of Molly, strumming lyres. Another perched before Molly's robed knee, rubbing scented oil into her feet and calves. From time to time Molly nibbled from a bag of Popchips that one of them thoughtfully tipped toward her. The birthday toasts were rolling right along, every detail of the party going off without a hitch. I looked around the cavern to really soak in the sight of so many wonderful people coming together to celebrate Molly, this larger-than-life force pulling us all together into something greater than ourselves. I had my vision board spread across my lap under the table, and I couldn't wait to unveil it. But as my gaze fell on the birthday girl gracefully reprimanding a nearly nude eunuch for spilling oil on Tim's notebook, something struck me as odd. That eunuch getting his ass handed to him looked really familiar. I caught his eye and mouthed, "Fernando?"

Fernando, clearly frightened, shot a quick look over at me as if to say "Shut up."

Something messed up had obviously happened to Fernando. First of all, he wasn't wearing anything other than a loose loincloth, and I happen to know he's extremely self-conscious about his body. So I knew he wasn't nearly nude by choice. He was also completely hairless. His hair, eyebrows, all of it was gone—and he'd been slathered with some kind of glittery lotion that made his skin look wet.

I "accidentally" dropped my roll on the floor and crawled toward him to retrieve it. "What happened to you?" I whispered.

A tear rolled down Fernando's pale, hairless cheek, and he shook his head. "I didn't get enough Pow Points."

I looked around at the other eunuchs. Holy crap. How had I not recognized them before? Yes, they were all bald and obese now—but I knew these people! There was Gigi, Molly's stepsister, gesturing mildly with her plump, clammy hands, explaining the bread service. The eunuch pouring the wine was Krista, Molly's friend from work. And—wow—the creamy ball fanning Molly with a palm frond was Kendall! Kendall freaking Siegler! I didn't know Kendall very well, in fact I mainly just saw her at Molly's birthday parties, but I had always really liked her. Kendall was a children's speech therapist, and I roomed with her for Molly's twenty-sixth birthday in Miami. I remember her wearing one of those stylish high-waisted two-piece bathing suits that I had seen Taylor Swift sporting in a magazine. Kendall had been incredibly fit, with long, flowing blond hair. She was completely hairless now and, although I truly believe all bodies are beautiful, severely overweight.

"Kendall freaking Siegler!" I blurted out. I couldn't help myself. I was in shock.

From her seat on her throne, Molly's gaze trained on us, and her eyes began to glow lime, neon lime, like the tip of Missy's vape pen. "I see you found the birthday girl," she said to Kendall, and at first I was confused. But then I was like, Awww. That was actually such a sweet moment.

Because in all the excitement, I really wasn't expecting anyone to mention my birthday.

Molly and I share one, but it rarely comes up. It's neat: we're both Leos, but of course there are different types of Leos, and Molly's the classic outgoing type, while I'm type two, which is more introverted and down-to-earth.

I asked Molly softly what Kendall did to deserve this.

Kendall froze, the palm frond in her hand quivering. A stream of urine ran down her leg and onto the floor of the cave. Molly cocked her head—intrigued by my boldness, maybe?—and took a step toward me.

"I called shotgun, and Kendall did not honor it," Molly said. She wasn't speaking in her normal voice anymore but an ancient, guttural moan that seemed to emanate from below the earth.

Holy wow, I thought, looking at eunuch Kendall with a newfound respect.

Molly wasn't finished. "Kendall also told my parents that I needed help overcoming my opioid addiction."

Holy *freaking* wow, I thought. Molly's opioid addiction was something she really, really didn't like talking about!

"Think that's badass, Hornstroth?" Molly asked, more like hissed, really, as she walked toward me.

Fernando threw himself down at Molly's feet, his hands clasped in supplication. "Let her go," he begged. "She's essentially brain-dead! She's just a stupid dummy! Let Hornstroth go!"

God, I love Fernando. My heart swelled as I watched him try to defend me—but then I was distracted, as Molly started to shriek and convulse, sending Fernando scurrying behind the throne. He looked on in horror and gasped. "Her birthday powers are increasing!"

I looked back at Molly and noticed that her head had started to pulse. It's hard to describe. It was kind of like the plates of her skull were separating and pulling her skin tight—her eyes were big lime-colored globes. It was pretty remarkable, so, instinctively, I took my phone out and started to take a video of it. Who knows, maybe I could make a GIF of it for her b-day invitation next year, like, "Don't be a 'monster' . . . and miss Molly's birthday!" I don't know. Something like that, but funnier. But then Molly—a bit rudely, if I may be so bold—incinerated my phone with a single searing glance. It burst into flames right in my hands.

I looked down at my singed, throbbing palms. Blistering, smoking. My hands. *My burning hands.* And, of course, that reminded me of something unpleasant. Something deeply upsetting, actually, that I'd pushed down in my mind for some time, but that now, in this moment of truth, shot right back up to the surface.

And that was the fact that, a basquillion thousand or however many miles away, Donovan might have eaten all my mini carrot cupcakes. Every single one. They really might be gone. Long gone. In fact, thinking back to how freaking delicious they looked, they probably were.

Well, that certainly put me in a mood. I started to feel a heat grow inside me.

I happened to glance at Fernando at that moment. In the midst of everything, he was staring longingly at a roll in the bread basket. My heart went out to the hairless, hungry blob that was my friend. Without consciously deciding to do it, I addressed Molly.

"Give Fernando that roll."

Everyone's necks snapped up toward Molly. Molly and I just stood there staring at each other. Finally, she spoke.

"He will have no roll," Molly bellowed. "And furthermore, there will be no build-your-own-poké-bowl station."

Now, wait a minute. No poké bowl station? Wait. One. Minute! I have a fairly photographic memory, and I thought back to the b-day schedule as it appeared on Tim's Evite.

"But the invitation clearly mentioned one."

Molly threw her head back and laughed demonically for some time. While muscle memory urged me to laugh alongside her for the duration of her mirth, I couldn't do it. I looked back at Fernando, sweet, weak Fernando, staring stupidly at his sandaled feet, his stomach rumbling. I thought of Donovan, stuffing that last mini carrot cupcake into his mouth. I thought of that fateful day my family went on that rafting trip, and then that other fateful day, yesterday, when they fire-suicided themselves. Then I thought of the cupcakes again. And *then* I thought: enough.

I looked down at my still swollen body in Molly's birthday T-shirt. What the heck was I doing? I'd been Molly's bitch for years, pruning my personality to be more attractive to her. But to what end? Just so I could eventually be conscripted into her ranks of hairless near-nudes? I was several hundred thousand dollars in debt. I didn't even have a freaking family anymore. The cost of being Molly's friend was high. Too high, I suddenly decided.

I threw my arm out dramatically and pointed at Fernando.

"How could you expect him to get twelve Pow Points? *It's a miracle he got the six he did!*" I yelled, my voice surprisingly strong and clear. "He was a low-tone baby. You knew that. *We all knew he was low-tone!*"

Fernando stared at me in awe. I could hear murmurs spreading up and down the candlelit banquet tables.

And I could feel my birthday powers growing.

"And what's up with the no build-your-own-poké-bowl station?" I went on, pacing now, picking up a little *Showtime at the Apollo* energy. "It said *right there on the invitation*. It's not like you have to have one, but if you're gonna put it there on the invitation—*where the fuck is it?*"

I have to be honest: this was *really* not like me. I felt uncorked! I took a swig from my vodka cranberry and felt the energy course through my newly thirty-four-year-old veins. I couldn't put a finger on precisely what had changed. Yes, I was a little drunk from cocktails on an empty tummy. Yes, I was jet-lagged. But this was the real me talking. For the first time all weekend, and perhaps all of my life, I felt in control. And so maybe that's why, this time, I saw the arm coming. When Molly threw her hand out to slap the glass from my lips, without even thinking, my hand flew up and blocked it.

Molly's eyes widened in surprise.

What happened next is a blur, but I'll describe it as best I can. I remember grabbing my last EpiPen and stabbing it in Molly's eyeball. As Molly clawed at the stick, a steaming yellow ooze gushing out of her socket, Tim dived across the floor and sank his teeth into my thigh. Mustering a strength I never knew I had, I grabbed Tim by the neck and flung him toward the center of the cavern, where he clattered against the mic stand and then scuttled off to cower among the stalagmites. Molly jumped onto my back then, wrapping the crook of her

elbow around my eyes and shoving a handful of something into my mouth. I couldn't see them, but I could
smell them: peanuts.

I spat them out.

"You . . . fucking . . . bitch," I said, pretty feisty now.
"You've been trying to kill me!"

Molly jumped off my back, and I spun around to face
her. Her eyes glittered as she drew a sword that I (incon-
veniently!) had not noticed.

"Took you long enough," she sneered. "How many
EpiPens have you been through?"

Fernando threw me a sword. I don't know how I knew
these fancy moves, maybe from watching hours of Molly's
fencing tournaments, but my hand immediately found an
assured grip, my posture straightened, and my feet moved
confidently as I parried Molly's lunge and then followed it
with a riposte that sank deep into her shoulder.

"*Yeoooaahaaaaaa!*" she screamed, kicking the weapon
from my hands. I was stunned by the unsportsmanlike nature of the gesture, and watched in shock for a moment as
the weapon clattered to the ground. It was a moment too
long. Molly dived toward me and knocked me down, then
wrapped her legs around my waist as she tried to force
more nuts into my mouth. I sucked my lips in between my
teeth as I uppercut her and wriggled free. I scrambled up,
and she came at me again—but this time I stepped aside
and used her momentum to swing her into the cave wall.
I heard a sick cracking noise, and then she slumped down
into the stalagmites and lay still.

Around this time, Missy screamed, "*Hornstroth, look
alive!*" and I noticed a sniper ready to fire. I swiveled back
to my seat for the vision board and flung it, ninja-star

fashion, at the shooter's neck. It sliced his jugular and he fumbled, dropping his rifle and gurgling blood.

There was a moment of deep quiet as we all caught our breath, and I swear you could have heard a pin drop inside that volcano. Everyone was just sitting there, jaws hanging open, looking at me like I was some kind of god.

I looked down and realized that at some point I had picked up the sniper's rifle. I cocked it with one hand.

"I'm the birthday girl now," I said softly.

Well, I wasn't really sure what to do at that point. I kind of felt like throwing my head back, emptying my lungs with a wild howl, and beating my hands over my chest—but the old me was seeping back in, and she didn't want to be "extra." Still, there was enough new birthday-girl energy surging inside me that I wasn't about to just sit back down at the table.

The instinct birdie whispered in my ear that I had to establish dominance.

I strode over to Tim, ripped his sweat-wicking performance clothes from his body, and raped him on the floor in front of everyone. While there wasn't a board to confirm it, I'm sure I earned several additional Pow Points.

When I was finished, I stood up to address the group. Panting and wiping the sweat off my brow, I noted with pleasure that the strategy had worked: I could see the fear and respect in their eyes.

Missy was the first to stir. She darted over to my side and began quickly braiding my hair. Fernando squatted down to groom my pubis. The other eunuchs disappeared deeper into the cave and returned wheeling a glistening sculpture toward me. As they brought it closer, I felt a wave of cold, refreshing air kiss my face—and I made out the tower they were rolling forth. It was the build-your-own-poké-bowl station. Deep bowls of perfectly cubed tuna and salmon were arranged in an artfully lit conch shell made of ice.

Tim hobbled over to the station, assembled a bowl, and crawled it toward me, head bowed low and arms outstretched, his exhausted penis hanging like a salted slug at his waist. Fernando unsheathed some chopsticks and, with a deep bow, presented them to me. I noticed Missy prying the EpiPen out of Molly's dead eye and looking up at me with a desperate, apelike grin as she wiped it off on her pants and lay it at my feet.

I reached down into Missy's pocket with my good hand, brought her vape pen to my lips, and took a deep, revitalizing drag as I assembled the perfect bite of poké. As I exhaled, a chunk of ruby-red fish glistening on my chopsticks, I looked over at the stalagmites, where I'd left Molly bleeding out.

Her body was gone.

"*Find her,*" I bellowed, and my slaves scattered. Some darted farther into the cave, others climbed up the walls to better survey. I strode to the center of the cave and watched in satisfaction as my minions did my bidding. Fernando and the other eunuchs scurried among the stalagmites while Missy crawled along a far wall, sniffing.

I felt a shadow pass overhead and tipped my head back to investigate.

Molly was perched on a ledge high above me, her ruined eyeball hanging down from its socket, her lips twisted into a sinister grin. Before I could even gurgle my surprise, she was plunging down, my tuberose candle lifted high in her one hand, poised to strike.

I stood frozen, sure in that moment that I was going to that big carrot cake cupcake in the sky.

The monkey's vagina whizzed millimeters from my face as it slammed onto Molly's one good eyeball, knocking her off course. As Molly stumbled around, blind and screaming, the big leader monkey tipped her head back and shrieked, summoning her soldiers.

They swung down into the cave from every direction, swarming onto Molly's body, biting and scratching like crazy. As Molly dropped to her knees, the big monkey wrapped her long, hairy arms around Molly's neck and snapped it with a single violent twist.

If you've never been anointed the god of an island nation before (I hadn't), heads up: it's *fun*! Like "you can't go back to the way things were because it's like you've unlocked a higher level of consciousness" fun. And guess what? You don't have to!

Once the monkeys unclamped from Molly's corpse, I presented the big one with a heaping platter of poké. Yeah, she'd tried to kill me a few days ago, but she'd also just saved my life, so we were square. She bowed her head slightly and bid her monkeys to mingle with my slaves. The pale, round minions and the lean hairy ones crouched among the rocks and began grooming each other.

As the party kicked back into gear, I thought about the plane leaving the next day at dawn, and about the person who would be on it. I thought about going back to my life in Allentown, to an empty house full of medical equipment that my family no longer needed, to a potentially half-full or even empty carrot cupcake container, to my small, lonely life.

And then I thought about staying here, on the island, and stepping fully into the New Me.

Looking out at my slaves, I knew exactly which life I was going to choose. I dragged Molly's corpse out from the stalagmites and whistled powerfully (I'm *whistling* now? *Cool beans!*) over to Missy.

"Bone saw," I growled, my eyes twin pools of liquid steel. Missy nodded and tossed it over.

This time, the work went much faster. I chopped up Molly's body and split the meat between my monkey and human minions, who gobbled it up noisily. I gave Missy the liver, and the big monkey the spleen. When I got to the heart, I removed it carefully and padded over to the ice sculpture, where I placed it in a bowl and dressed it with spicy mayo, avocado cubes, and crispy shallots: the ultimate build-your-own poké bowl.

As I settled into my throne, I thought about sharing it with Fernando, or my new monkey sister. But that wouldn't be right. This was a treat that should be consumed only by the rightful birthday girl.

After all, I thought, bringing a juicy red chopstick-full to my lips: there can only be one.

My Dearest Caroline

3 September 1861, Fairfax

My Dearest Caroline,

The general has indicated we will move tomorrow, and it is widely believed that the fighting will be fierce. Their force is rumored to be superior both in training and in number. While I still nurse hope that God and Providence will allow me to return home to you, I feel compelled to write a few lines now, in case it is not to be. My sweet Caroline, you have been a model wife and mother in all ways. And it is out of respect for our union that I must confess something to you now: I have not always been faithful. You have, however, always been my greatest love and I beg you to forgive me my indiscretions.

Please live a long life and raise our son Josiah to fear
God.

Your ever loving,

Abraham

5 September 1861, Fairfax

My Dearest Caroline,

Hallelujah! My sweet one, can you believe it? I am alive!
It is nothing short of a miracle. I do not want to worry
you unduly, but it is only by God's grace that I write to
you today.

The battle was indeed fierce. We defended our line for
nearly three hours under heavy fire. Bullets whizzed by
me and my uniform was shot through! Yet somehow I es-
caped without so much as a scratch.

About that "faithful" remark. I hope you did not mis-
understand. I simply meant that I haven't always been
faithful in the sense that, several times when away on
business, I allowed colleagues to persuade me to visit
dancing-halls, where I drank, and occasionally danced.
Nothing more. In any case, I tarry too long on this unremarkable topic.

All my love to you and to my dearest boy, our beloved
son Josiah.

Your ever loving,

Abraham

7 September 1861, Fairfax

My Dearest Caroline,

Our situation has darkened. The general has called for a
surprise strike on the enemy's flank, but we are severely
outnumbered and are not due to receive enforcements
for several days. Still, we've been ordered to ready ourselves for the signal to move, which could sound at any
time. The odds are grim, dearest, and I fear the worst. I
must make this brief.

Caroline, you have been my rock. And you deserve to
know all. My dearest one, I have lain with other women.
But they didn't mean anything. It was just sex. As I hear
my fellow soldiers readying their weapons, I must also
tell you this: one of those women was your sister Ade-
laide. Never in our bed, dearest! I have kept that place sacred. Never in a bed at all, actually. Closets, mainly. If it
was nice out, a gazebo. Once in a sleigh. But, my darling,
know that you were always foremost in my thoughts.
Not during the act itself, but you understand what I
mean.

There—the signal! Oh, dearest one, please, forgive me
my many faults. Yes, I am flawed, but I adore you above
all else and still implore you to raise our son Josiah to
love the Lord and fear Him.

I will await you in heaven, if the Almighty One sees fit
to admit me there.

Your ever loving,

Abraham

P.S. When I said "sister," I meant "sisters."

8 September 1861, Fairfax

My Dearest Caroline,

Hello.

How are you? I hope you are well. I myself am doing very well. Still alive, which is certainly unexpected, but great. I hope our son Josiah is also well.

Oh, I almost forgot. This might sound random, but if you haven't opened my last letter yet, don't even bother. You see, the strangest thing happened last night. Before we even got the signal to decamp and head to our next battle, a horde of wild Indians broke into camp. You think Yankees are bad! These men were frightening to behold. They ran around with tomahawks chanting all sorts of witchy incantations and then forced us to smoke of their enchanted pipe. Crazy, right? And it gets stranger: they made us put pen to paper and write— I think to keep us distracted while they robbed us. Well, we all wrote letters, but we were addled by the redskins' pipe and recorded the most bizarre ramblings. I have no recollection of what I penned, but I assure you it was full of fantastical, drug-addled ravings and you should throw it promptly in the fire.

Anyway, I continue to love you very much. Remember that restaurant we went to last summer for your birthday? That was a great time, wasn't it? We will do it again for your next birthday. And this time we'll . . . stay at an inn overnight! Wouldn't that be enjoyable?

Hug Josiah for me.

Your loving,

Abraham

14 September 1861, Fairfax

My Dearest Caroline,

This is the end. I have been shot and am bleeding out at the bottom of a ditch. All is lost, dearest. Yet, in my final moments on this earth, thinking of your face brings me comfort.

Here's when I hit rock bottom: June 25th, 1859. I was at the office, as I called it in those days—Madame Xi's opium den. But that day, in the back room, it wasn't a pipe they were passing around. It was me. I had a cock in my hand and another in my mouth. I hadn't yet looked at the boy I was sucking off, but when my eyes rolled back in a moment of dope-addled ecstasy, I saw he resembled our young Josiah. And that's when I realized: I was so high, I wouldn't even know it if I was sucking off my own son.

Your father saw me when I stumbled into the house that night, covered in the juices of other men. He said he cursed the day we married, that I wasn't fit to lick your boots, and that our son would turn out to be just as lowly as myself. Well, do you recall how I said that a horde of wild Indians broke into the house that day and killed your father? And even relieved themselves on the floor next to his body? Alas, dearest, you may divine where this is going.

My vision is fading. Darling, I am slipping. Please—live a long life. Marry, and do not wait for me in heaven. I know it is that other, hotter place for which my soul is bound.

P.S. I am fairly sure you have syphilis. You need to get that checked out immediately, my darling.

16 September 1861, Fairfax

My Dearest Caroline,

I know what you're thinking. And it's true. Miracles
abound!!!

Caroline—it is truly a wonder! I am alive, darling one!
In fact, I have even earned the nickname "Unkillable
Abe"! After the last battle, there is now a song they sing
about me in the ranks. It is set to the tune of "Yankee
Doodle Dandy."

> *Abraham a-went to battle*
>   *riding on a pony.*
> *Blades and bullets whizzed right by him,*
>   *then he fucked his pony.*

A ribald (and baseless) turn at the last line, to be sure,
but I believe the rest of the ditty captures the general
sentiment of awe surrounding my time on the battlefield.
In any case, here is the update: I was indeed shot in the
shoulder, but it was a flesh wound. My cousin Zachariah
carried me from the battlefield to the ambulance. I was
taken to a hospital in Fredericksburg and it is from my
hospital bed that I write to you now.

And you will not believe what I discovered.

Zachariah divulged it. You see, one of my fellow soldiers, a fellow named Jamison, is quite the prankster. To
pass the time, the little devil has made a habit of imper-
sonating his fellow infantrymen's handwriting and writing "prank" letters home. Apparently it is a popular
young man's game nowadays, and Jamison went to
Princeton. You know Princeton men, the brutes.

I have reported Jamison's infernal meddling to the General, and rest assured, he will be disciplined.

By the way, have you heard of "the couples cure"? Apparently, it is the latest fad in medical science. It is a treatment for married couples, whereby through simply talking, you "heal" your relationship. Some fancy city doctors cooked it up. Anyway. Perhaps it is something we should try.

Now, Caroline—my physician says that in order for me to heal, I must not receive any upsetting news. So if you can, my darling, let's please try to keep the letters upbeat.

Love,

Your still living but very weak and vulnerable,

Abraham

19 September 1861, Fairfax

To Mrs. Caroline Ellison,

It is with the deepest regret that I write to inform you of your husband's passing. He fought valiantly on the field of honor, but succumbed to his wounds this morning.

He takes his place in an esteemed line of patriots who have paid the highest price, that liberty might endure.

With deepest sympathy,

General William Barrett

22 September 1861, Fairfax

My Dearest Caroline,

I've had the most extraordinary four and twenty hours.

You are not going to believe this, but by Jove, I live! At this point, my darling, one simply has to laugh.

Apparently I was pronounced dead around dawn this morning. I can recall the priest reading me my last rites. I remember that part distinctly, because, of all places, I actually recognized the man from Madame Xi's Opium—never mind.

Darling, I know this sounds incredible, but I did die briefly. I remember rising toward the heavenly plane, and suddenly I was in the kingdom of light. You might imagine my surprise as the Lord God greeted me with outstretched hands—but he told me it wasn't my time yet, and bid me go back to the earthly realm, and to cherish my loved ones, and be a better man.

And that is exactly what I am going to do. I am coming home to you, darling! I live for the moment when we shall be reunited and I can devote myself to you as a faithful husband.

Your loving,

Abraham

P.S. While in heaven, I may have had celestial relations with one to four cherubim. I swear, darling, they only appear to be children. In point of fact, they are ageless beings and their appetites are fully mature.

The Adventure of the Mistaken Right Swipe

When I glance over the pages I've devoted to my adventures in the dating world, I'm faced with so many strange and peculiar incidents that it is difficult to select one as the most unusual. There is, however, one episode so remarkable in its particulars that it bears special mention. This strange interlude began, if I'm not mistaken, on an inclement winter's night, when my friends started bugging me to get on Smush.

You see, Tia and Steph had been riding me about getting back out there ever since I broke up with Rob, but the idea of condensing myself into a couple of pictures and a two-line bio felt gross and overwhelming. So one night they came over to my place, got bombed on Franzia, and made me a profile.

With the hard part over, I couldn't believe how easy it all was. I swiped left on the first couple of guys I saw: a guy with a crazy-long beard, and another whose pictures were all of him rock climbing. The first guy I swiped right on was this cute, academic-looking thirty-five-year-old in a tweed blazer. He was wearing a hat that was definitely "a choice," which gave me pause, and I wondered what kind of a name Holmes was. But his apartment was full of books and had a working fireplace. I decided he was at least worth meeting in person.

That Thursday we met for a drink. Right away, there were red flags. First of all, it was obvious he'd used old pics. He looked way older than thirty-five. Also, he had a friend with him, this guy Watson. Yeah. So, right away I'm like, Sorry, not my thing. But he just said, "It's not like that. He's my roommate." (So you lied about your age and you have a roommate? Jackpot.) I decided to just get the date over with, so I knuckled down, took a gulp of my drink, and asked him what he did for work. He told me he was a freelance homicide detective. I tried to keep a straight face, but he must have noticed something, because he said, "I detect . . . that you want to leave." I laughed. I mean, he was right. And it actually broke the ice. After that, I started to have a really good time.

It turns out "freelance homicide detective" actually is a job, and he's super good at it.

He told me about a few of his recent cases: one where he recovered some compromising letters for a copper heiress, and another where an earl killed his Punjabi manservant in a rage. The police hired him regularly as an expert consultant. I thought that was pretty cool. For background: my ex-boyfriend worked as a party motivator for corporate gigs and bar mitzvahs. So you can understand why I was intrigued.

By my second Aperol Spritz I was having such a blast I

was ready to suggest grabbing dinner, but all of a sudden he stood up and said he had to go meet a divorced woman about a pearl. That was a turn-on. I mean, here's a guy with real shit going on. Again, I guess that just shows how low the bar was for me at that point. Anyway, he left quickly, but Watson stayed a little longer, taking care of the check and saying that Holmes would be in touch.

The first time Holmes and I had sex, Watson was there. He was reading a book called *New Techniques in Wound Drainage,* but we made eye contact a few times.

Holmes definitely knew what he was doing. I liked how focused he was, how much he paid attention to what I was into. I told him I liked it when guys talk during sex—so when he put his mouth up to my ear, I was like, Hell yeah—but then he just told me he'd deduced that I played the cello and had once lived on a boat. He was right, and ordinarily I would have been really impressed; it's just that he was also inside me at that point. Overall, though, he was a really generous lover. Super into oral. I asked him how he was so good at it, and he replied modestly that whatever skill he had was acquired after perusing a monograph called *The Anatomy of the Pygmy Female.*

It wasn't completely smooth sailing in bed, however. Like, I'm almost sure he never came. At a certain point he'd just pull out and start taking notes. The first time, I asked him if everything was okay, and he nodded, took out a magnifying glass, and examined my vagina for forty-five minutes. But he seemed pretty happy with that.

And I tried sexting him a couple times, but we never really found a groove with it. Like, this one time, I sent him a picture of me topless—and then followed it up by texting, "Can you deduce what I'm thinking about [wink emoji]." After several minutes, he replied, "No. Any deductions drawn would rely on mere speculation." I gave him one more chance, a layup. I spread out on the couch, stuck my hand in my panties, and sent that—but he just texted back, "Based on visual evidence in your immediate environs, I deduce that you've recently mailed a letter." So that was the end of that experiment.

But as dense as he could be at times, he could also be super thoughtful and refreshingly unpredictable. He stayed ahead of you. It was exciting. Take that day when I was home sick from work. Holmes knew I was super stressed about this presentation I had to give to our investors on the West Coast, and two days before my flight, I came down with this awful flu. So, there I am at the apartment, sick as a dog, trying to work. And I get a knock on my door, and it's my super, Gabor, this old Romanian dude. He says he has to look at my kitchen sink because there's water damage on the ceiling below me. So I'm like, "Sure."

Gabor goes to the kitchen, and I stay in the living room, camped out on the couch with my laptop. A couple minutes later he comes out with a tray of steaming chicken noodle soup and I'm like, "Oh my god, Gabor, *what?* This is too kind of you!" And then he sets the tray down and starts doing this little twirl, and he keeps twirling and twirling—and it's Holmes! In a wig and some kind of nose prosthetic, and a lot of fake moles. It was extremely impressive, except that in the moment before I knew it was him, I started to scream because I was thinking, This is how I die, Gabor is going to murder me and probably eat my body.

After I stopped shaking, though, I realized that it was super sweet and spontaneous. He surprised me in other disguises, too; once, he was the sushi delivery guy, and another time he was this middle-aged Turkish electrician who actually fixed the track lighting in my hallway. Sometimes we'd even spice it up, and he'd leave the costume on. There was definitely a memorable night when I slept with a Caribbean Jehovah's Witness named Theresa— I ripped off her wig as I was riding "her," to reveal Holmes in ecstasy.

And then there was an even more memorable night, when I seduced Darvin, the cable guy. I had just assumed he was Holmes, but when I pulled his dreads, they didn't budge. I never mentioned that one to Holmes, but if he ever found out, he really couldn't blame me.

It all went up in flames when my parents came to visit. Even though the relationship was super new, things were going so well that I invited him to join us for dinner. He seemed really touched. That night, he presented me with a monograph entitled *Upon the Distinction Between the Varietals of Ink*. The dedication page said "To Sarah—a woman who needs no ink to add color," with a little smiley face. I made a big thing of displaying the book on my mantel, but honestly, I was disappointed. I mean, we've never talked about ink once. I don't have any strong feelings about ink, one way or the other. It seemed like it was just a gift for him, you know? But at that point I was just like, Cut him some slack, let's see what he does for my birthday.

In the days leading up to my parents' visit, Holmes seemed relaxed enough. But then when we were on the subway headed over to the restaurant, I could tell he was nervous. He kept fiddling with the chain of his pocket watch and tapping his pipe against his leg. He'd obviously just done a huge amount of cocaine. Did I like the drug habit? No, but again, my bar was low. Anyway, when we got out at Christopher Street, he abruptly announced that he had to go work on something.

"What is it this time, babe?" I straightened his scarf and kissed him on the cheek. "A pearl?"

"No," he said, his wheels turning, clearly buying time. "It's . . . the Case of the Amber Brooch."

"Nice try. You solved that one last week. Don't you remember telling me about it at Sweetgreen? The boatswain did it."

He reddened. "Ah. Quite so, quite so." He took out a handkerchief and dabbed his forehead. "I'm kind of really fucking high right now."

"It'll be fine," I said, squeezing his hand. "They're going to love you."

We walked over to Ladle and Fork, a quiet farm-to-table restaurant I'd found in the West Village, and saw my parents seated at the far end of a communal table. My dad excitedly waved us over, then gave us bear hugs as my mom clapped her hands in delight. She leaned into Holmes conspiratorially. "So. You're the mysterious Holmes!"

Holmes was sweating. A lot. I tugged his scarf playfully, and gave his knee a reassuring squeeze. He didn't answer, so I chimed in. "Yup!"

My dad gestured to the line of strangers seated alongside us at the table. "I guess these one-big-table places are pretty hip right now, huh? In my day we used to call this a soup kitchen!"

My mom elbowed him playfully. "Oh, Rich."

"I'm just saying, if this is what you're into, there's a Salvation Army three blocks away. You could save me a lot of cash!"

"It's elementary: you had a homosexual relationship in college," Holmes began, his eyes trained intensely on my father. "Your brother died in an automobile accident and you have a secret family with a JetBlue flight attendant named Natasha."

My parents stared at Holmes. My mom looked down and started fiddling with the fringe on her blazer.

"The fuck are you doing?" I hissed into Holmes's ear.

Holmes trained his eyes on me, visibly concentrating as he spoke slowly and deliberately.

"It's elementary: you're mad at me for the things I just said about your father," he began.

I turned to my parents and tried to laugh off the moment. "Sorry, guys. I guess he's just nervous. That's insane!"

But no one joined me in my laughter. My dad took a somber sip of beer, and my mom was staring down at the table, suddenly looking really tired. Finally, my dad spoke.

"Natasha has advanced Lyme disease," he said. "Having a child certainly wasn't the plan. I tried to break it off, but when she got pregnant, it made her feel like she finally had something to live for." He looked away then, trying not to cry.

We sat in silence while I waited for him to say "Just kidding." When that didn't happen, I swiveled over to my mom.

"*Mom?*"

She grabbed my hand and squeezed it. "No marriage is perfect, honey."

I couldn't believe what I was hearing. I looked around the restaurant at the other diners, who were still laughing, talking, enjoying their evenings. That's when I noticed Watson sitting at the end of the table reading a treatise on the properties of ether. We made eye contact, and I mouthed "bathroom." He nodded.

He was waiting for me inside the handicap stall, which had a little sink. I grabbed onto the porcelain and stared hard at my reflection in the mirror. "This was such a huge mistake."

Watson pulled me in for a hug. I sobbed into his shoulder. "My dad has a secret family. With a woman who has advanced Lyme disease."

"Even late-stage Lyme can be treated with antibiotics," he murmured, swaying us gently. "As long as it's given intravenously, Natasha has the same shot at survival as—"

"I don't care about Natasha's fucking survival!" I yelled, breaking out of the embrace. I turned on the faucet, bent over, and splashed some water on my face. Watson stroked my back soothingly. Finally, I grabbed a handful of paper towels and dried off.

"This is just a lot to take in, you know?"

Watson nodded. "I know."

Just then, a woman stepped out of the middle stall. I couldn't see her, but she sounded older, and I could see she was wearing orthopedic dress shoes.

"I've lived with Lyme for twenty-nine years," she began. "And let me tell you, it hasn't been a picnic. But with the help of my medical team and family, I've flourished. With the right treatment, so can your friend." We were silent as the woman washed her hands quietly and left.

I turned to Watson in despair. "Well, what the hell am I supposed to do now? This night is beyond fucked."

Watson sighed. "Just give him a chance. I've never seen

him as nervous as he was on the way here. He obviously really likes you, he's just spectrum-y."

"Yeah, but I didn't think he actually had autism."

"Are you serious? The guy has an encyclopedic knowledge of blood spatters but he doesn't even know you love *Frasier*."

I laughed. "How do you know I love *Frasier*?"

"You always put it on when you're getting ready for bed. And when you laugh, you get this little dimple in your right cheek."

There was an awkward pause as the implications of that sunk in, but frankly, I didn't have the bandwidth to deal with it.

"Anyway," I said. "This is a disaster. I mean, I'm thirty-two. If my dad has a secret family, at this point I don't even want to know."

He nodded sympathetically. "Totally. But, look, Holmes's relationships *never* last long enough to meet the parents. He's just new at this. He's trying to impress them, and he's stumbling."

I zhuzhed my hair in the mirror, trying to get ahold of myself, then remembered. "Hey, do you have a tampon?" I asked.

"I do, actually," he said, reaching into his vest and handing one over.

When I got back to the table, Holmes was gone.

"Your friend went outside for a pipe," my mom said. My dad's eyes were red. He had obviously been crying.

"I'm sorry," he muttered. "You have a half sister. Her name is Madeleine and she's eight and she wants to be a biologist."

My parents and I sat in silence for a few minutes. Then Holmes rushed back into the restaurant, carrying his violin. He leaned into my ear. "I'm cleaning this up," he whispered, touching the bow to the strings. "Trust me."

Holmes started playing the familiar, doleful melody that I recognized as Wagner's *Faust Overture,* the music he put on during sex.

My parents listened politely, but it was obviously getting him nowhere, and he knew it. When he got to the second movement, he put down the instrument and ran a hand through his hair.

"Great Scott!" he said, feigning inspiration. "I've just realized a flaw in my deduction: Mr. Weinbaum, you *don't* have a secret family. So it follows that you didn't have a homosexual relationship in college, and you're not seventy thousand dollars in the hole for your colonial coin addiction."

The mom of the family next to us at the communal table perked up. "You didn't say anything about a colonial coin addiction the first time."

Holmes loosened his scarf and visibly gulped.

My mom glared. "So *that's* why I couldn't get the loan for my catering business?"

My dad was staring at a groove in the table, silently imploding. Finally, he lifted his head. "I am not in control," he said, his voice unsteady. "And I need help."

He bit his lip, on the verge of more tears. I reflexively looked away and hated myself for it. Jesus. What the hell were we all going to talk about *now*? I had a hundred questions about my dad's second family, about the emotional toll that had taken on my mom, on him. How often did he see my half sister? And where the hell was he holding $70,000 worth of colonial coins? I was emotionally over-whelmed.

"You guys watch *Succession*?" Holmes asked.

My mom picked an olive from the little bowl our wait-ress had set down a while ago. A few beats passed in si-lence. He continued.

"Took a while to warm up, but once it got going, hoo boy."

"I think you should leave," my mom said, finally look-ing at him again.

"Quite," Holmes said, clearly hurt but trying to play it off. "Quite. I'll see you soon," he said to me, giving me a peck on the cheek. Then he grabbed his phone, swung on his cape, and walked quickly out of the restaurant.

To my parents' credit, once Holmes was actually gone, they looked at each other and, God bless them, laughed a little. Man, that was a relief. I even joined in. I mean, I was still shell-shocked from The News, and of course it was depressing that my "boyfriend" turned out to be a disas-ter. I'd obviously have to end things. But I could already see that this night was going to make an epic story.

My dad rubbed my mom's back, and when the waitress came by a little later and started reading off the specials, we actually listened. It felt sort of insane to stay and eat, but at the same time, we were hungry, so what the hell. When I asked if she could repeat the risotto special, she suddenly started to sputter and cough—then doubled over, hacking up something. My dad moved behind her to give her the Heimlich, but then she threw off her scarf and stood up tall. Holmes was wearing another nose pros-thetic and a lot of foundation—he had disguised himself as a thirtysomething Korean woman—but it was clearly him. I looked over at Watson, who was motioning for his check and giving off a very clear "don't involve me" vibe.

My parents just stared. A young Asian American couple who happened to be seated farther down the table stared, too. "Not cool," the husband said.

"A fair conclusion," Holmes replied, wiping at his face with a napkin. "But entirely immaterial to its effectiveness as a disguise."

"What the hell is wrong with you?" I shouted, finally losing it. I'm really not one to make a scene. I'm not a big yeller. So I think it was scary for Holmes to see me go to eleven. I was disgusted. Mainly with myself, for making such a rookie mistake. How could I introduce my parents to a guy I had just started seeing a month ago? What kind of move was that?

And what the hell was he trying to do with the waitress bit? It was all pouring out of me now. "Yellow face? *Yellow face* will make it better?"

Now it was his turn to lose it. His face got all splotchy, and he slammed his hands into the table. "What is this, a seminar at fucking Oberlin?" My parents looked at me then like, Whoa, we hope you aren't serious with this person. Holmes pulled back quickly and wiped some more makeup off his face with the back of his jacket. "Sorry. Sorry. That's not me," he muttered. My dad started peeling bills out of his wallet and tossed a few on the table. Holmes nodded back toward the kitchen: "So, should I put in the risotto for you?" I stared at him as he refilled our waters. My parents were already standing, holding their coats.

I turned to my mom. "How about I meet you guys for

breakfast at the hotel?" They nodded, and I motioned for the check.

In the cab home, as I watched Holmes dart out at a red light to collect a soil sample from a nearby flower bed, I reflected on our time together. Yes, we had fun when it was just the two of us. Or, rather, when it was just me and "Theresa, the Jehovah's Witness" or when "Mayor de Blasio" came canvassing door to door. But that wasn't enough to keep a relationship going. I don't want to be with someone that I have to take care of in a group. If a simple dinner with my parents was too much for him to handle, the writing was on the wall.

As we got closer to my building, Holmes casually mentioned that he'd been reading more monographs on the anatomy of the Pygmy female—that's how oblivious he was to the damage he'd done. When we got to my place I told him I just wanted to be alone.

The next morning I texted him that we'd jumped into everything too soon, that I needed more time to get over my ex. I wish he'd written back something weird, to make it easier, but all he texted was "I understand." I offered to bring his stuff back—the monograph on inks, some of his wigs, a napkin where he'd written "warships of the future" with a bunch of diagrams—but he said I was welcome to keep them. I threw them out that day.

Sometimes Holmes texts me, just to stay in touch, I guess. Usually they're deductions. On my birthday he deduced that I'd had a good time at ABC Cocina—which I assume he saw on my Instagram. Once, he just texted "pearl handle," which was weird. Was he reminding me of our first date? Or did he mean to send that to someone else?

I haven't seen Holmes since, but I did end up going on one date with Watson. It was weird. First of all, he's married. I had no idea. He said keeping it open is the best thing they ever did for their sex life, which was a lot to dump on me on a first date. The other thing was, without Holmes there, we didn't have a lot in common. We just ended up talking about his knee surgeries. He's had like nine of them.

Monster Goo

Zack Mercer pulled his Knicks cap low over his floppy blond hair and shot a basketball at the hoop in his driveway. It hit the backboard with a *thwack* and bounced off into the grass. Zack scowled as he dragged his sneakers across the pavement to retrieve it, his favorite song blaring from his boom box.

Welcome to the Space Jam
Here's your chance, do your dance at the Space Jam
Alrightalrightalright

Zack was in a bad mood. He'd found a note from his mom on the kitchen table saying she might be home late, which meant he'd have to babysit his little sister, Meezy.

"Yuck!" Zack had said out loud. His mom, Cindy, was a real drill sergeant. She was used to bossing people around in her law firm, and when she came home, Zack thought she liked to boss him around just for fun!

Come on and slam, and welcome to the jam!
Come on and slam, if you want to jam!

Meezy was so annoying. She was loud. She was weird looking, with frizzy blond hair that made it look like she'd just stuck her finger in a light socket. And to top it all off, she was always doing these stupid science experiments in their basement.

Zack missed another basket. He was pretty bad at sports—unlike Seth, his tall, athletic best friend. Girls always giggled around Seth, but they didn't even look at Zack. Zack groaned as he jogged over to get the ball. Just then, Meezy burst out of the screen door and ran over to him, holding a big bowl of grape Jell-O. She was wearing her cherry-red high-tops, pink shorts, an oversized orange T-shirt, and Zack's favorite Knicks cap—the one he saved for game days.

"Take that off!" Zack shouted as he ran over and tried to grab the hat off his sister's head. Meezy darted away, causing her to spill some of the Jell-O. It fell onto the driveway with a loud *plop*.

Zack scrunched up his face like he was grossed out, but really, he was scared. The jiggly mess on the pavement reminded him of something Meezy had concocted during one of her stupid experiments. She'd called it "monster goo"—and the sticky purple slime seemed to have a mind of its own.

Zack shuddered as he thought back to that afternoon.

Meezy had had the bright idea to feed Corduroy, the family cat, a tiny dollop of the goo. Within seconds, the animal had grown into a huge, slobbering beast. It had chased Zack all around the living room and almost eaten him alive before Meezy stabbed it with a kitchen knife dipped in "shrinking juice"—another one of her crazy inventions. Instantly, Corduroy had returned to normal size, and their parents were never the wiser. But Zack still had nightmares about the day Meezy made that purple goo.

"My experiment!" Meezy shrieked as Zack finally grabbed his Knicks hat. Then she stomped her foot. "Why can't you *share?*" Zack tucked the cap into the waistband of his shorts, turned on his heel, and shot another basket. It missed the hoop by a foot.

Drop it, rock it, down the room
Shake it, quake it, space kaboom—

The music cut out suddenly as Meezy punched the power button on Zack's boom box.

"Ha-ha!" Meezy squealed. Boy, she really was annoying.

"Whatever," Zack grumbled. He was tired of missing baskets anyway. "I'm going inside for a snack."

Zack turned and jogged to the back porch, opening the rusty screen door with a loud *creeaaakkk*.

He headed for the pantry, where he found a new bag of Fritos—his favorite. Meezy followed close behind, yipping at his heels.

"Wanna play checkers? Wanna play Sega? Wanna build a fort?"

Zack poured a big pile of chips into a bowl. "Here's a

game for you, Meezy." He popped a chip into his mouth. "Solitaire!"

Meezy stuck her tongue out at Zack. "Fine! Then I'm going to make pudding and you're not getting a spoonful!" Meezy darted off toward the pantry.

Zack shrugged. "Knock yourself out." But as he glanced after her, his eyes widened.

It couldn't be . . . but . . . it *was*!

There, behind her, a hairy black monster was rising up.

"Meezy! Watch out!" Zack shouted.

But then something strange happened. The monster started . . . giggling!

"Gotcha!" Seth yelled as he pulled off the King Kong mask he'd been wearing.

Zack let out a big sigh of relief.

Seth laughed. "Isn't it dope? It's my Halloween costume!" Seth looked at the mask proudly. He was wearing black Converse sneakers, a backward Yankees cap, baggy brown shorts, and a neon-green T-shirt.

"That wasn't funny, Seth!" Zack said.

"I thought it was pretty funny!" Meezy giggled. "Hey, Seth, I'm making pudding! Want some?"

"Sounds rad." Seth shrugged, sticking his hand in Zack's chip bowl. But then he raised his eyebrows at Zack. "Hey. Isn't pudding a lot like . . ." He lifted his arms up, zombie-style. *"Monster goooooo?"*

Zack shuddered. "Don't even say that."

The boys went back out to the driveway to shoot hoops, leaving Meezy alone in the kitchen. Seth dribbled around Zack and made an easy layup. "Hey. Is your dad still giving you a dollar for every A you get on your report card?"

Seth was jealous of Zack's deal with his dad, Neil. Zack was saving up for a banana-yellow Sony Sports Walkman, and he only needed seven more A's before he'd have enough to go to the mall and pick it out. Zack knew Seth thought Neil was kind of a nerd—he was a doctor who worked at the university, looking for cures for cancer—but that it was cool how he always helped Zack get the newest gadgets.

Zack nodded, grinning. "Yup. And I've been studying for Mrs. Manley's algebra test all week. If I ace that, hel-looooo, Walkman!" He picked up the basketball and stepped back to take a shot.

Seth snatched the ball and did some fancy dribbling. "Whatever. You can listen to your Walkman—while I take Chrissy to the dance!"

Zack scowled. Chrissy was his crush—or at least, he liked talking to Chrissy. She was funny. So he guessed that counted as a crush. The thing was, girls usually never talked to Zack. Girls liked Seth, because he was tall, and funny, and good at sports. And good-looking. Zack looked at Seth as he dribbled the ball around the driveway, at his sunburned nose, the muscles working in his golden forearms, his look of concentration as he sank the basketball with a neat *swish*. Zack felt the tickly feeling in his stomach that sometimes bubbled up, like, *bloopbloop*, when he was with Seth, but he smooshed the feeling down deep inside.

Meanwhile, in the kitchen, Meezy stirred the pudding mix and milk in a big bowl until it was thick and gloppy. Then she paused. A mischievous grin crept over her face, and she ran down to the basement—to her lab.

Outside, Seth shouted, "Nothin' but net!" as he sank

another basket. He hoisted one triumphant fist in the air. "Did you see that? It was dope!"

"Lucky shot," Zack said.

"Pudding's ready!" Meezy called. She ran outside smiling, holding a big, jiggly bowl. Only . . . something was wrong with the pudding. It looked like it was . . . growing!

Zack's eyes narrowed, then grew big with fear. "Meezy . . . that pudding doesn't look right."

Seth laughed. "What, you're scared of a little pudding? Come on, Zack!" Seth strode over to Meezy and the bowl of weirdo pudding and grabbed a handful of it, throwing a big gloppy fistful of the stuff right in Zack's face. "Nothin' but net!"

Zack Mercer felt the wet goo hit his face with a sickening *thlupp!* Sputtering, he wiped it out of his eyes and spit it out of his mouth as fast as he could. But it was too late.

He felt his heart start to pound. And then his head. His muscles felt achy, and he got a tingly feeling all over his skin. He closed his eyes and felt a breeze start to whip around his body. It sounded like his bones were going *pop* and his insides were pushing against his skin, making it feel tight, tight, tight! When he opened his eyes again, he heard some faint, tinny voices shouting his name. He looked around, but all he saw was the roof of his house and the treetops. Then he looked down and saw Seth and Meezy. They were so small—as small as Corduroy!

Seth and Meezy looked up at Zack in wonder.

Seth shouted at him. "Holy cow, Zack—you're huge!"

Zack wiped his face and stared in horror at the monster goo on his hand. Then he looked down again. Holy cow! he thought. I must be fifty feet tall!

Zack felt panic start to build inside him. He spotted Meezy way down there on the lawn, staring up at him with her frizzy dumb hair flying.

"Meezy! What have you done?" Zack bellowed. *"How could you make more monster goo?"*

Meezy squeaked up at him. She looked scared. "Zack, I'm sorry! Don't worry! I can make the shrink juice!"

Zack sat on the ground and cried—his tears falling in big bucketfuls on his naked chest and thighs. He had burst right through his clothes, and now they were lying around him in little ribbons!

Seth climbed up onto a fence and shouted to him.

"Don't cry, buddy," Seth shouted. "We'll fix you!"

But Zack Mercer kept crying. It was scary being so big. "If we don't get me normal sized again, Mom's gonna *kill* me!"

Seth slapped his hand over his forehead. "Cindy is gonna *freak!*"

"This is really bad," Zack wailed. "I'm big! I'm big and I'm naked!"

"Hey! Look on the bright side!" Seth shouted. "Now you can probably make the team!"

Seth threw the basketball up at Zack. It hit Zack's palm, and he just closed his hand over it, then dropped the ball into the hoop like a coin into a slot. It was so easy!

"That was kind of fun," Zack said, wiping some tears off his huge cheek.

"Do another one!" Meezy shrieked.

And Zack did. He dropped in a couple more baskets, and even yelled, "Nothin' but net!" as Seth and Meezy covered their ears. His voice was so loud!

"Wait 'til Coach Harvey sees you at school!" Seth yelled.

School. Zack's stomach did a flip-flop. If Zack couldn't get normal sized again, he couldn't even *fit* in his school. And if he couldn't go to school, he'd miss his tests this week. And then he wouldn't make A's on his report card—which meant one thing: bye-bye, Walkman!

Zack's head whipped around as he heard Cindy's black car snaking up the driveway. She parked the car and got out. Cindy was wearing a gray pantsuit, a blue silk scarf, and pearl earrings. She was carrying a couple of pizza boxes and a briefcase. When she saw her giant, naked son sitting on her front lawn, she dropped the pizzas and the briefcase. Papers flew out and the pizza pies plopped down with a yucky *thwuccck!*

Cindy and Zack locked eyes in terror.

Cindy Mercer stared out over the frozen lake, took a deep drag on her vape pen, and blew it out with a *whoosh*. It wasn't as good as a menthol, but Cindy was used to making do with pale comparisons. Giving up cigarettes was the least of the sacrifices she'd had to make in the last three years. Ever since Zack ate the monster goo.

Cindy was wearing blue jeans, a big gray sweatshirt, and an extra thirty pounds. She didn't go in to the office anymore. Now she took care of Zack full-time. She was an "attorney-at-large," she thought to herself. Large. Ha.

Cindy was sad all the time, and she coped with food, getting up in the middle of the night to raid the fridge. She would gobble up leftover takeout or sometimes even just plain hot dog buns and Reddi-wip, if that was all she had around, like, *nyum nyum nyum*. When Cindy was eating, she wasn't thinking. And Cindy needed these little vacations from her brain, because the scary reality of her life often punched her in the stomach and made her go, *Oof!*

Zack was seventeen now. He still had the same floppy hair, and he was still a Knicks fan. But almost everything else had changed. The Mercers now lived in an airplane hangar outside of town. It was the only structure large enough to fit Zack's massive body. They'd sold their Scarsdale colonial to cover Zack's never-ending medical expenses, and tried to make the hangar into something like a home. There was a "cis-sized" kitchen, Cindy's preferred term, with a standard refrigerator. Then there was Zack's refrigerator—an eighteen-foot-deep meat locker stocked with beef sides and cases of whole chickens. Zack needed two hundred pounds of protein a day to live. *"Oink oink!"* Neil would say to his son, trying to lighten the mood as another shank bone clattered into the dumpster.

Neil, too, had reorganized his life around Zack. He'd left his job as head of pediatric oncology at White Plains Hospital and built his own home lab, to focus on his son full-time. After three years of research, he finally had a working theory of what had happened to Zack: an acid in the monster goo had triggered a benign tumor in his pituitary gland, causing a flood of growth hormone and turning him into the biggest fourteen-year-old boy ever. But for all that he'd learned, Neil was still nowhere close to finding a cure.

Meezy, meanwhile, refused to go to school, insisting on staying home and trying to make the shrink juice. Despite thousands of attempts, she'd never been able to re-create the formula. After her last failed attempt, she'd stopped talking. Her parents thought that was about erasing herself: making herself small to offset Zack's hugeness.

Cindy took another drag from her vape pen and thought about fixing herself a drink. She looked at her phone: 9:46 A.M. She had to leave soon for couples therapy. She could chew gum on the ride over, but they'd still smell the booze. More ammo for Neil.

Cindy pocketed the vape pen and headed for the family "car"—a big-rig semi. It was the only vehicle Zack could fit in. If he lay flat on his back in the trailer with his knees up against his chest, they could haul him around to his doctor and therapy appointments. Arriving at the rig, Cindy saw that Zack had already loaded himself in. She slapped the back of the truck to let him know they were about to go. As the huge wheels rolled over their gravel driveway with a satisfying *crunnnnncch,* Cindy muttered, "Fuck it," opened the glove compartment, and reached for her flask. *Glug-glug-glug.*

Zack couldn't fit inside the waiting room, so he sat outside while his parents had their counseling session. Afterwards, Cindy would take him to Costco, where she would buy parachutes to sew into T-shirts.

The accident had strained Cindy and Neil's marriage. And although Zack waited for his parents across the street, he could still hear everything coming out of the therapist's open window. His eardrums were as big as boulders!

Inside the therapist's office, Cindy grabbed a Kleenex from the box on the coffee table. The therapist was a nice older lady with short white hair, a fuzzy peach sweater, and glasses that hung on a zebra chain. Her voice was gentle. "When was the last time you had sex?"

Cindy looked down at her hands. Neil cleared his throat. "I've, uh, had trouble performing. Since the monster goo."

Zack reached for his banana-yellow Walkman, desperate to drown out what he was hearing. His father had given it to him as a cheer-me-up gift that first week in the hospital. But in his current state, the Walkman was actually quite hard for Zack to operate. His huge fingers couldn't help but mash multiple buttons at once, and the normal-human-sized headphones were tiny next to the cavern of his ear canal. Zack carefully pressed Play and turned the volume on the Walkman all the way up. He knew it wouldn't do much, but it was worth a shot.

"Do you still touch each other? Hold each other, kiss . . . ?" the therapist asked.

"I've tried," Cindy said. "We've tried. It's just that, well, every time, Neil, um . . ."

"Well, thanks, Cindy. I guess it's all my fault."

"Come on. I didn't mean it like—"

"No, no, it's all Neil's fault. Neil can't make the goo come out of his monster!"

Zack pressed the Walkman hard against his ear and shut his eyes. He didn't even notice when Seth rode up on his bike and joined him.

A moment later Neil's voice could be heard shouting through the open window.

"I can't help my son! I can't talk to my daughter! I can't even fuck my wife!"

Seth shook his head. "Man, that does not sound rad."
Zack scrunched his eyes closed and focused on the music.

Wave your hands in the air if you feel fine
We're gonna take it into overtime
Welcome to the Space Jam
Here's your chance do your dance at the Space Jam—

Seth still hung out with Zack all the time. He said it was just because they were friends, but Zack knew the truth: he felt responsible for what had happened to Zack. After all, Seth was the one who threw the monster goo in Zack's mouth. It was an accident, sure, but still. Seth seemed pretty surprised that Zack still wanted to talk to him at all! But Zack didn't hold it against Seth. Seth was the only friend who still hung out with him, and Zack was happy to have him around. Also, Zack still got that fluttery feeling in his stomach whenever he was with Seth. And even when he wasn't around, when Zack just thought about Seth, at night, in his bed—an Olympic-sized pool tarp strung up between goal posts.

Zack knew he was gay. But he wasn't ready to fully own that part of himself. He couldn't be big *and* gay, he thought. His parents already had to deal with the big part! And it wasn't just the big part, either. The goo had so many side effects. Acne, constipation, epilepsy. Cindy and Neil spent most of their time arguing with health insurance companies on the phone. He couldn't lay the gay thing on them, too.

Zack's father had hooked the family computer up to a

homemade, giant-sized keypad that Zack could use to navigate the World Wide Web. The monitor fed through a projector, which beamed onto an old movie screen Neil had bought from a drive-in and set up outside for Zack. One night, Zack tapped out a question on the keyboard, then looked up at the giant screen where it appeared in fifteen-foot letters:

HOW TO STOP BEING GAY

Just then, Cindy came in driving the forklift she used to handle Zack's laundry. She looked up at the screen, then at her son.

Once again, Cindy and Zack locked eyes in terror.

Meezy walked by the train tracks behind the hangar, her frizzy blond hair floofing out in the afternoon breeze. She was wearing a black crop top, black cargo pants, a black studded collar, and black lipstick.

Seth jogged up and dribbled silently by her side for a few minutes. Finally, Meezy spoke. Seth was the only person she allowed herself to speak to.

"I feel so bad, Seth. I feel bad for what happened to Zack."

"Meezy, you were a little kid. It was *my* fault. I threw the monster goo!"

"Want to get high?" Meezy asked, taking two ecstasy pills out of her cargo pants.

"Nothin' but net," Seth said, sucking a pill off her finger.

And then they did what they often did by the train

tracks, while Zack napped and Neil worked at his lab and Cindy drank: Seth and Meezy fucked the pain away.

Seth's basketball rolled slowly away from their bodies as a train went zooming past, horns blaring. *Choooochooooo!*

Zack bit down onto his fist as Nico worked the harpoon under his skin. Nico was a really nice tattoo artist. He had a big, spiky purple mohawk and a tongue cut in two like a lizard. Zack thought he looked rad.

Nico shouted up at Zack. "Almost done with the *e*, buddy, then you're out of here."

Zack was getting "Wave your hands in the air if you feel fine" inked onto his chest. He was working his way through the entire lyrics to "Space Jam." The song had become Zack's battle cry, a positive, can-do mantra to help him face his many, ahem, *big* challenges. As soon as one line healed, Zack went to Nico to start on the next.

One lyric in particular, "Everybody get up it's time to slam now / We got a real jam goin' down," had taken on a special meaning for him.

Everybody had problems. Some small, some big. Zack's problem was certainly big. But it was time for him to figuratively "get up" and "slam," or, put another way—face his problems and deal with them energetically and head-on. Because "we got a real jam goin' down," or in other words, only one life to live, and "here's your chance"—the here and now. Zack knew he had to "slam" confidently in the direction of his dreams if he wanted to truly "jam"—live a full, happy life despite the challenges posed by his size. So what if he was gay? So what if he weighed four thousand pounds? So what if the arthritis in his hands meant he had to use a giant apparatus made of duct-taped hula hoops to masturbate? The Knicks were winning, Neil said he was getting closer and closer to a cure, and if Zack ever truly needed a rip cord, euthanasia was going to be legalized in the Netherlands any day now.

> *Get wild and lose your mind*
> *Take this thing into overtime!*

That spring, over at the lab, Neil was getting closer. So close he could taste it.

The monster goo samples he'd recovered from the lawn the day of Zack's accident had been helpful. In the past three years he'd infected hundreds of mice with "sudden-onset gigantism," the term he'd invented for what happened when you ate monster goo. He then tested his various shrink treatments on the gigantic mice. He was assisted in these trials by Seth, whose guilt drove him to help Neil in the lab whenever he could.

One night, Neil and Seth had a breakthrough. They managed to turn a teenage mouse with SOG back to normal size!

> *Alrightalrightalrightalright!*

But the treatment had several drawbacks. For one thing, the mouse died. Also, while the mouse's skin and bones did shrink back to normal size—*score!*—its organs stayed gigantic, popping out of its skeleton, tearing through its fur and shredding its genitals. *Crud.*

Seth shook his head, wiping mouse gore off his lab coat.

He trudged over to his computer, logged the details of the subject's grisly death, and, with a frustrated sigh, assigned an SNR rating to that particular treatment: super not rad.

Neil grabbed his baseball bat and lab goggles in a huff and stalked away to the storage room, which his assistants kept stocked with a stream of Salvation Army desks, chairs, and old computer monitors. Destruction sessions in his pain palace helped Neil channel his fury without hurting himself or others.

As Neil raged, his bat crashing down on the furniture with ear-splitting *crrrraaack*s, Seth grabbed his basketball and dribbled distractedly, already troubleshooting the next antidote.

Cindy made eye contact with the scruffy blond guy in the AA meeting. He was just a kid. Twenty, twenty-five, tops. He kind of reminded her of Seth.

He glanced toward the bathroom.

After the meeting, she found him waiting for her in the last stall.

Cindy reached for his belt.

When Cindy was eating, she wasn't thinking. *Glug-glug-glug.*

In the beginning, there had been so much interest in Zack's case. Anderson Cooper had spent three full days living with the family for a special on CNN. The Obamas produced a six-episode Netflix documentary about Zack's disease, and Michael Bloomberg made a million-dollar contribution to the GoFundMe that was set up to cover

Zack's medical costs. There was even an offer for Zack to walk in the Macy's Thanksgiving Day Parade.

Then there were the other offers. Offers that Zack's parents never wanted him to know about. Zack heard them whispering about them in their bedroom at night. He couldn't help it. Those pesky eardrums picked up everything.

"You wouldn't believe the one I got today," Cindy said angrily as she tore up yet another letter. "They offered a million dollars for Zack to have sex with a whale. How do you even do that?"

"A million dollars, huh?" Neil said.

"I mean, really—what would that even look like!"

"Yeah." He nodded. But Cindy didn't like the faraway look in his eyes.

The whale offer wasn't even the craziest one. There were offers for Zack to have sex with a car wash. Offers for Zack to have sex with the Dallas Cowgirls. One offer that read, simply, "Gulliver's Anal Travels." And one from Bahrain that offered eight figures: "Giant Troll Fills Giant's Hole."

The Mercers ignored them all.

But as Zack's medical expenses piled up, deleting the emails and voicemails became harder and harder.

One night, when Neil brought Seth home for dinner—Thai takeout for the "cis folks" and a sixty-quart cooler of venison for Zack—Cindy climbed onto the hydraulic cherry picker they used when they wanted to speak with their son at eye level. There was an energy in Cindy's voice that hadn't been there in years. It sounded like when she used to try out her closing statements for Neil, back when she still took cases to trial.

"Who wants a little hors d'oeuvre?" she called out cheerily.

Cindy was holding something behind her back. Meezy and Zack exchanged worried looks and tried to figure out what it was as Cindy rose higher and higher in the air.

"What's going on, Cind?" Neil called up to his wife.

"I've figured it out. I've figured it out!" Her cheeks were flushed, like they got when she'd been drinking. She looked down at her family. Neil, Seth, and Meezy were in cis-sized chairs, and Zack was sitting on a hill they'd had carved into an ergonomic, chairlike design. She took her hands from behind her back and held up a mixing bowl. It was filled with something like rice pudding. Rice pudding that was—moving?

Neil jumped back. "Christ, Cindy, is that—"

"Monster goo!" She held the bowl high over her head. "See, if we eat the monster goo, we'll *all* be big. And we can be big together. We can be a family again!"

"Under the table!" Neil screamed at the kids. Meezy and Seth dived underneath the dining room table. Zack stood up and backed away in fear.

Using a takeout container to shield his head, Neil shouted up at his wife.

"Cindy. *Please*. Put that down right—"

"Don't you see, Neil? The goo is the way!" And then Cindy dropped her head back, opened her mouth, and started tipping the bowl over her head.

"Mom, don't!" Zack yelled—scared and frozen to the spot.

Neil sprang into action, diving for the cherry picker's hydraulic arm. He body-slammed into it with an *"Arghhhh!"*—causing the platform to lurch and the bowl to fall out of Cindy's hands. It clattered to the ground, and the monster goo plopped out with an icky *gloooop*—but only onto the concrete floor. *Phew!*

Underneath the table, Meezy was sobbing. Seth wrapped her in a hug and held her tight.

Neil kicked the bowl across the concrete floor. *Scrrrr!*

Cindy scrambled off the cherry picker and made a dash for the spilled goo, but Neil blocked her path.

"Cindy. What the hell are you *doing*?!"

"I'm eating this fucking goo, and I'm living life with my son."

Neil shook her. "You have a daughter. What about her? What about me?"

Cindy looked pained and hung her head. Her hair fell over her face, making her seem younger, helpless. She sniffed. "We all have to eat the goo."

Neil pulled Cindy in close, rocking her back and forth. *"Shhhh. Shhhh.* It's okay. It's okay." Zack, Meezy, and Seth looked on as Cindy broke down, sobbing with an abandon that scared them.

"Zack's gone. Meezy's gone. You're gone . . ."

"I'm right here, Cindy," Neil said, pulling her in tightly and putting his mouth on her ear, through her hair. "I'm right here."

Zack needed another bone marrow transplant. A transplant for someone Zack's size required so much marrow, it was like paying for a thousand regular-sized transplants.

The Mercers didn't have the money. But if he didn't have the operation, Zack would totally die.

Cindy and Neil had mortgaged the hangar three times, and the GoFundMe had dried up long ago. They were desperate for cash. The time had come to talk to Zack about the Offers.

Neil sat down at his computer, opened his email, and forced himself to type a word into the search bar: "Troll."

Then he hooked his computer monitor up to Zack's movie screen so he could read the email subject heading for himself.

Zack sat down on his tarp, and Cindy and Neil climbed onto the cherry picker. They could see Zack's enormous lips moving as he read the subject heading silently to himself. He looked confused, and turned to his parents. "Am I the hole?"

Cindy and Neil locked eyes in terror.

Meezy walked along the rail of the train tracks, dipping her foot down and skimming it as close to the ties as she could get without touching. It was a dumb game she liked to play. She liked that she could do it alone. Meezy liked being alone.

A train whistled behind her, and she jumped off the tracks and walked beside it as it rushed past. If a train ran over her, she'd get smooshed. And then she'd be small. So small that she wouldn't matter.

Meezy thought back to that bad afternoon. In a way, they had all eaten the monster goo. Because they had all turned into freaks. Cindy used to be so elegant, so powerful and strong. Now she was a sloppy drunk. Neil was like a mean caricature of the dad she once knew. In a funny way, Zack was the only one who hadn't turned into a scary monster. He was still so gentle and sweet. It was just that now, when he went to the bathroom, he had to do it in a landfill that Neil and Cindy had zoned off behind the hangar.

Meezy thought about going to the lab and waiting for Seth. Sometimes they used the room where her dad beat the crap out of stuff. She'd gotten a few splinters in her back the last time. Seth had picked them out for her, then dabbed the tiny puncture wounds with peroxide. It burned, but the pain made her feel clean.

But Meezy didn't turn back to the lab. She just kept walking, toward nothing. She pulled a pill out of her pocket.

Choooo chooooooo.

Seth was there later that night when the squad car lights flickered on the bifold hangar door. The policemen were holding their hats in their hands, just like in the movies. Zack fell to his knees with a thud, causing the hangar to shake like a leaf.

Seth comforted Zack at the funeral, holding his basketball respectfully still under one arm. He put his hand on Zack's calf as they approached the casket. Cindy and Neil had fought about whether or not to leave the casket open. Cindy wanted it open—to show everyone "what the world did to my beautiful daughter." Neil had called Cindy a ghoul and slept out on the cherry picker that night. In the end, Neil had won, and the casket stayed closed.

Zack felt hot tears rushing down his face as he laid his

best Knicks cap, the one he saved for game days, on the casket. His big tears fell onto the shiny wood with a *splatch, splatch, splatch.* He loved his little sister, who was now gone forever. He loved his best friend. He wanted to kiss his best friend. Aw, come on! Zack thought. Stop being gay. Stop being gay in front of your dead sister, you big, dumb monster boy!

That night, Zack asked Seth if he would sleep over. Seth snuggled into the pocket of Zack's T-shirt, and the boys fell asleep crying. Seth's tears seeped through the cotton onto Zack's chest.

In the middle of the night, Zack woke to see Seth sitting Indian-style on his sternum, staring into his eyes. Zack's huge eyeballs looked down Seth's body and saw that Seth had removed his Taxi Cab boxers.

Zack reached his pinkie out and traced Seth's nipples.

Seth's erection was visible as he crawled up Zack's torso, pushed his face up to his friend's giant ears and whispered, hoarsely but clearly, "Get the hula hoops."

Over the next eleven months, Zack starred in over sixty adult films.

Cindy insisted on accompanying her son to the set.

After a particularly not-awesome shoot where a "horny robot" (a telephone pole strapped to a tunnel-boring drill) fucked Zack until he became "part machine," Zack sat his parents down in the open field outside the airplane hangar. He had asked Seth to join them.

"I'm moving to Rotterdam," Zack told his loved ones. "I want to establish residence there so I can legally euthanize myself."

Seth slammed his basketball into the grass with an angry *"Arrrrggggh!"* Zack looked down at his best friend and felt bad. Seth had always been there for him, and he knew it felt like he was giving up on their friendship. But he had made a decision.

Neil dropped his face into his hands. Cindy just started shaking her head no. Zack pressed on.

"It took me a long time to come to a place of peace. But once I got here, I realized that this is what I want. It's what I need. It's what we all need."

Cindy broke down crying, but when Zack looked to his dad, Neil's eyes were dry. He looked broken. Actually—and this made Zack's heart ache—he thought that his father looked relieved. A part of Zack was mad about that. But another part couldn't blame his dad for wanting this nightmare to be over.

Neil reached up and rubbed his son's ankle. Cindy shook her head violently and shimmied up Zack's leg, clinging to his thigh as she wailed into it. "No, Zack. *No!* This family never talks about euthanasia again."

Zack used the tip of a pinkie finger to stroke his mother's back as she sobbed.

Zack's euthanasia was scheduled for five P.M. on his nineteenth birthday.

They decided to call the weekend a "monster life celebration," and it would just be family: Neil, Cindy, and Zack. Seth had assigned an SNR rating to Zack's decision and chose not to join them in Rotterdam, where they had Airbnb'd a circus tent to use for the final goodbye.

When the time came, Cindy, Neil, and Jan (the care-taker they had hired to administer Zack's painless, lethal drugs) gathered around Zack. Five years after getting big from the monster goo, Zack was choosing to die by assisted suicide. The medicine bags filled with poison hung on an IV stand nearby, ready to be pumped into Zack's Broviac port, the disc in his chest that would bring the life-stopping chemicals to his heart.

Suddenly, a scary monster lumbered into the circus tent.

"Whoa!" Zack yelled, pointing at the hairy black creature and shielding his parents and caretaker with his body. *"Look out—"*

But then the monster took his face off with a flourish—and it was Seth! Wearing his King Kong mask! *"Wait!"* Seth screamed, grinning, rushing into the tent and doubling over with his hands on his knees, panting, trying to catch his breath.

Zack let out a big, relieved sigh. He had to admit, the mask was still pretty dope.

Seth tossed his basketball up and spun it desperately on one finger. "I've found the cure!"

Cindy shot up from her chair as Neil swiveled toward Seth, his face frozen in disbelief.

"But the antibodies—"

"Fuck the antibodies," Seth said, triumphant, pulling out a beaker of blue liquid. "You were careful, Neil. Too careful. *Behold.* The shrink juice!"

We got a real jam going down
Welcome to the Space Jam

Zack's eyes welled up with tears. Seth's dedication was touching. The shrink juice was so tempting. But he was ready. He would not try the juice.

Except . . . what if it worked?

Here's your chance, do your dance at the Space Jam

His parents had given up their lives taking care of him. Wasn't this the only way to repay them? To give them their lives back?

Cindy walked over to Zack and squeezed a tiny part of his hand. "Don't you dare think it's too late for this."

Alrightalrightalright

Seth uncorked the beaker. Exposed to the air, the shrink juice started to bubble and hiss.

Drop it, rock it, down the room
Shake it, quake it, space kaboom

Seth thrust the blue liquid up toward his giant friend. *"Drink!"*

Zack wiped the juice from his mouth with the back of his hand, and saw his parents and Seth staring at him intensely. Waiting.

And waiting.

And *waiting*!

But nothing happened.

Finally, the tension left everyone's face. Cindy started to

sob. Neil put his arm around her, and Zack stroked her back with the tip of his pinkie knuckle. Seth looked at the empty beaker in disbelief.

Zack and Jan made eye contact, and Zack nodded. Jan bowed, and picked up the industrial squeegee he had dipped in alcohol to sterilize the skin over Zack's Broviac port.

But as Zack was walking over to the IV stand, he felt a funny feeling in his stomach. His skin started to itch. And his heart did flip-flops in his chest. All of a sudden he felt woozy. His vision went black. And then his bones felt tight—so tight—like they were squeezing back into themselves! And he felt the air on his face whoosh past as he went down, down, down!

So fast!

He was just above Neil's and Cindy's heads—and now he was looking right into their eyes! Their big, happy, tears-of-joy-filled eyes!

He was exactly at eye level with his parents! Just like he should be!

Cindy threw herself into Zack's normal-sized arms and wailed, and Neil gave him a bear hug. Seth hung a hoop on Zack's IV stand and shot a celebratory basket into it, then kissed Zack passionately on the lips. Cindy and Neil weren't upset or surprised. Instead, they just high-fived, overcome with happiness!

Seth cupped Zack's neck in his hand and brought their foreheads together to touch.

"Nothin' but *neeeeeeeeeettttttt . . .*"

But suddenly, Zack heard Seth's words coming from far away. He could see Neil screaming and Cindy jutting out her hand to grab him. . . .

Air whipped Zack's cheeks as he sank lower and lower . . . he saw the undersides of the tables and chairs . . . and then he landed on his bottom with a *thunk*.

Zack opened his eyes and saw shoes. Gigantic, hulking shoes. He looked up and saw the shoes were attached to legs . . . giant legs . . . Cindy and Neil and Seth were giants! A cockroach strolled by. It was just as tall as Zack! It paused to eat a crumb, then walked on.

Neil, Seth, and Cindy were on all fours now, their huge eyeballs staring down at him. The last thing Zack saw was Seth's face contorting in horror as he lost grip of his basketball. Cindy's and Neil's faces were terrified as they scrambled to grab it, but they were too late, and as the dark shadow of the plummeting ball grew bigger and bigger, Zack closed his eyes tight. He wished he had just let Meezy wear the dumb Knicks cap! He wished he had played Sega with her! He wished he had told Seth he loved him, that he'd told his mom that she was his best friend and his dad that he was his hero. Then he opened his mouth and sang at the top of his pin-drop lungs:

Welcome to the Space Jam!
Here's your chance, do your dance at the space jam!
Alrightalrightalrightal—

One Thousand and
One Nights

The desert moon sat high and fat in the night sky, casting an eerie glow over the magnificent domes of the sultan's palace—and also over a slightly smaller, slightly less magnificent building a couple domes away, where the sultan's vizier sat before a fire, lost in thought.

As he was the sultan's right hand, the vizier's job was to advise him on a variety of matters. Everything from affairs of state to battle strategy to which tunics were flattering for the sultan's age and build. It wasn't always easy—the sultan could be impulsive and stubborn—but the vizier performed his job well, taking pride in the stability he helped bring to the kingdom.

Now, though, he had a serious problem on his hands.

It stemmed from an unfortunate episode a few years back, when the sultan caught his then-wife cheating on him. He had popped into the royal kitchen to request a special cake for his wife's birthday and found her and the cook nude, intertwined on the kitchen floor, laughing in Allah's face as they made a mockery of the marital covenant. Before that moment, the sultan had been a wise and benevolent ruler, but his wife's betrayal turned him into a madman. He ordered the vizier to chop off their genitals, burn them in front of their eyes, and make their next bed in hell. The vizier suggested that the sultan consider couples counseling and a seaside getaway, but it was no use. The sultan's thirst for vengeance was strong. After personally executing his wife and the cook, the sultan announced that he had lost faith in womankind. He began a campaign of taking a new virgin wife every day and ordering her executed the next morning. The vizier pleaded with him to reconsider, reminding him that none of these women had cheated on him, that he was sapping the kingdom's vitality by killing so many people, and that sex with virgins was usually below average and more than you bargained for emotionally. But the sultan just started yelling about his honor, the depravity of all women, and some really racist stuff about Bedouins that might have made sense if the cook was Bedouin, but he wasn't, he was just really tan. The sultan was grasping at straws.

The end result was that over the last couple years, the vizier's responsibilities had boiled down to a grisly two-pronged task: finding virgins for the sultan to marry, and then executing them the next morning.

At the sultan's direction, the deaths were not swift.

First, the virgin was tied to a post and whipped moderately. Then her limbs were tied to the feet of four different donkeys, and the donkeys were made to scatter. But the animals often refused to move, or simply walked around aimlessly, chewing on brush. During this portion of the execution, the virgins tended to sleep. Then the virgins were buried in sand up to their necks and pelted with dates that were a day or two past their expiration, but not so off that they didn't eat a couple. Finally, the virgins were beheaded. And the beautiful, raven-haired heads of the virgins were then placed on spikes ringing the sultan's palace.

Around the two-day mark, the virgin heads started to reek. Eventually they dried out, but there were always fresh ones to replace them. Whenever the vizier would go outside to douse the rotting heads in vinegar, he couldn't help but sigh and think, "I majored in comparative literature at the University of Damascus." Then he'd wipe off his hands, duck into the harem, and drag another screaming victim to the chamber of death.

Earlier that evening, the vizier had dropped off the kingdom's very last virgin to the sultan's suite. Tomorrow, he would show up empty-handed. And he would have to face the sultan's wrath.

The vizier started tossing figs into the fire, paying no attention to the snake charmer and flutist and other entertainers performing for his pleasure. The figs were a nervous habit. He liked to watch them twist and crackle as they burned. Their quick, tiny deaths were a soothing reminder that someday all would perish in the flames of eternity. He drained his mind and focused on the calming notion of death claiming all. And when that stopped working he began to mutter to himself, "Fuck, shit, fuck fuck shit."

The vizier's daughter, Scheherazade, sat on a nearby divan, reading. She was an exceptionally accomplished woman, a speaker of many languages, with the nimble mind of a scholar and an elbow crease like a dolphin's vagina. At least, that was the word around the kingdom—a disturbing comment that the vizier often wished he had not overheard. The vizier wasn't up on young-people trends, and he supposed elbow intercourse wasn't the worst. When he was a teen, he remembered something called the cardamom challenge—this stupid thing where you had to inhale a spoonful of ground cardamom without sneezing, and then kill a wolf with your hands. At any rate, he wished his daughter a happy romantic life, but he didn't want to know anything about it.

The vizier's eyes were focused on the fire, but he had run out of figs, so he started doing the thing he did when he was really stressed out: jabbing his hand into the open flame to see how long he could keep it there. Scheherazade watched him with growing concern. On the third jab, she made up her mind. The vizier didn't even notice as she slipped out of the room.

When Scheherazade returned and announced her news, the entire chamber was stunned into silence: the parrot dancer froze, the snake charmer paused his flute mid blow. All eyes turned to the vizier. After some stuttering, he exploded.

"You're going to marry the sultan? You're mad!"

The entertainers packed up and scuttled away. Scheherazade began tossing books and clothes into a bag. "Don't worry, father," she said, smiling mysteriously. "I have a plan."

"Oh, fuck this," the vizier muttered, reverting back to his outer-borough Damascus accent, as he always did in anger. He dug his hands through his luxuriant gray hair as he paced, then wheeled around to face his daughter. "That guy's a maniac. He's going to order you killed. And I'm going to have to watch!"

Scheherazade ignored him as she continued gathering her things. Finally, the vizier sank onto a pillow. "What's your plan?"

Scheherazade took a seat next to him. "I'm going to keep the sultan so entertained that he will keep me alive for another night. And then another. And another."

A grimace passed over the vizier's face as he recalled the elbow comment. "I'm your father. Do we have to go there?"

"Not with my body," Scheherazade said. "With my words. I will entertain him with stories."

The vizier nodded slowly, breaking eye contact.

Scheherazade bristled. "What? You don't think I'm a compelling storyteller?"

"No, no. Of course I think you're a compelling story-teller," the vizier said, repeating her words in an obvious bid to buy time.

The fact was, no one had supported Scheherazade's aspirations as a writer/performer more than the vizier. After all, who had footed the bill for her fancy dramatic writing MFA? Who'd paid for her clowning classes? The vizier had actually spent three sacks of dinars to send Scheherazade to something called a "writer's colony" in upstate Samaria for three weeks so she could finish a play. But it was a brutal business. He'd hoped that after she got her degree, she'd feel like she'd gotten it out of her system and would return home to resume her place as his trusted counselor and assistant.

But the day after graduating, Scheherazade insisted on moving to Ur. Within a few weeks, she pigeoned home that she had nabbed a writer's assistant position, working for a popular poet who drew big crowds reciting in the palace gardens. She explained that it was really hard to get a writer's assistant gig. "Everyone" (her word) tried to get one because it helped you break into the poet's writer's room. But Scheherazade never did make the leap to staff writer. She was promoted to script coordinator, which sounded pretty impressive to the vizier, but apparently that was more of an administrative job. After a series of pigeons from the vizier where he hinted heavily that she could always just come home and regroup, a deflated Scheherazade moved back to the palace, two years after graduating.

Watching her pack now, hours away from certain death, the vizier begged her again to reconsider. But he knew it was in vain. Just like grad school, and Ur. When Scheherazade had her heart set on something, Allah Himself couldn't stop her. So the next evening, at sundown, he filled his goblet with honey wine and began gulping it down as Scheherazade strode confidently down the marble hallway to the sultan's bedchamber.

The vizier didn't sleep that night. He just sat in front of the fire, throwing shit in. He'd made it through a waist-high basket of pistachios and was starting in on the hand-jabbing by the time dawn crept through his latticed windows. Seeing the sun's rays, the vizier braced himself for the inevitable knock on the door, his signal to repair to the sultan's quarters and begin the dreaded execution. But the knock never came.

Finally he mustered the strength to peek out of his chamber, and then to sneak down the long marble hallway to the sultan's suite. There—to his unspeakable relief—he saw the guard idly whittling outside the sultan's door. Cautiously ecstatic, the vizier held a finger up to shush him while he peered through the keyhole—and beheld a shocking tableau. The sultan sat on his throne, transfixed, as Scheherazade knelt before him, talking and gesticulating gracefully. And as the vizier settled in and listened to his daughter entrance the sultan, his eyes widened in amazement.

One thousand and one nights passed, in peace and prosperity.

Against all odds, Scheherazade was able to make good on her plan: she told the sultan a new story each night, but refused to finish it 'til the following evening—thereby securing her life for one more sunrise. She mesmerized the sultan with such tales as "The Hammam-Keeper and the Thief," "The Caliph and His Seven Slave Girls," and "The Magical Garment," about a pair of jeans that inexplicably fit four best friends perfectly.

But on the thousand and first night, something changed.

That evening, Scheherazade began as usual, by wrapping up the previous night's tale, this one about a barber and his treacherous monkey. But before she could begin a new story, the sultan waved his hand, cutting her off. He picked up a large ruby from the glittering bowl of jewels by his side and ran it through his fingers as he watched her belly dance nude, which she always did as she spun her tales. She found it helped warm up her audience; a useful strategy she'd picked up at her MFA, when it was her turn to be workshopped.

Beneath his shimmering robes, spun of the finest silk

and woven from a thousand threads of gold, under a night of a million stars, Scheherazade could see that the sultan had exactly one erection.

"Think I'm good on the stories tonight," the sultan said, rubbing himself through his silks. "Why don't you come over to Papa."

Scheherazade looked at him seductively, twisting her hips in a slinky, swirling motion, then bent her arms to show off her elbow creases to advantage. That drove him wild. But despite her impressive track record, she knew that to lose his attention and lay with him would mean certain death.

"Are you sure you don't want to hear one last little story?"

The sultan's lips parted. He was breathing heavily. "I want your vagina on my face."

"Well, it's funny you say that," she cooed. "Because this new story's about a vagina."

The sultan raised his eyebrows. "No shit," he said, genuinely curious. "Really?"

She nodded and turned in a slow circle, looking over her shoulder at him as she did so. "In a way."

The sultan narrowed his eyes. "I don't love the 'in a way.'"

"It's about one woman's fight to put women's reproductive destiny in their own hands," Scheherazade began, channeling her best new-tale energy. "This is the story . . . of Margaret Sanger!"

The sultan rolled his eyes. "I don't want another inspirational narrative about a feminist trailblazer."

Scheherazade silently cursed herself as she continued to undulate her hips. What was she thinking? She had done

Martha Gellhorn two nights ago. "All right, different story. Really good story," she said. "This one's about an immigrant family grappling with love and loss in 1930s Brooklyn."

"Let me guess," the sultan said, strolling over to a platter of halvah and popping a square in his mouth, his erection waning. "It's a soaring tearjerker that's ultimately a love letter to the spirit of immigrant America."

Scheherazade winced. At almost three years in, it was getting hard to stay ahead of him. In the beginning, she'd been able to dazzle him with the stupidest shit. Like, the first three months, she'd just told him a bunch of stories about a boy and his dog. They'd get into a scrape, there'd be some insanely thin B story, like the neighbor lady makes a pie, literally that thin, and then she'd wrap it up with a smile, a tear, and a moral. She'd squeezed an entire week out of one story where the dog runs away because the boy ignores him after getting a new chemistry set. And when the sultan got tired of the dog, she'd told him a bunch of stories about a helpful dolphin who assisted a widower and his sons in a marine park in Key Largo.

But the animal stuff hadn't cut it for years. Now, to stay interested, he needed violence, sex, intrigue, and humor all at once. On the plus side, it kept her at the top of her game. It was creatively fulfilling to push the envelope in this way, but also a huge challenge to keep topping herself. In the past few months, she'd cycled through her edgiest content yet. A serial killer who only kills serial killers. A mild-mannered chemistry teacher who becomes a ruthless drug kingpin. And perhaps the edgiest tale of all: four women over sixty living and loving in Miami.

As she mentally scrolled through her repertoire, Scheherazade was so distracted that she didn't even notice the sultan approach her, hiding something in his hand.

"Scheherazade," he began, his voice soft. "You're amazing. You've made me see that there is good in womankind. You've made me look forward to tomorrow, to feel hope in this world. I want to ask you a question."

Scheherazade nodded, surprised by the tears that sprung to her eyes. "Yes. I will be your wife."

The sultan looked up, confused, and opened his palm to reveal three miniature portraits. "Oh. Um. I was actually just going to ask you which of these princesses is the hottest. I'm gonna marry one of them."

"But you just said—you just said you wanted my vagina on your face," Scheherazade said, stumbling, confused.

"Yeah," the sultan said, embarrassed, rubbing the back of his neck. "The thing is, the more I think about it, the more I realize that this works better as a friends thing."

And then the sultan began to tell her a story. It was one Scheherazade had heard before—a thousand and one times.

"Look, Scheherazade," he said. "You're super cool. You're smart, you're confident. Obviously, you're an amazing storyteller." He took a deep breath. "It's just, *I* want to drive, you know? You're a lot. Does that make sense?"

Scheherazade's face started to crumple. Guys only said this to mask a harsher truth: that they just weren't attracted to you. "You don't think I'm pretty," Scheherazade said.

"You're super pretty," the sultan said. "You're so pretty. It's not that. It's a vibe thing."

Scheherazade raised an eyebrow. "So, how does this end? Hakim drags me off to be whipped and buried alive?"

They glanced at the bulky silhouette of Hakim. He'd been standing at the ready every night for the past three years, holding a thick cord of rope, ready to drag Scheherazade away to the vizier for executing. He bowed slightly.

"Personally, I would love to hear the tale of Margaret Sanger," the guard said gently.

The sultan brought Scheherazade in for a bear hug, clearly relieved that he'd gotten this far. "Of course I'm not going to have you killed. I was actually hoping we could meet up in a couple weeks. Check in."

He motioned over her shoulder, and a servant materialized with Scheherazade's clothes already neatly folded in a basket. "You're awesome," the sultan called out as the servant threw a thin shawl over her shoulders and escorted her away, the enormous lattice doors sliding closed behind her. "Seriously, let's be friends!"

Scheherazade padded across the palace to the vizier's quarters in the silent predawn. She slipped quietly into her father's rooms and sank onto a cushion near the fire. Then she let herself cry. Unmarried, unemployed, on the wrong side of seventeen; she grabbed a handful of pistachios from a platter and hurled them into the flames.

Suddenly a large, heavy object thunked down in front of her. Scheherazade wiped her eyes and saw that it was a book, bound in handsome emerald leather. Startled, she glanced up. Her father was gazing down at her, his eyes shining with love.

As Scheherazade opened the book and flipped through it, her confusion melted into happy shock. She recognized her father's handwriting; the illustrations were pictures she'd seen in her mind. The vizier had painstakingly transcribed each of his daughter's thousand and one tales.

Even the emotionally manipulative crap about the friendly dolphin and the widower.

The vizier knelt down next to his daughter and brushed one of her tears away. "To hell with the sultan," he said, giddy, laughing at the sheer joy of being in her presence again. "To hell with his tiny ego—and his tiny penis!"

Scheherazade joined her father's laughter. "How did you know about the sultan's penis, father?"

The vizier stopped laughing. "Wait a second," the vizier said. "How do *you* know?"

"I mean, we didn't—technically," Scheherazade began, stumbling. The sultan shuddered as he accidentally made eye contact with her elbow.

"Anyway," he began, shaking off the image. "One day you'll meet a marvelous man who will appreciate you for all your gifts. But it's not going to be here."

"He's banished me?" Scheherazade said, her eyes wide.

"No, no," the vizier said. Then he explained. How she couldn't stay in the kingdom and waste her talent. How he'd written to a friend of his cousin's ex-wife's stepson who works in the Industry, and how the guy had agreed to read Scheherazade's stories and sit down with her for coffee. How she had to give Ur another try.

For once, Scheherazade was speechless.

As the morning light filtered through the palace and the sultan bathed happily, excited to meet his hot new princess, Scheherazade mounted her camel. The vizier watched her from his window, wiping away a tear as his brilliant daughter rode confidently toward her destiny, toward a thousand and one crazy possibilities. He threw a pigeon into the air with a welcome message so that she'd have some mail as soon as she got to the big city. It read, simply, "*Ur* gonna be great!" He scowled as the pigeon flew away, realizing a beat too late how lame that was. He probably should have spent a little more time on that. Whatever, he shrugged. She's the writer.

As her camel dipped out of sight behind a sand dune, the vizier wished his daughter wild success. He wished her the fulfillment of dreams she didn't even know she had. And turning back to his quarters, to the well-worn grooves of his life and all his responsibilities, he wished, as he often did, that he had never overheard the elbow thing.

First Kid, Second Kid

I love both my kids equally, but I have to admit there's some truth to that old saying, "You're a different mom the second time around." Now that they're both grown, it's funny to think back on how my parenting style changed from kid number one to kid number two.

Snack Time

Whenever Julie, my firstborn, wanted a snack, I'd wash and peel an organic, locally grown apple. I'd arrange the slices in a pleasing fan shape around a dollop of home-ground almond butter and serve it to her with a glass of oat milk.

When Jane, my second, wanted a snack, I'd bite off half a Snickers and spit it into her pen.

Bathing

When Julie needed a bath, I would fill a crystal bowl with Himalayan rainwater. After meditating over the water for two hours, I would pack her on my back and trek to a field of ripe lavender, so that she could commune with nature as I bathed her.

When Jane needed a bath, I put her in a salad bowl and slid it out onto the fire escape during a storm.

Bad Dreams

When Julie had a bad dream, I'd listen as she told me all about it. I'd rub her back and tell her that the monster with the scary teeth and the one big eye was only in her imagination, and that there weren't any monsters, period. Then I would sing her a lullaby until she drifted back to sleep.

When Jane had a bad dream, I'd tell her the monster she was scared of wasn't real. "But you know who was real?" I'd say. "Aileen Wuornos. Aileen was scared of monsters, too, until she became one herself—a hitchhiking hooker who murdered seven johns in a rage. She ended up being executed by lethal injection. Some of those drugs can take hours to kill." Then I'd say good night and lock the door.

Athletic Achievements

When Julie passed her swim test and graduated to the level of Rainbow Fish, I gave her a high five and took her out to her favorite frozen yogurt shop for a celebratory treat.

When Jane became a Rainbow Fish, I woke her in the middle of the night and drove her out to the river, where I loaded her into a motorboat. I steered us out to a remote inlet and dropped her in the water. "Swim home, bitch!" I yelled as I gunned it back.

Keeping the Peace

Whenever my husband and I argued in front of Julie, I would do my best to lower my voice or continue the conversation in a different room.

When we argued in front of Jane, I'd still go into a different room. But this time, it was to retrieve my blade. Then I'd tell Jane to go for daddy's knees while I targeted his face and neck.

Birthdays

When Julie said she wanted to dress up as Elsa from *Frozen* for her birthday, I took her to a fancy costume shop and bought her a top-of-the-line Elsa costume with real satin lining and Swarovski crystal detailing on the cape.

And when Jane told me she wanted to dress up as Dora the Explorer for her birthday, I did the right thing for once. I went to that same costume store and I bought her a top-of-the-line Dora outfit. I just did it fourteen years after she asked me to.

See, I hadn't spoken to Jane much since she'd run away from boarding school her sophomore year. I paid a PI to track her down, but when I finally found her, she was working the fryer at Uno's and refused to come home. On the eve of her eighteenth birthday, all my guilt about her hit me in a suffocating pang—so I drove down to the mall, got the Dora outfit, and took it to the house she lived in with her thirty-nine-year-old boyfriend.

They lived in tract housing out in Rankin, a colorless little neighborhood ringing a strip mall off Route 48. I'd driven by half a dozen times before, but had never worked up the nerve to go and knock on her door. Today I did.

Jane was smoking when she answered, her enormous, pregnant belly pushing through a mesh tank top. As I took in her face, my eyes welled with tears.

I couldn't believe my daughter was in there. Sunken eyes, hollowed-out cheeks. Her hair was straggly and thin. Her left eye was green and purple from a fading bruise. Beyond her in the messy darkness, an open laptop was blaring the laugh track from a sitcom.

We stood facing each other in silence.

"It's your birthday," I said finally, choking back a sob.

She glanced at the Dora costume. My hands were trembling. I knew a tic like that might set her off, but I couldn't stop. Every muscle in my body tensed as I waited for her to react. Maybe she'd kick me. She'd done it before. Slap me, spit on me—when she was in one of her rages, all bets were off, and her bursts of violence could strike with the suddenness of a thunderstorm. But now she just turned around, leaving the door standing open, and walked slowly back inside. Relief flooded through me. The last time I confronted her, she'd held a Swiss Army knife up to her throat and threatened to kill herself if I kept stalking her.

I followed Jane back into the dark house. Underneath the overpowering mildew smell, I noticed another scent. It was acrid, sour and sweet at the same time, probably an animal decaying in the walls. Shuffling behind her, zeroing in on a small bald spot on the back of her head, I felt my foot tap something on the ground. I looked down and saw I'd accidentally kicked over an empty cup of Easy Mac, smeared neon orange, filled with cigarette ash.

"Don't touch anything," Jane snarled. She walked into the living room and slumped down onto the couch, a pink heating pad on her back. The cord from the pad wasn't long enough, so it stretched in a straight line to the outlet. After adjusting the heating pad, she hoisted her feet up onto the coffee table, laying them on a folded purple-and-orange checkerboard afghan. I remember that blanket. She'd knitted it at Deep Creek, the special school we sent her to when she started self-harming and nothing we could do or say could get her to stop.

"What happened to your eye?" I asked.

Annoyance flickered on her face. "Fucking Marshalls cashier," she said, rolling her eyes and exhaling. "They're all fucking racists at Marshalls."

I nodded, uncomprehending. I had recently taken an online course with Julie about reckoning with our whiteness. I thought about mentioning this, but then of course said nothing.

Jane packed a glass pipe with marijuana and lit the bowl. I looked around the room at the traces of their lives. Several halfway-colored-in coloring books lay on a side table, along with a pack of cigarettes, an empty family-sized bag of salt and vinegar chips, and a Magic 8-Ball. My eyes stopped on the neon-pink lava lamp in the block glass window. We bought her that lava lamp on a family trip to Paris. Jane saw it in a variety shop in the Marais on our first day and begged for it; I tried to explain to her (and Dave) that we could get the exact same thing back home, where we wouldn't have to lug it around in a suitcase for ten days—but Dave was putty in her hands. He'd do anything to avoid a meltdown.

A man's voice called down from upstairs.

"Hey, babe! Jasper's hungry. We have any more mice?"

"In the cooler," Jane shouted back. She stuffed her hand into an open box of gingersnaps, grabbed a few, and pressed them into her mouth. I almost felt like smiling. I went through boxes and boxes of them when I was pregnant with her.

Our therapist had said the only thing we could do was to "keep the door open." Let her know that we were there. I was supposed to be warm, loving, and accepting—no judgment, no expectations. I was not supposed to plead. But then I remembered that little bald spot on the back of her head, the white skin of her scalp, and I blurted out that I was sorry. That I wanted a second chance. I said I knew I was a shitty mom, and that I felt horrible for treating her differently than her sister. I begged her to let me try again. She sucked on the bowl deeply, blew a cloud of smoke in my face, and told me to go fuck myself.

I tried to hand her the Dora costume, but her eyes were already back on the screen. She was done. I shuffled to the front door and let myself out, closing it softly behind me. A dog barked a few houses over and then went silent, replaced by the buzzing of the fluorescent street lamps, which had come on when I was inside. I placed the Dora costume on the stoop and was halfway down the walkway when I heard Jane rip open the door behind me. She screamed that if I knew what was good for me, I would stay the fuck away from her and her baby. That I was toxic. That her psychic said I was a witch. And that she couldn't wait to give her kid a better life than she'd had.

She slammed the door again, and as I walked back to my car I thought, Well, sure. That's your first kid.

The Boyfriend Identity

The man wakes up woozy and bandaged on a cot, head throbbing. He has the sensation he's on a boat, but otherwise his mind is blank, pounding with unformed questions he doesn't have answers to. As his eyes adjust to the dank little room, he becomes aware of voices outside. Men's voices. They sound upset about something. Stressed, tired. The man strains to make out the words. They're bickering over who was supposed to wash the dishes, whose turn it is to make breakfast. In a flash, the man knows exactly what he must do.

He flies off the cot and out the door, stunning the fishermen who stand talking in the kitchen. Before they can even react, the man is at the sink. He washes the dishes, whips up perfect omelettes with goat cheese and dill, and then settles in to give the fishermen back rubs—and he doesn't phone them in, either. He's super present for it, intently focused on giving a relaxing, stress-melting massage.

Afterward, the fishermen are dumbfounded. They hadn't thought this man was going to survive, much less give them a morning off they didn't know they needed.

As he dries the second round of dishes by hand, the man tentatively questions the fishermen. He learns that he's on an American fishing trawler off the coast of Long Island. That the crew found him floating in the water three days earlier with twin gunshot wounds in his back, an iPhone still wedged in his pocket. That they'd patched him up, poured some whiskey down his throat, and left him to live or die.

They ask him who he is, what he does for work, what kind of trouble he's in—but the man is at a loss. He has no idea about any of it, not even his name. Only one thing is crystal clear to everyone: this man possesses advanced boyfriend skills.

A day later the trawler stops to refuel. The man goes ashore so he can walk and think, and also buy some flowers for the crew—just because. It's while he's bending down to inspect a bunch of tulips in a stand outside a grocery store that he feels a click against his left kneecap. He kneels, rolls up his pant leg, and investigates. There, just below the skin: a small, hard object. He slips a knife from his pocket, flicks out the smallest blade, and makes an incision. He works the tiny cylinder out from beneath his skin, then cauterizes the wound using a lighter and the blade of his knife.

What the hell? the man thinks as he squints at the bloody piece of metal. He turns it in his fingers; it seems to be engraved with something. Holding it between his thumb and forefinger to get a closer look, he notices a tiny green light shining from a lens on its surface. He aims the light at the side of a flower bucket and reads the flickering letters it projects there:

FOX AND FIG
103 GREENWICH AVE.
RESERVATIONS: 212-478-1839

He racks his brain, but the words mean nothing to him. Taking out his phone, he punches in the number and listens to it ring, once, twice.

"Fox and Fig reservations line, this is Mara," says a voice. She sounds pretty, early twenties. The man fights the urge to ask her how her day's going and really listen to the answer.

"I need to make a reservation," he says, unsure but hiding it.

"Of course, Mr. Anderson. We can accommodate you at any time."

Anderson. So that's his name. Well, it's a start. The man checks his phone, calculates the time it'll take him to get into the city, and makes a reservation for six o'clock.

An hour later he's on a bus to New York. He is shivering, having given his sweatshirt to a middle-aged woman who said she was cold. But his mind is burning as he peers at the logo engraved on the cylinder: +1. What could it mean?

Thousands of miles away, on a wild, forested island off the coast of Seattle, an octagonal compound made entirely of black glass juts up against the sky.

A golden eagle soars over the sleek fortress. As it glides down to its nest, its wing tips momentarily into the hundred-foot radius of the building. The next instant it's gone, incinerated in a cloud of fire. Sizzling feathers rain down on the glass below.

This is the headquarters of the Plus One Project.

Deep inside the compound, in a secure room, a dozen agents sit in silence around a conference table. The air crackles with tension as they watch a shimmering projection in the middle of the room: grainy surveillance footage showing a man buying flowers outside a grocery store in Greenport, then stooping down to examine something on his knee.

A woman in her midfifties sits at the head of the table, watching the footage from behind black designer sunglasses. Her austere platinum bob and high cheekbones, together with the glasses, give her face a remote, mannequin-like appearance. She raises a hand and makes a quick, deft gesture with her fingers. The footage freezes. She gestures again and the image zooms in to reveal the man's face, his brow furrowed in confusion. There's a long pause, and then the woman removes her sunglasses, revealing piercing blue eyes fixed on the image in front of her. When she speaks, her voice is terrifyingly soft.

"What am I looking at?"

The agents sitting around the table are silent. Their fear is palpable. A trim man in wire-rim frames to her right shakes visibly.

"I know I can't be looking at a rogue unit," the woman continues, calmly folding her hands on the table. Only the twitch in her eye betrays her rage. "Because that would mean this entire operation is compromised."

"Barnes." She addresses the shaking man in glasses. "He was your problem."

Barnes sputters to life. "I had verification. I had eyes on. That fucker was dead!"

The woman gets up, paces, rubs her face. She turns away from the agents and stares out of the floor-to-ceiling windows at the fog snaking through the treetops.

"How do we stay alive?"

The agents glance at one another. Is she leading them down some theoretical line of thought? You never know with Imogen. One thing they do know is to keep their mouths shut.

"Why do we get a blind eye from the feds? Why do we consistently beat back competitors? Because we execute flawlessly. No surprises. No mess. We've never had a fuckup." Imogen turns back to her team, her voice an icy singsong. "Until now."

At this point Barnes is noticeably sweating. He clenches his jaw to stop his teeth from chattering.

A young woman with a pixie cut punches a few keys on her laptop. "We have close to a billion dollars in contracts slated for the next eighteen months. We have to contain this."

Imogen nods, solemn. "Plus One has a one-strike policy. It applies to our units. It applies to management as well."

Tears stream down Barnes's face as she turns to him, shakes her head sadly, then nods to a pair of guards standing at attention by the door. Without a word, they stride over to Barnes, lift him up by the shoulders, and drag him away.

The other agents look down. Somebody coughs. A tear

rolls down the pixie-cut woman's cheek. Imogen keeps her back to the room, staring out at the wilderness.

A moment later, one of the guards pops his head back in. "Just wanted to *triple*-check—"

Imogen swivels his way. "Kill him by shooting his head with a gun and then throw his dead body in the sound."

The guard makes a clicking noise and snaps. "Yep. Copy that!"

Imogen turns back to the surveillance footage and stares into the man's eyes.

"I'm cleaning this up myself."

Walking down to the Village from Port Authority, the man catches sight of his reflection in the glass façade of an office building. He pauses, taking in his square jaw, big, soulful blue eyes, sensual mouth, and five o'clock shadow. He looks at his broad shoulders, sculpted arms, and flat stomach. "Alright, Mr. Anderson. Who are you? A trainer?" he thinks. "A professional soccer player?" All he knows is that he's handsome, muscular, empathetic, and he's often had orgasms simply from performing oral sex on women, during which time flies by and fifty-six minutes actually doesn't feel long at all.

A buzz on his thigh jolts him back to the present. He'd thought his phone was dead, but when he pulls it from his pocket there's a text from someone named Katie.

"Where are you, baby? You missed brunch! [Crying emoji, kiss emoji, heart emoji.]"

The man's mind races. Who is Katie? Should he respond to her text? If so, what should he say? Is she someone he can trust, or is this some kind of a trap?

He pockets his phone, deciding to reconsider his options after Fox and Fig, whatever that is.

Walking up to Fox and Fig, the man sees that it's a restaurant. He steps cautiously inside and is greeted warmly by a beautiful young woman in a cream-colored suit. As she smiles at him, an image flashes in his mind of the two of them lazily browsing a farmer's market for rhubarb. He pushes it away, not trusting it, but returns her smile automatically. Have they met before?

Without a word, the woman ushers him into a private room and waves him through a body scan, watching a monitor as he passes through. Shit, he thinks. Is she going to notice that he dug out the cylinder? But the woman just nods, satisfied, and opens a second door on the back wall, motioning for him to enter. Then she leaves.

The man passes through slowly and peers inside the small room. There's a single chair, and a table with a steel case a little bigger than a shoebox sitting smack in the middle of it. The man studies the engraving on the lid: +1. Here goes nothing, he thinks, and opens the box.

The first thing he notices is the cash. Huge bundles of fifty-dollar bills, with labels on the bands. He flips through the stacks of bills: "One-Month Anniversaries," "Two-Month Anniversaries," "Birthdays," and "Just Cuz." Below the money, several jewel tone V-neck cashmere sweaters. A worn, annotated *New York* magazine article titled, "The Perfect Afternoon in the West Village." A list of maître d's names and emails. And a full stack of driver's licenses, from all over the country. His head spins as he reads the different aliases. There's Michael Anderson, from Denver; Ben Schwartz, from Michigan; Dave Seiger, from Illinois; Dan Carson, from California. And beneath the stack of

IDs, the man finds something even more disturbing: a stack of photos.

There are at least thirty, all of him with different women. He blinks at one where he's standing on a dock, arm-in-arm with a redhead. On the back is written "Mike + Maggie, 8/7/20." Neither he nor the woman are wearing rings.

"I have a girlfriend named Maggie," the man says slowly. He stares at her face, trying hard to remember anything. His mind is blank. "Maggie," he repeats, determined for it to spark a memory.

The next photo shows him and an African American woman on a swing set with their backs to the camera, laughing as they turn to face the photographer. "Dan and Lauren," the note on the back reads. Next is "Ben" and an Asian woman clinking margaritas at a Mexican restaurant with a mariachi band playing behind them. There's "John" with his arm around an older blond woman in a sports car. And dozens more, all of him with different women of various shapes, sizes, and colors—all apparently at the same exhilarating-yet-cozy three-month mark of a relationship.

The man feels his sense of reality collapsing around him. What were these pictures? Who were all these women? And why did he feel the urge to make them homemade birthday cards?

He shuffles through the photos again, checking the inscriptions for "Katie." There aren't any. He closes his eyes, thinks "Katie" . . . and has a dim recollection of an apple orchard . . . a thirtysomething woman with ombré hair . . . he knows what ombré hair is . . . why does he know what that is? . . . but beyond that, nothing.

Suddenly the man feels an urgent need to get out of this

place. In the bottom of the box is a Ralph Lauren gym bag; he shakes it open and dumps the contents of the box inside, then zips it shut. Trying to control his breathing, he steps out of the room holding the bag—and notices the woman in the cream-colored suit eyeing him strangely. She smiles and waves him over. "Hey, there's a spider in the bathroom," she coos. "Can you kill it for me?"

He nods, and her look of gratitude is like a heroin injection straight to his heart. It feels so good he almost doesn't notice her reach under her desk and press a little red button.

The man locks eyes with the woman as her expression changes to a cold, dead stare. He backs away, stumbles, then turns and sprints for the exit, just as a SWAT team bursts through a set of doors at the other end of the dining room, spraying bullets.

Terrified patrons scream and take cover as the man somersaults out the door and dashes across the street, setting off car horns as he goes. He bounds onto a taxi and then leaps to the roof of a passing box truck, just as the SWAT team spills out of the Fox and Fig entrance. Flattening himself against the roof with the gym bag dangling off the side, the man hears their shouts fade as the truck drives away. Soon it slows to a stop and reverses into a gigantic garage door. Raising his head, the man sees that he's in some kind of loading bay. He drops silently down and disappears through a set of swinging doors into the building.

Inside, he pauses to take in his new surroundings. Fluorescent lights. Pallet trucks. Colorful boxes of food. He peers down an aisle and sees two people chatting, both wearing Hawaiian shirts.

Holy shit—he knows this place. Knows it well. Trader Joe's on Sixth and Spring.

He's still too close to Fox and Fig. He should put more distance between himself and his pursuers, knows that, but suddenly he's walking quickly forward, into the store. He grabs a basket, heads to the refrigerated section, swipes a bunch of vanilla nonfat Greek yogurts into it, then scans the produce section for Honeycrisp apples and firm red grapes—the harder the better. Finally he heads for the special case near the flowers, knowing instinctively that's where the kombuchas will be. But when he gets there, he notices that—oh, shit, something's wrong, something's seriously fucked here—they're out of the rainbow bottles.

A Trader Joe's employee, a large, cheerful woman with a gray buzz cut and a Fitbit, looks up from stocking a nearby shelf with breakfast bars. "Can I help ya find something?"

"Kombucha," the man barks, his voice hoarse. "The ones with the rainbow-y label."

She trots over to a stack of cardboard boxes, riffles through a few, and then shakes her head apologetically.

"Drat. Looks like we're—"

The man's face is now inches from her own. *"Check in the back."*

The woman staggers back in surprise. "Okay, buddy, okay. Calm down. Just wait right here."

But he follows her into the storage room and hovers. Panting. Circuits misfiring. Memories returning in flashes. Lauren eating the yogurt on the couch. Allison dunking Honeycrisp slices into almond butter. Mimi washing the hard red grapes, popping one into her mouth . . .

She turns to him, a rainbow kombucha in each hand. "How many do you need?"

He looks up at her, fuzzy. "They're not for me. They're for Katie."

The employee nods cheerfully. "Cool beans. How many we talking?"

His mind goes blank. He tries to think. Tries to summon Katie's face. Can't do it. What the fuck is he even doing here?

"I don't know . . . I don't know how many Katie wants."

"Well, maybe ask her?" the woman says gently.

". . . I don't know who Katie is. I don't know who *I* am!"

The man breaks down crying. He looks at the employee's name tag. "Joy?"

Joy nods.

The man wipes his nose with the back of his sleeve. "*I don't even know my name.* But I know the yogurt is for Lauren. The grapes are for Mimi. She likes to freeze them . . . says they're a healthy treat . . . but no carbs after eight P.M. . . ." At this point, he is sobbing uncontrollably. "No carbs after eight P.M. . . ."

"Okay, buddy, okay," Joy says, putting her hand on the man's back, guiding him to a seat at a desk covered in papers, a slinky, and a dog-a-day calendar. "Let me get you some tea. Would that be okay? Hold on. Just sit tight." Joy putters around the office kitchen and returns a few moments later with a steaming mug.

"Rooibos. The South African healer," she says, jolly, handing it over. "It's my favorite of our yummy herbal chillax teas." She pops open a box of Joe-Joe's and tips it toward him. He takes one and nods weakly. Joy helps her-

self to a couple and sits looking at him, munching sympathetically.

The man eats and sips. He doesn't know why, but he
feels safe around this woman. He lets down his guard.
Fills her in on the trawler. The laser projector with the
weird logo. His mysterious skill set.

"I know which Le Labo diffuser oils go best in which
rooms. In a woman's shower, I can always tell which
shampoo I'm not supposed to use. When I look at a menu,
I ignore my own preferences and wait to be told what to
order. Why?"

Joy looks at him with kind eyes. "You might just be an
observant, caring person," she says, helping herself to another cookie.

The man shakes his head. "It's more than that." He
nods to a middle-aged man opening a file cabinet on the
far side of the office. "That guy over there is wearing a
sweater that he thinks complements his coloring and
build. It doesn't. He'd be better in a maroon three-quarter
zip." Joy stops chewing. "I can tell you the UPC numbers
for every item in the West Elm catalog. I know the delivery
dates of every goldendoodle breeder in the tristate area. I
don't have any fucking cuticles. My pubic hair is perfectly
groomed. And I'm straight." His eyes burn with despera-
tion. "Now, why is that?"

Joy sits frozen, a half-eaten Joe-Joe in her mouth. She
wipes away some crumbs, speechless.

"What's a three-quarter zip?" asks the middle-aged
man across the room.

Just then, the man's phone buzzes again. Another text
from Katie.

"Still coming to my Dad's seventieth, right boo? Bring a jacket tonight it's gonna be fancy! My cousins are so excited to meet my hunky 'plus one,' lol."

"Plus one." The phrase rings a bell. He closes his eyes and remembers the engraving on the laser projector. The logo on the steel case.

Joy tilts her head. "Bad news?"

He ignores her, shuts his eyes again, concentrates harder. Apparently, Katie's his current girlfriend . . . but what does that mean? Is she a real person? He thinks so, but even if she is, there's something very wrong with the relationship. Something not even a weekend upstate bingeing *Frasier* can fix. Because he's sure of it now: he's being hunted.

The dozens of girlfriend photos. The feeling that he's not in control of his own actions . . .

All at once he knows what he needs to do. He opens his eyes and texts back: "Can't wait, baby" with a heart emoji and three kiss emojis. Hits Send and waits to see that it's delivered. Then he turns to Joy.

"Can you drive me to the airport? I need to be on Martha's Vineyard by dusk."

Joy looks at the wall clock, concerned. "Sorry, bud, my shift isn't over 'til—"

He reaches inside the gym bag and plunks a brick of cash down on the table. "Twenty thousand now. Twenty thousand when we get there."

Joy puts her hand on her carabiner of keys. "The Cube's outside," she says, nervous. "Sure hope you don't mind dog hair!"

. . .

Slicing through the clear, freezing air at 38,000 feet, Imogen sits back in her plush white leather recliner and scowls at the iPad in front of her. It shows a spreadsheet with the most up-to-date stats on her current units: a few dozen good-looking men in a rainbow of colors, all between the ages of twenty-seven and thirty-five.

Scanning the list, she notes a few subpar BMIs, three appearances of love handles, and several abysmally low COB scores (Compliments Out of the Blue). She frowns. She'll have to bring those units in for emergency retraining. As if she has time for that.

Suddenly, the blond-pixie-cut woman appears, wearing a satisfied smile. "The client's playing ball. She sent the Vineyard text. He's on his way."

Imogen nods. "Deploy an agent to meet him on the plane." She gazes out the window. "Use Cobra. He's the best we've got."

Pixie Cut smirks. "Sounds like our rebel's in for one bumpy ride."

She disappears through the curtains, but returns a few moments later. "Just to be crystal clear—"

"Our agent who is named Cobra should kill him on the plane and throw his body off the plane."

"Pree-cisely. Noted!" chirps Pixie Cut, shooting Imogen a fearful thumbs-up as she darts back through the curtains.

Imogen turns to the chiseled man in the navy three-quarter zip seated across from her.

"Sometimes I feel so alone. You know?"

"I know, baby. I know," he replies, rubbing her knee thoughtfully.

Imogen looks at him silently for a moment, then jots a few performance notes on her iPad. He had missed an Opportunity to Ask a Follow-Up Question, as well as an Opportunity to Pile On, where he could have joined her in shitting on whomever she was venting about. But those are easy fixes, she thinks, stroking his face lovingly.

He's almost ready for the field.

As Joy's Cube squeals up to the JetBlue terminal at JFK, the man riffles through his gym bag for the remaining $20,000. He blushes. "It seems I've miscalculated, Joy," he says sheepishly. "There's only like nine hundred dollars here."

Joy waves him off. "You know what? I was thinking. Don't even worry about the bucks. You seem like a good guy, you're in a bind. And I think you might need that cash more than me."

The man puts his hand on Joy's arm and squeezes.

Joy pulls out a Trader Joe's bag. "I brought along some provisions for your journey," she says, handing it to him. "Some Joe-Joe's, a box of rooibos, a couple Honeycrisps. And, of course, a rainbow kombucha."

He takes the bag from her, barely able to meet her eyes. "Thanks, Joy."

She watches him walk through the sliding doors into the terminal, his broad, muscled shoulders rippling underneath his T-shirt. Then he turns back and jogs to the car. "Sorry, the plane might be chilly. Do you have a jacket I can borrow?"

Ninety minutes later, the man pulls Joy's hoodie back from his face as the coastline of Martha's Vineyard comes into view outside the window of the Cessna 9K. The man watches it, knowing he'll need every ounce of strength for what lies ahead. Pulling an apple from the Joy bag on his lap, he takes a big, satisfying bite—and is suddenly flooded with memories. Apple trees. A folding table with cider donuts. A group of laughing thirtysomethings. A guy his age named Dan, who worked in biotech. Super boring dude. He was supposed to make conversation with that guy! Right! And Katie . . . there was Katie at last, smiling at him over her shoulder, her blond hair falling over a black backpack with a +1 sewn onto it—

The force of the cord around his windpipe rips the man instantly back to reality. Someone sitting behind him has slipped it over his head and is pulling, hard, so expertly that he can't even make a sound. Blood collects behind the man's eyes as his hands fly frantically forward in search of a weapon.

There's only one.

He yanks the rainbow kombucha out of the Joy bag and smashes it backward into his attacker's forehead. It connects, and he hears a surprised grunt. The cord loosens only for a moment, but it's enough for the man to work his fingers behind it, then push forward and up. This he does with such force that the attacker behind him is catapulted into the air, slamming into the ceiling of the plane. Passengers scream and cower in their seats as the two men roll into the tiny aisle, fighting to the death.

The attacker gets a grip on the man's neck and starts to choke him. Desperate, the man deploys his most powerful move. He looks deep into his attacker's eyes, modulates his voice to a gentle, thoughtful tone, and asks sincerely, "How was your day?"

The assailant's eyes go wide with surprise. But then his face softens, his eyes smile. He makes the man feel like he's the most important person in the whole world. "My day was wonderful. Because I knew I was coming home to you."

Holy shit. An equal. The man is taken aback. He's on the verge of asking "Really?" when the attacker drops his sincerity like a mask and headbutts the man. He falls backward, vision blurred, and recognizes the broken kombucha bottle out of the corner of his eye. He grips it and swipes wildly outward, feels the glass tear through flesh, sees blood spray, watches the hulking shape in front of him collapse.

The man kneels over his attacker, who is now on his back and bleeding badly. *"Who are you?"* the man screams down at him.

The dying attacker lets out a rueful, blood-choked laugh. "You must have fucked up bad," he says, coughing, struggling to stay on the surface. "Plus One . . . one-strike policy . . . totally fucked."

The man brings his face down close to the attacker's. *"What is Plus One!?"*

The dying man doesn't seem to hear. He spits up blood. Then slowly, his eyes drift up to meet the man's. "Do you get the emails?" he asks.

Stunned, the man loosens his grip. He's never talked to anyone about the emails.

"From the fucking restaurants and spas and pop-ups the girlfriends make us go to?"

The man nods.

The agent's body shakes; he's almost at the end. "Must

have unsubscribed from eight thousand fucking listservs," he gasps. "I like . . . a clean . . . in-box."

"Me too," the man says. They share a deep, knowing look.

The assassin closes his eyes and whispers. "I ate a bath bomb once . . . thought it was a cupcake . . . they didn't teach us the difference. . . ."

And then he's gone. The man is left staring at a lifeless face.

Goddammit. He'd been so close.

He lifts his eyes and takes in the terrified passengers clustered around him. "Everybody okay?" he asks.

They stare back at him, silent, their faces contorted in shock.

For a beat, he just sits there, panting. Then he gropes for Joy's bag, reaches into it, and tips the box toward the onlookers.

"Joe-Joe?"

When the plane lands, the man turns himself over to the police. Handcuffed in the back of a squad car, he contemplates life behind bars. It doesn't actually sound that bad compared to the house of mirrors he's currently living in. But before he can process his situation any further, the door is abruptly opened. A young woman in a blazer with a pixie cut stands next to a uniformed officer, who removes the man's handcuffs.

"You're lucky you have friends in high places," the cop says gruffly. "This is only temporary."

"Katie's dad sent me from the hotel to pick you up," says the pixie-cut woman, extending a hand. "Sorry it's been so crazy for you getting here!" She leads him over to a sleek, black SUV waiting on the tarmac, and opens the door for him.

"Who are you?" asks the man.

"I'm Charlotte," she says. "The hotel sent me. Everybody's so excited for you to get there!"

Hotel? The man narrows his eyes at her. She's taking in the Trader Joe's bag in his hand.

"Respect," she says. "TJ's is life."

What the fuck is going on? thinks the man to himself. But he doesn't see any option other than going with her. He climbs into the back seat of the SUV as she hops in front, next to a burly driver—who immediately child-locks the car.

They pull out of the airport and drive east along a two-lane road with the sun setting behind them. The man watches a gourmet grocery store pass by and fights the urge to ask the driver to stop for a bottle of wine to bring as a gift. Then, up ahead, he catches sight of something familiar: a big shingled house with a sign over the porch that reads MORNING GLORY FARM.

And in that moment it all comes back to him. The apple orchard. His assignment. A three-month contract with Katie that was almost up the weekend he joined her and her friends on the Vineyard to pick apples. He remembers that morning, the moment he got the email with his next assignment: an interior decorator named Allison, somewhere in the Florida Panhandle . . .

He remembers the feeling of panic he'd had as he chatted with Katie's brother-in-law about GMOs; how he knew he'd never be allowed to move beyond these meaningless surface-level conversations with friends of his girlfriend, never have friends of his own. How he'd fixed his hopes on a desperate idea that he knew deep down was too crazy to work.

He'd waited until he was alone with Katie in the orchard to pass her the note. He'd taught himself to read using their Anthropologie catalogs. He'd take the forbidden pages into the bathroom at night, and by the glow of a Jo Malone candle, he'd stumble through the words. "Max . . . i . . . dress. Flor . . . al . . . romp . . . er." It took years. But he'd done it.

He'd watched the blood drain from Katie's face as she read the note. Read that he wanted out. That he wanted her to buy his freedom. It would be steep; he knew that. He was a top-performing asset. But he'd promised to pay her back eventually. He just needed some time and space to pursue his dreams. He had mentioned grad school, maybe art history. Hiking the Trans-Catalina Trail. Trekking with the silverback gorillas of Rwanda.

He remembers the way Katie looked at him then. It was the same look he'd gotten from the woman in the cream-colored suit. But Katie, too, had covered it with a smile and brought him in for a kiss. Behind his back, she'd pressed the panic button on her phone.

Ninety seconds later, a squad of Plus One helicopters thundered overhead.

He'd fled. Knocked over a table of cider donuts. Zigzagged his way through the orchard with the helicopters following him until he'd reached the coast. As he dived into the water he felt the bullets rip into his back and thought, "Finally. I'm free."

· · ·

The SUV pulls up outside the hotel entrance, and the man hears the doors unlock. "Have fun!" the pixie-cut woman says cheerfully.

The man gets out and closes the door behind him. Party sounds float over from an open courtyard on one side of the hotel. He hears jazz music, people talking and laughing, the clink of glasses and plates. He buttons his cardigan—Joy's cardigan, actually—tries to slap some of the dog hair out of it, and then walks the stone path to the courtyard entrance.

The brightly lit courtyard is completely empty save for a single chair at its center. In it, a fiftysomething woman in designer sunglasses sits with her legs crossed. She raises her hand and flicks her wrist. The party sounds abruptly stop; the man realizes they had been piped through speakers set up around the lawn.

"Hello, John," the woman says nonchalantly, removing her glasses. "It's been a while."

Seeing her face, his memory flashes back to one of the pictures from the steel box. The older blond woman in the sports car. The one he had his arm around. He steps closer, narrowing his eyes.

"Who are you?"

She laughs. "Come on, John," she says, pursing her lips. "You remember. *Zzzzhhhhh. Zhhhhhh.*"

The weird whirring sound jolts him back. The training in her pristine white condo. The whirring sound of the dishwasher. *Zhhhhh. Zhhhh.* Run. Unload. Load. Run. Unload. Load.

He'd learned her takeout orders. Dressing on the side. No cilantro. *No cilantro.* Then, the flash cards. Hours of flash cards. "Do you think she's pretty?"/"No." "Would

you mind running over to CVS to get [blank]"/"Sure."
"Don't you hate when [blank] does [blank]?"/"Yes, I hate
when [blank] does [blank], and here's another thing I
hate that [blank] does." When he messed up or stuttered
she'd slammed the pillowcase of rocks against his legs.
Never the face. She wouldn't dare touch his face.

She'd broken him. And rebuilt him.

Imogen lights a cigarette. Tucks a lock of platinum hair
behind her ear. "You're my best work. So you see how this
is personal for me."

Part of him wants to bash her brains in. But another
part wants to go home with her, put on their schlumpies,
order Thai food, and watch three hours of *Shark Tank*. He
grits his teeth, strangles the impulse. He needs answers.

"Who am I?"

As she gets up and saunters toward him, he sees she's
holding a gun.

"You really don't know?" She cocks her head. "You're a
billion-dollar lab diamond. The very first military-grade
boyfriend. The ultimate"—she pauses for effect—"Plus
One."

The words hit him like a punch in the gut. He fights to
stay on his feet. She continues.

"Do you know how hard it is to find a good boyfriend?
Emotional support. Intellectual stimulation. Sexual satisfaction. Tallness. They've never occurred together in the
wild. Until you. Until I made you."

He gulps. "Made me?"

She's just a few feet away now, but for some reason he
can't will his body to move. He stands frozen, staring at
her.

Imogen smiles. "I remember the night I found you in

that foster home. You were eleven years old—just a kid, but the potential was there. So I watched you. I watched you for years."

"You watched a kid in a foster home for years?"

"On your seventeenth birthday, do you know how much I paid your foster family for you? Two grand. They were broke. I brought you back to my apartment and trained you myself. Broke you down. Built you back up. You're my top-performing executive companion, John."

Imogen is now standing directly in front of him, the gun pointed at his chest. "It's not too late to patch things up, you know," she says quietly. "You're only thirty-one. You still have a lot of great years ahead of you. Travel . . . parties . . . women and men who adore you. You're going to make one hell of a zaddy."

The man feels his last bit of strength leaving him. He'd come here to end this, but now he feels too tired to fight. He sinks to his knees and stares at the grass. "Whatever you wanna do is fine."

A cruel smile creeps across Imogen's face. "Really? Thanks, babe. You're the best."

Imogen slips a syringe out of her blazer, uncaps it. Tilts his head toward his shoulder to expose the length of his neck. "I think we'll just take you back to the lab, remove those pesky parts of your brain that keep thinking. Let Mommy put you down for a nap."

Just as Imogen is about to drive in the syringe, a carabiner of keys slices through the air, nailing her in the side of the head. She stumbles.

"The fuck—?"

The man hears a familiar voice call out from the shadows.

"C'mon, buddy! You got this!"

As Imogen rubs her head, trying to make sense of what happened, the man's eyes dart over to the sound, and there's Joy, wearing a fleece pullover blanketed in dog hair.

"Don't give up! You're more than just some rented dick!" Joy shouts. "You're one cool dude!"

A smile spreads over the man's face, and suddenly, he twists his body around and uses his leg to sweep Imogen's feet. As she crashes to the ground, he lunges forward and grabs the gun from her, then pulls her body up to use as a shield, knowing there must be snipers posted around the courtyard.

He grabs the carabiner and throws it back to Joy. "Get the Cube!" he yells as he backs toward the entrance, holding Imogen in front of him in a headlock.

"You're really fucking this up, John," she hisses through clenched teeth. But he only tightens his elbow around her neck and keeps going.

They make it out of the courtyard just as Joy's Cube screeches up. The man drags Imogen up to the back door, brings his mouth to her ear, and spits out the words, though it takes every ounce of his being: "No . . . I will *not* . . . make a CVS run . . . for more Lubriderm . . . and almond milk . . . and cotton balls." Then he snaps her neck, chucks her body, and jumps into Joy's Cube. They zoom off into the night, bullets peppering the rear windshield.

"What are you doing here?" the man gasps from the back seat.

"I figured you could use some backup," Joy says, her eyes locked on the road ahead. "So I kept driving."

He beams at her. "The keys . . . that was incredible."

She chuckles. "Just a little move I picked up at work. Sundays in the TJ's checkout line can get pretty crazy. You gotta know how to defend yourself." She winks and tips a box of Joe-Joe's toward him.

John digs his hand into the box and turns his face away to hide his tears.

In the fuzzy predawn outside Freeport, Joy finds an all-night diner on the side of the highway.

John looks down at the menu. Scans it, concentrates hard. Tries to make a decision on his own. His eyes stop on the buffalo pizza. The wings. The steak sliders. Something flutters inside him, but he tamps it down. He looks up at Joy expectantly, hoping she'll tell him what he should order—but she's busy looking at the menu herself.

The waitress approaches the table.

"Know what you'd like?"

"Uh, I think I'll have the quinoa bowl and an iced tea," he hears himself say. But it doesn't feel right.

Joy shrugs and orders a grilled cheese.

The waitress nods, scribbles it down, then adds, "Oh, I forgot to mention, we have a special on sliders tonight. Three for five bucks. And fifty-cent wings with Alabama white sauce. Just FYI."

That all sounds so good. He looks up at her, his face full of gratitude. "Yeah, you know what? Forget the quinoa thing. I'll do the sliders and wings. Dozen wings. Thank you."

"Ooh, make that two!" Joy squeals. "And eighty-six the sandwich."

When the wings come, Joy picks out a meaty drumstick and takes a bite. Her eyes go wide.

"These flavors are incredible!" she exclaims, taking out her phone and making a note on the flavor profile. "I'm going to have to bring them back to the team!"

John laughs. He's had countless girlfriends before. But he's never had a girl . . . friend.

The Secret Meeting of
the Women's Club

S ince the dawn of humankind, the elders had gathered
this way: once a year, on a moonless night, always in
total secrecy. In the early days they'd come by foot, camel,
and horseback, but now they arrived in private jets, helicopters, and limousines, emerging from gleaming cabins
to join the silent procession to the entrance of the Lair. As
they walked, their gazes were calm but resolute. They
were the Most Powerful Women on Earth, united in the
ancient cause of female world domination.

There was Oprah, Sheryl Sandberg, Angela Merkel, and
many others—each a giant of her industry, each a spiritual
descendant of the female warriors who'd walked before,
and each sworn to the ultimate purpose: womankind's do-
minion over man. One by one they passed into the hidden
crevasse in the earth's surface, floated down the long spiral staircase, and took their places around the Sacred

Table—a single slab of obsidian mined from the riverbed of the Euphrates.

Selena Gomez shifted nervously in her seat. It was her first meeting, and the pop singer and former Disney star was wondering if her invitation had been a mistake. As she looked around the table, none of the women said so much as hello. She thought about turning to Margaret Atwood and complimenting her scarf, or making eye contact with Michelle Obama and mouthing, "Big fan," but the formal hush in the room told her to hang back. Plus, the women were drumming on the table, swaying to a strange rhythm.

Selena picked up the beat and drummed along softly. Taking another glance around the room, she kicked herself for wearing the wrong thing. The invitation hadn't mentioned attire, so she'd played it safe by opting for dressy-casual: cigarette pants, a black velvet blazer, and her lucky Louboutin stilettos. But the other women were all wearing long, pointed leather slippers and brown muslin robes.

Suddenly, the drumming stopped, and all eyes turned to a figure who rose at the far end of the table, her face obscured in shadow. Dramatically, the master of ceremonies pulled back her hood, her beautiful face aglow from the light of the torches ringing the hall. Selena knew it was somebody famous; was it that lady from the exercise videos? She wanted to say Joanne?

Jane Fonda hit the welcome gong with a somber grace.

"Welcome to the annual meeting of the Women's Underground Resistance Consortium, or, WURC." She snapped her fingers in a flourish. "I understand that as a white woman I can do the snapping part, but not the neck roll, and I embrace these limits."

Ava DuVernay nodded. Fonda continued. "Ladies, you may remove your expressions of pleasant interest."

The women groaned with pleasure, grimacing, rubbing their cheeks until their faces settled into mildly irritated scowls.

Fonda spoke again. "You may take out your monster penises."

Again, the women groaned, shifting in their seats, and laid their gray, scaly eight-foot penises on the black stone.

Selena Gomez had never once talked about her retractable monster penis. In fact, before this moment, she'd thought she was the only person on earth who had one. With a mounting glee, she uncoiled it from its cavity and placed it gently on the table. It grazed Nancy Pelosi's, and the House Speaker gracefully but coldly shifted away from her.

Fonda again addressed the room. "All in favor of continuing to not let men know that we have serpent penises that shoot venom, in order to preserve the element of surprise when we enslave them?"

"Let it be so," the women responded gravely. Somehow, Selena knew to say it too—the words were right there on her lips.

Gloria Steinem rose and stared out at the women ringing the table, a quiet fire in her eyes. "The time has come to destroy mankind and begin anew," said the feminist icon of the 1960s and '70s. "Every year we vote to keep concealing our monster penises and defer our mastery over mankind. But the time to strike is now. Waiting any longer would be fatal."

A shocked murmur rippled along the table.

"I'm with Citizen Steinem," said a voice from farther

down the table. She leaned forward into a pool of light, and Selena gasped. Demi Lovato!

"I agree that we should annihilate mankind with our dick venom," said the singer/songwriter/actress born in 1992. "Tomorrow. Midnight. We blind and castrate every single man, then harvest their organs and rebuild them as a servant race in our image."

A beat of silence followed as several of the women exchanged looks. Anna Wintour removed her spotless sunglasses to buff them. Michelle Obama coughed. Kate Middleton crouched behind Queen Elizabeth and began to groom her. Finally, Angela Merkel spoke. "Who are you?"

The pop star rose gracefully from her seat.

"My name is Demi Lovato," she said, taking instant command of the room. "I am one of the most popular recording artists in the world. My music has an uplifting feminist message, and I use my battles with addiction to inform my art and activism."

She waited for the recognition to come. When it did not, she continued. "How do you not know who I am, but you know Selena Gomez?" Demi motioned toward the former Disney star.

Elizabeth Warren, startled, clutched the lapel of her purple blazer and regarded Selena for the first time. "My god. I thought that was a purse."

Selena Gomez shrunk in her seat, and Fonda struck the gong once more for order.

"Young blood is necessary to ensure longevity and strength," she said. "And rest assured, Citizens Steinem and Lovato: we will strike. In good time."

Steinem leaned forward, fists clenched on the table.

"But we're running out of time. Our rights are under assault. Our leaders are openly sexist, and there are rumors of a new *Transformers* movie."

Malala Yousafzai cracked her neck. "Not under my watch."

Reese Witherspoon brushed a wisp of blond hair from her face. "Respectfully, I'd like to highlight the gains we've made this year. We've fully assimilated yoga pants into office wear. BarkThins snacking chocolates now come in convenient single-serving bags. They're called 'Snackable Singles.'" Witherspoon produced a sample and presented it proudly to the group. When no one responded, she shuffled some papers, flustered, grasping for more hard wins. "Olivia Colman . . ."

Steinem waved her off. "We must go nuclear. It's the only way we can achieve our ultimate goal of world domination."

Jennifer Lawrence cocked her head. "World domination? I thought we were just trying to, you know, achieve equality with men."

"Yes, young feminist," Steinem said. "Equality. That's what I meant."

A few women snickered. Elena Kagan and Iman exchanged a knowing glance.

Fonda reclaimed the floor. "We'll never achieve world domination if we go off half-cocked. We need a focused, actionable plan of attack. Sheryl Sandberg, let's review our targets."

Sheryl Sandberg produced a remote from her robes and beamed a PowerPoint onto the cinderblock wall. "These are the primary challenges facing women today:

- Workplace harassment
- Unequal pay
- Husband kills you
- Boyfriend kills you
- Tampon rolls out of purse in meeting
- Rape as a weapon of war
- Honor killings, domestic violence, female circumcision
- Low-rise jeans make comeback

The last bullet point drew shrieks and groans. Sonia Sotomayor slammed her fist onto the table.

"Come now," piped up Swedish climate change activist Greta Thunberg. "Low-rise jeans aren't a problem. All bodies are beautiful."

Justice Sotomayor took a swig from her thigh flask and regarded the teen with an icy stare. "You're embarrassing yourself."

Fonda continued. "The revolution will be pointless unless we've mastered the ability to reproduce. Where are we on asexual reproduction?"

Sheryl Sandberg shook her head sadly. "Recent breakthroughs in testing with mice made us overconfident. We beta tested a program that resulted in a litter of web-footed Kylie Jenners. They've been terminated, but we'll need to be more careful going forward."

The women booed, and Sandberg raised her voice to regain order.

"We did find a silver lining, however. During the course of our research we accidentally invented a new type of carbohydrate. It's a cross between a bagel and a crêpe. We're calling it a brêpe, and preliminary testing shows that it's delicious."

"Excellent news," Jane Fonda said, and then looked around the room. "I'd like to do a celebratory dab. Is that all right?"

Gayle King shook her head no. Fonda slumped in her seat, miffed.

Oprah rose and produced a ram's horn from her robes. "Let this clarion call rouse us from our sleep," she announced. Then she brought the horn to her lips and blew mightily. Selena hadn't heard anything like it before; its piercing cry was both haunting and exuberant. "For too long we have slumbered. Let the clear, strong notes of truth and justice—"

"Oh, screw the horn," Steinem said. "Where has it gotten us? We're still murdered. Assaulted—"

"Also, hold on." Fonda gave her hair a toss. "Hold on. How is it not okay for me to dab, but you can blow a shofar? It's a Jewish ceremonial trumpet." Fonda was clearly still smarting. "How is *that* not appropriation?"

Taylor Swift took a sip of eco-friendly boxed water and turned to Fonda. "Dabbing recalls minstrelsy, when African Americans were called on to perform for slave masters. African Americans reclaimed this vestige of slave culture. Jews weren't enslaved, so it's different. Don't say Egypt. Egypt doesn't count."

"Oh? Well how about the Holocaust?" Fonda said, getting louder. "Does that count?"

Taylor Swift examined her nails. Fonda looked at her, incredulous.

"Are you saying the Holocaust didn't happen, Taylor Swift?"

Swift produced a small mirrored compact from her purse, reapplied her trademark red lipstick, and snapped it shut.

"Enough," Sandberg broke in, holding up a stack of papers. "I have focus group data that says infighting will destroy us." Sandberg looked out over the table. "The revolution needs male allies. Where are we on our cloning program? Honorary Woman Justin Trudeau?"

Justin Trudeau removed his hood. "We're making progress, but our test subjects are losing strength in captivity. It's compromising their ability to withstand the cloning process." He gestured above him to where a frightened Chris Hemsworth hung in a wicker cage.

Chris cleared his throat. "Please. I have three children. Their names are Sasha, India, and—"

Doris Kearns Goodwin banged her fist on the table. "Dammit, I'm sick and tired of waiting on this!"

Sandberg forged on. "What other progress do we have to report?"

Reese Witherspoon's face lit up. "Ooh, I almost forgot! After decades of campaigning, it's finally going to happen: A *First Wives Club* sequel."

Reanimated Harriet Tubman pointed a finger at Witherspoon, the emotion catching in her throat. "Original cast?"

Witherspoon looked around the room, savoring the moment. Then she nodded.

The room erupted into cheers, and tears streamed down Harriet Tubman's face. At long last, her work was done. Reese then surreptitiously dashed off an email to her agent saying she was pulling out of the "New 'Untitled New First Wives Project'" and to "get the original cast. Probably cheaper that way, anyhow."

Michelle Obama looked up from the book she was writing about the magic of community. "I want to circle back to something that was brought up earlier. For those in favor of starting the revolution, how do you propose we trigger it?"

Demi Lovato clapped her hands. "Great question. Malala, wanna take this?"

Malala smiled and held up a flash drive. "Behold: the virus."

The women gasped. Selena broke out in a cold sweat. What exactly was she being asked to join here?

Malala placed a laptop on the table, inserted the USB, and turned the screen triumphantly toward the women. The video was a four-second GIF of Kate Upton in a string bikini doing a silly sex dance.

"When we activate the virus, every screen across the globe will play this GIF on a loop. As the men are frozen, transfixed by the jiggling glandular and fatty tissues, we will annihilate them with our monster penises and begin the New World."

For a beat, no one spoke.

Michelle Obama broke the silence. "That's insane. How can we assume this video will transfix all men? What about gay men?"

Malala smirked. "Look closer," she said, punching a few keys on the laptop.

The women leaned forward in their chairs and watched a slo-mo version of Kate Upton jiggling. This time, however, they noticed something flashing in between the frames, so fast you almost couldn't see it.

"Idris Elba holding a teacup Pomeranian," Michelle Obama murmured.

Justin Trudeau looked concerned. "What does it mean if you see both?"

Diane von Furstenberg waved a bangled wrist, shrugging elegantly. "Ladies, this is all beside the point. Why bother with this war at all? Earth is a wasteland. We should just accelerate plans for the new planet."

Reese Witherspoon scowled and shook her head. "There's a problem with the backsplash on the rocket. We still haven't ironed things out with the contractor, and I just want it to be really special when we begin the voyage."

Von Furstenberg sighed. "Well, when we *are* ready, I've developed the perfect garment for our pioneers to wear on their journey. It's a simple, versatile wrap dress, one that takes the modern woman from day to night."

"A versatile wrap dress isn't the answer to everything, Diane," Anna Wintour said softly, smoothing her cloak across her lap.

Von Furstenberg fixed Wintour with a stare. "Turtle-looking motherfucker," said the septuagenarian Belgian entrepreneur.

Wintour shot back. "You wanna go? I'll go right now," she said, swiftly removing her pearl drop earrings.

"Please!" Sheryl Sandberg pleaded. "We can't turn on each other. This isn't the comment section of a *Jezebel* article about whether Lena Dunham is racist!"

Lena Dunham nodded vigorously. "Great point, Sheryl. Solidarity is key, as is interrogating our whiteness and empowering female artists of color. Toward that end, I've written a one-woman play from the perspective of an eighteenth-century Jamaican slave named Ranata, and I would love to perform it for you all now, providing that—"

The sound of the shofar split the air once again, and Lena fell silent. Michelle Obama set the ram's horn gracefully back down and turned back to her book.

Dunham nodded. "Great point, Michelle. One that, I hope, jump-starts a much-needed dialogue about boundaries and inclusion."

Madonna, who'd been uncharacteristically silent all evening, reached out and grabbed a donut from the salver in the middle of the table. She took a bite. "Sorry, guys. Shouldn't we stay on track? We were talking about how we're going to enslave all the men."

Total, sudden silence descended on the Lair. Even Selena Gomez clocked Madonna's mistake.

Gloria Steinem's eyes flashed. "What did you just say?"

Madonna stopped mid bite. "Uhh . . . just that, you know, we should stay focused?"

"No, before that." Jane Fonda smiled. "You said 'sorry.' "

Madonna looked around the table, nervous.

"Prefacing your comment with an apology is forbidden," Fonda continued. She paused. "Are you enjoying that normal, not-gluten-free donut?"

Madonna wiped some crumbs from her face. "Um . . . yes? Wait. Were these for later?"

Nancy Pelosi's monster penis shot up and wrestled Madonna to the floor. The House Speaker rooted the jagged tip of her serpent genitals under the pop star's scalp, pulling it off to reveal—

Selena gasped. It was that old guy you sometimes see with Hillary Clinton. She wanted to say, Bruce?

"Bill Clinton!" the women gasped.

Clinton's eyes were full of fear. "I'm on a listening tour," he said softly, gulping down the last of his donut.

"I thought it was weird that she had a normal male penis," Malala Yousafzai said. "But I just figured it might be one of her new evolutions as an artist. She's such a chameleon."

Demi Lovato grabbed her monster penis and aimed its venom hole at Clinton's face, but Fonda's penis shot out and swatted it down.

"We need information," Fonda hissed at Lovato, who growled in frustration. Fonda strode over to Clinton, grabbed his hair, and kneed him hard in the stomach. "Who are you working for?"

Clinton's bloodshot eyes darted around the room. "I'm here alone," he said.

"Bullshit." Michelle Obama strode over to Clinton and smacked him hard in the face with her penis. "Talk, fuckhead."

Clinton groaned and spit out a tooth. "I swear . . . alone . . ."

Fonda ensnared the former president with her serpent dick, squeezing until tears of pain streamed down his face.

"Okay!" he gasped. "I'll tell!"

Fonda relaxed her grip and the women all leaned in to listen.

Clinton panted as he caught his breath. "Who are we *all* working for, dipshits?"

There was a silence, and then he and Michelle Obama spoke the words at the same time: "Jeff Bezos."

The shock of this revelation caused Jane Fonda's monster penis to retract involuntarily. Clinton sagged to the floor, but then suddenly pulled a laser gun from his ass and waved it wildly around the room.

"I'm on a data-mining mission for Bezos!" he screamed.

"And if I do good, he says I can go to Mars with him. Everyone in Colony Zero gets a new body! And he made Alexa real. She's hot. Bezos says I can have her!"

He aimed the gun at Fonda and fired, disintegrating her serpent penis. Then he shot it at Elena Kagan—and her penis disintegrated as well.

The women screamed.

Selena Gomez grabbed Malala Yousafzai's laptop and turned the screen toward him. *"Bruce!"* she shouted.

Clinton caught sight of the GIF, and his eyes glazed over instantly.

"Glandular . . . fatty . . . tissues," he murmured to himself, mouth open, dropping the laser gun as his hands floated up toward the screen. "Glandular . . . fatty . . ."

Malala Yousafzai looked around the Lair triumphantly. "The virus!"

The women gasped as they realized the scope of their power.

As Clinton toddled toward the laptop, Selena Gomez calmly slipped off a Louboutin and chucked it at his neck, piercing his jugular.

"Agghhh!" Clinton screamed, squeezing his neck and sinking down to his knees. Blood spurted from the wound in little bursts.

For the first time that evening, every woman looked at Selena Gomez. And they smiled. Margaret Atwood gave Selena Gomez a mischievous wink, and Michelle Obama caught her eyes and mouthed, "Big fan."

Moaning, in a rapidly growing pool of his own blood, Bill Clinton clawed at Fonda's robes. "Please. My foundation brought healthcare to thousands of Malawi women.

We foster women's leadership in the renewable energy sector." He took a strained breath. "I have a daughter."

At this, a pair of sentries who'd been standing silently by the door stepped forward, removing their hoods as they did. Clinton stared up at them in horror.

"She'll be fine," Hillary Clinton said as she and Chelsea gave Selena a final nod. Then all the women watched, rapt, as Selena Gomez removed her remaining stiletto, walked around the table, and tomahawked it into Bill Clinton's heart.

"Just kiss it," Clinton gurgled as his eyes rolled back. Then he was dead.

Selena withdrew the bloody Louboutin, accepted a wet wipe from Hillary, and quietly cleaned the blood spatter from her face as she returned to her seat. Then she smiled, grabbed a donut from the platter, and started to giggle. The women passed the platter around the ancient table, eating donuts and laughing, their monster penises quaking with pleasure as they did.

The Tale of Mr. Mittlebury, Millennial Pig

There once was a pig named Mr. Mittlebury, who lived in the mossy clearing of a sun-dappled glen with his mother and father, despite the fact that he was thirty-four.

Mr. Mittlebury was a plucky little pig with a soft, rosy snout and shiny black eyes who loved nothing more than rolling about in the mud and rooting around for scraps. The very best days were the days when Mr. Mittlebury found a crab-apple, or a bit of honeycomb, or a scrumptious tuber. Oh, those were the merriest days, indeed. For when Mr. Mittlebury was munching a bit of tuber, it was easier to forget that Mr. Mittlebury owed $94,000 in student loan debt!

What a very large number 94,000 was! Sometimes Mr. Mittlebury would lie awake at night and try to make sense of it. He would think of the Ripplings, the rabbit family who lived down the lane. There were so very many Rippling rabbits, all packed together snug in their warren. Still, there couldn't be more than sixty. So Mr. Mittlebury would think of the clover in the glen: were there 94,000 clovers in the glen where he romped? And then Mr. Mittlebury would begin to sweat.

And when Mr. Mittlebury worked himself into such a state, he often found it difficult to fall asleep. Indeed, sometimes he would find it necessary to sing himself a little lullaby.

Acorns and pine cones and babbling brooks,
There sleeps a robin warm in his rook.
When the sun rises o'er the glen,
The robin will sing and be merry again.

And when the lullaby didn't work, Mr. Mittlebury masturbated himself to orgasm.

One day, Mr. Mittlebury was scampering about the glen, rooting around for a few larvae before lunch. Mr. Mittlebury's improv-show was scheduled for later that evening, and he had invited his friends Tristan the Right Honorable Tadpole and Mr. Plumpton, a monocled cricket. But Mr. Mittlebury's improv-team had to bring in an audience of at least ten, or else the theater would cancel that evening's performance. Mr. Mittlebury knew that the other gentleman on his two-man team, Sir Pipsley, a bushy-tailed brown squirrel, could be counted upon to bring several friends. Still, that might not be enough. Mr. Mittlebury sniffed out a plump, juicy larva and chewed it as he pondered his predicament.

The larva was tasty. He found another. And then another. If only larvae counted as audience members, Mr. Mittlebury thought. Oh my. *Whomever* could he invite to that evening's show?

Mr. Mittlebury ate and pondered, but no solution presented itself. So Mr. Mittlebury did what he always did when he worked himself into a state: he sang himself a little ditty.

Junebugs and raindrops and high-leaping frogs,
there sits a red robin 'top of a bog—

This time, however, Mr. Mittlebury didn't even make it halfway through the song before he began masturbating himself to orgasm.

Masturbation had become something of a crutch for Mr. Mittlebury, a quick and satisfying rip cord he could pull whenever he felt the urge to escape reality, which seemed to be happening more and more frequently. Mr. Mittlebury hadn't been in a serious relationship since the tabby cat Miss Gwendolyn, and that was in college. The last time he'd had sex was all the way back to Little Rumple Thumple, an otter who hit on him at the Del Close Marathon. He hadn't even had a crush since that pheasant from his co-working space. Mr. Mittlebury shuddered. Masturbation wasn't even sexual for Mr. Mittlebury anymore; it was simply a release valve. So great was his anxiety over his dry spell that he doubted he could even achieve an erection with a female, let alone satisfy her.

Just as Mr. Mittlebury had finished cleaning himself, up scampered his little sisters, Tippy-Toppy and Tappy.

"Hello, Mr. Mittlebury! Shall you be joining us for lunch today?"

Mr. Mittlebury was glad for the diversion. "Why, yes, sisters. Indeed I shall." Mr. Mittlebury was looking forward to the meal. Especially since his mother was making his favorite treat, nettleberry pie. Mmm, he could taste the toothsome nettleberries now! But it certainly wouldn't be toothsome letting his parents know that he would need help with his student loans this month. He would save that conversation for after the pie.

Tippy-Toppy clapped her hooves in delight. "Oh goody. We have someone special we'd like you to meet!"

Mr. Mittlebury sighed. Here we go, he thought. Another awkward setup. Last week it was Madame Cuttlesworth, a vole who'd recently lost her husband. Mr. Mittlebury walked her back to her burrow and held her paw as she wept. She had seventy-two children. Madame Cuttlesworth was perfectly nice, but she was grieving. The evening had been uncomfortable.

"Oh, Tippy. I wish you wouldn't bother."

But the sisters merely giggled, and skipped off to the midday meal.

When Mr. Mittlebury arrived presently at the sty, he looked about his parents' table and was perplexed. Sitting in the chair reserved for guests was no eligible female but a fortysomething gentleman badger.

Mr. Mittlebury's mother, Middums, cleared her throat. "Mr. Mittlebury, may we present Blantyre the Badger."

My god, Mr. Mittlebury thought to himself. It's been so long since my family has seen me with a female that they think I'm gay. Mr. Mittlebury's cheeks burned rosy with shame.

"Pleased to meet you," Mr. Mittlebury said.

"The pleasure is mine," said the badger.

Mr. Mittlebury picked up a large bowl of slop. "I believe this needs a bit of seasoning. Tappy, would you join me in the larder?"

Mr. Mittlebury waited until the larder door was well closed before he whispered to his sister. "Tappy, I am not gay."

Tappy laughed. "Of course not, Mr. Mittlebury! We're not trying to 'set you up' with Blantyre. Blantyre is a life-coach."

Mr. Mittlebury felt his cheeks burn even rosier with shame.

"I see. So I'm some loser who needs fixing?"

"No, no, of course not. It's just that everyone can use a little help now and again!"

"Except for you and Tippy-Toppy and fucking David, right?"

David was Mr. Mittlebury's elder brother, a black-spotted pig who worked as an executive vice president of Zooples, a marketing firm on a nearby lily pad. Mr. Mittlebury let out an exasperated grunt and smashed his hoof into a sack of acorns.

Tappy glanced nervously toward the larder door, beyond which their family and guest waited patiently to sup. "You're making a scene."

"I can't believe this," Mr. Mittlebury fumed. He let a few moments pass in angry silence.

"Are you even aware that you're eating right now?"

Actually, Mr. Mittlebury hadn't noticed that he was eating. He'd been feeding loudly from the slop bowl. He wiped his snout bashfully.

Tappy put her little hoof on Mr. Mittlebury's shoulder. "Look. We're just worried about you."

"You shouldn't be. I'm fine!" And with that, Mr. Mittlebury went back to the dining room.

As Mr. Mittlebury took his seat at the table, his parents, Middums and Diddums, looked worriedly at each other. Tappy nervously spread slop on a biscuit. David appeared bored. Blantyre smiled at Mr. Mittlebury.

"So. I hear you do stand-up comedy?"

"Improv, actually."

"Ah! I see."

David popped some acorns in his mouth and chewed them loudly. "Tell him your team name."

Mr. Mittlebury glared at his brother.

Tappy cleared her throat. "Is there extra rubbish in this slop, mother? It is tremendously delicious."

Blantyre tasted his slop. "I must second the compliment. This must be some of the tastiest—"

"Martin Van Urine."

The badger looked at Mr. Mittlebury, confused. "I'm sorry?"

"My improv team name."

"Get it?" David said. "Like the American president Martin Van Buren, except *urine*."

"Ah. Well, that's clever indeed! Thank you for sharing that with me, Mr. Mittlebury."

Mr. Mittlebury's cheeks flushed once more as he excused himself and hurried to the bathroom. This time Mr. Mittlebury simply sang his little rhyme as he masturbated, quickly and brutally. There was no pleasure in the spasm that rocked Mr. Mittlebury's plump, plucky little body; only a moment without pain.

As Mr. Mittlebury was cleaning himself up, he suddenly remembered the unpleasant task of asking his parents for help with his loan. Mr. Mittlebury furrowed his brow. He simply could not face the quandary at present.

Mr. Mittlebury returned to the dining room and bid his family a hasty good-bye. "Thank you for the lunch, Mother. I'm afraid I must leave now; there is some business at the office that requires my attention."

David rolled his eyes. Middums looked pleadingly at her son. "Will you have some nettleberry pie at supper, then?"

"I'm afraid not—I have my improv-show this evening. Seven-thirty at the Gallery Loft!" And with that, Mr. Mittlebury trotted quickly out the front door.

"See you there," David called out sarcastically. Mr. Mittlebury could hear Tappy tittering anxiously as he scampered away through the clover.

The office was the shared workspace Mr. Mittlebury rented by the nut bushes that grew on the banks of the brook. Mr. Mittlebury used this space as his base of operations for his novelty T-shirt business, his primary source of income besides the cricket cakes he occasionally sold at market.

Several years ago Mr. Mittlebury struck upon the rather clever idea of a T-shirt with a picture of a slice of pizza, and underneath it the quotation "I hate pizza—said no one ever." Riding the wave of energy this fit of inspiration afforded him, Mr. Mittlebury emailed a T-shirt manufacturing company, ordered several dozen pizza shirts, and quickly sold the lot. Word spread of Mr. Mittlebury's pizza shirt, and suddenly Mr. Mittlebury had dozens more orders to fill. But that was years ago. Mr. Mittlebury still sold a pizza T-shirt every now and again, but the orders had more or less dried up. He needed a new idea for a T-shirt. Yet Mr. Mittlebury was suffering from a prolonged bout of writer's block.

Mr. Mittlebury sat down on his work log, retrieved a pencil and notebook from his knapsack, and reviewed the notes from his previous work session.

—Pizza Rules
—A burrito with the caption "I hate burritos—said no one ever"
—Rue McClanahan's face with the caption "Carte Blanche"
—Jeb! 2024

Mr. Mittlebury chewed upon his pencil. None of these ideas were terribly good. He tried something else:

—I owe $94,000 in Student-Loan-Debt and I'm Overwhelmed and Ashamed

Mr. Mittlebury crossed that out and began to sweat.

He looked around the workspace. There was the neatly dressed fox who kept to himself, the owl who had installed his own standing desk, and—yes, how lovely!—Miss Baxter, the plump pheasant whom Mr. Mittlebury had a crush on. He believed she freelanced for Mashable.

Mr. Mittlebury felt the familiar stirrings of panic. Under his breath, so as not to disturb the others, Mr. Mittlebury sung himself a calming ditty.

Hickamore, hackamore, tiddly-riddly-dee,
there sat a robin-bird flat 'pon my knee

At this point, merely humming the opening strains of the tune made Mr. Mittlebury rock-hard.

Mr. Mittlebury shook his head. He had no desire to masturbate, and yet here he was. Mr. Mittlebury looked toward the bathroom. It was occupied. He cast his attention back upon his notebook. Perhaps he could will his erection away with renewed focus!

Mr. Mittlebury concentrated very hard indeed. He took up the pencil and scribbled hesitantly, "Pizza . . . is my girlfriend."

Presently, the pheasant appeared beside him. "Hello, Mr. Mittlebury!"

Mr. Mittlebury jumped and covered his erection with his small hooves. "Miss Baxter! How do you do?"

The beautiful fowl smiled at him. Mr. Mittlebury was dumbfounded. Miss Baxter knew his name? He stole a quick glance at his lap. Mercifully, his penis was limp from fear.

"Haven't seen you around here in a while. Are you designing another T-shirt? You must let me be the first to order it! I'm cross that I neglected to order the pizza one."

Mr. Mittlebury was still overcoming his shock. "I'm working on a new one. It has to do with tacos." Wherever did that come from, Mr. Mittlebury wondered. "Would you like one?"

"I would indeed!"

Mr. Mittlebury fumbled for another topic of conversation. "You're at Mashable, right?"

The pheasant shrugged her soft, lustrous wings. "I edit their Hollywood section."

"How splendid!"

Just then, the bathroom door swung open—and out walked David! He sauntered over to Mr. Mittlebury.

"Shitter's free if you want to beat it."

Mr. Mittlebury was too surprised to feel shame. "David, what in heaven's name are you doing at my co-working space?"

David eyed Miss Baxter, and then leaned in to Mr. Mittlebury. "Look, maybe we should talk about this privately."

Mr. Mittlebury began to sweat. He looked at Miss Baxter, then picked up his notebook.

"Why, surely, David, if you feel that would be—"

"You know what, I don't have a lot of time. Listen. I know you're hard up this month. I'll pay your loan. But you have to get a real job. Come work for me at Zooples. You can be a customer service rep or some shit."

Mr. Mittlebury looked over at the neatly dressed fox working on his laptop. The gentleman met Mr. Mittlebury's gaze and then glanced toward a sign that read, "This is a silent workspace."

Mr. Mittlebury lowered his voice to a whisper. "Look, can we just talk about this after my show tonight?"

Miss Baxter's ears perked up. "You have a show tonight?"

David turned to Miss Baxter. "Yeah. Wanna go with me?"

Again, Mr. Mittlebury was shocked. He couldn't hide the hope in his voice.

"You want to see my show, David?"

David chuckled. "I want to see *her* see your show."

Mr. Mittlebury looked down at his pink, plucky little lap and nodded. David was cruel, but he was right. Mr. Mittlebury was, it must be said, a loser. He could feel his eyes well up with tears.

Just then, Miss Baxter piped up. "I'd love to see your show, Mr. Mittlebury."

Mr. Mittlebury looked into her beautiful, kind brown eyes. "How lovely! How perfectly splendid!"

"It's settled then," David said to Miss Baxter. "I'll pick you up at six-thirty, and we can grab drinks. Trust me, you'll need the booze."

Mr. Mittlebury didn't mind David's insult. He squealed with glee.

The gentleman fox closed his laptop and threw up his paws. "What the hell," he said. "I'll come, too."

Mr. Mittlebury left his workspace that evening walking on air. It didn't even matter that David had humiliated him in front of Miss Baxter and the gentleman fox, or moreover, that David was taking Miss Baxter out on a date. She was coming to his improv-show! For the first time in months, Mr. Mittlebury felt a bit of pep in his step. He went home to sup and dress for the evening.

His mother had left out a large slice of nettleberry pie and a fat, juicy beetle. He popped the beetle in his mouth, poured himself a glass of goat's milk, and sat his generous bottom upon a stool to better enjoy the pie. But when he picked up the plate, he noticed something unusual underneath it.

It was a letter. Mr. Mittlebury squinted at the envelope; it was addressed to him in his father's handwriting. His father rarely left letters. Mr. Mittlebury opened it.

Dear Son,

I know you are the creative one. I do not mean to presume that you would use my ideas. But I had some suggestions.

"King of the Sty"

"Nettleberry Pie? Yes, Please"

"2 Bowls of Slop? How about 3?"

Love,

Dad

Mr. Mittlebury cleared his throat and put the note in his vest pocket. It occurred to Mr. Mittlebury that he was alone in the sty and that he could masturbate without disturbance. With a heavy heart, Mr. Mittlebury realized that he was going to masturbate, whether he wanted to or not. He stared down at the nettleberry pie and felt sad.

Suddenly he thought of Miss Baxter, and how lovely her voice was. And then Mr. Mittlebury did something very unusual indeed. He lay down on his back and began doing sit-ups.

His belly was round as could be, and it bunched up in big, hard rolls as he strained to lift his pudgy neck, but he grunted with satisfaction at the effort. He decided he would do ninety-four. He quickly revised his number to a nice, round nine, and by the time he'd finished, Mr. Mittlebury had forgotten all about masturbating himself to orgasm.

That night at the Gallery Loft, Mr. Mittlebury bounded onto the stage with confidence. He introduced himself and Sir Pipsley and asked the audience for a suggestion of anything at all to get started.

"How about 'Life is a banquet of second chances!'"

Mr. Mittlebury looked out into the audience. It was Blantyre, the life-coach badger! He was seated next to Mr. Mittlebury's parents!

"Thanks, Blantyre—but we just need a suggestion of a single word."

"Failure," called out David. He sat next to Miss Baxter, who looked ravishing in a lavender beret. Mr. Mittlebury looked down at his hooves.

"Taco!" cried Miss Baxter.

Sir Pipsley stepped up to the lip of the stage. "Thank you—I heard 'taco.'"

With that, they began. Mr. Mittlebury started a scene with an unusually strong initiation. When he brought back his one-eyed janitor character for a callback in the second beat, he got his first laugh of the night.

Mr. Mittlebury loosened up. He played a Gypsy attended by trained monkeys, and whenever the monkeys pleased him, he did his Cotton-Eyed Joe dance. It made sense in the scene. The audience lapped it up, and Mr. Mittlebury was having a splendid, altogether stupendous night!

Just then, Mr. Mittlebury heard something strange. A soft, relaxing sound. It was the lullaby he used to relax himself. Someone was whistling it.

Mr. Mittlebury scanned the audience until his shiny little eyes rested on David, who sat whistling. Cold fear washed over Mr. Mittlebury as he felt a familiar stirring inside of him. No, he thought. Please, please no.

But it was no use. Mr. Mittlebury's penis was suddenly and extremely erect.

Panicked, he looked out into the crowd. The gentleman fox had his head in his paws. Tappy anxiously spread slop on a biscuit. David smirked. Only Miss Baxter met his eyes, and hers were full of sympathy.

Mr. Mittlebury stepped forward, his taut, engorged genitals bouncing as he did. He was propelled by a force he did not recognize.

"Ladies and gentlemen," he began. "I have a problem. I

use masturbation to cope with stress. But it has become such a habit that now even mild anxiety triggers erections. I'm not in control, and it's scary. I'm sorry."

There was a horrible silence. His mother started to sob. David chuckled, and there were a few other nervous laughs. Mr. Mittlebury realized he had made a terrible mistake. But then, a bolt of pure inspiration struck him. He leaned into the audience.

". . . said no one ever."

And then Mr. Mittlebury heard a glorious sound: Miss Baxter laughed. And then others joined in.

Sir Pipsley stepped forward.

"Whatever, sir. You want fries with that?" Sir Pipsley mimed adjusting a microphone in front of his mouth. An even greater laugh surged through the audience. Sir Pipsley was placing the scene at a drive-through restaurant—transforming Mr. Mittlebury into an over-sharing customer!

"Why, yes I do! I'll have fries with that. This is a drive-through, after all!"

And Mr. Mittlebury mimed driving a car, and he "drove" up to the window! And how the audience laughed! Mr. Mittlebury's limp little member swung jauntily as he trotted to the improvised drive-through. Out of the corner of his eye, he saw David sitting stone-faced as Miss Baxter clapped, laughing.

In fact, all the rest of the audience was clapping, too! Mr. Mittlebury tried to count the number—but he couldn't! Why, there might as well have been 94,000!

And suddenly 94,000 didn't really seem like such a very bad number, after all!

Big Time

Look, I'm not gonna sugarcoat it for you. Hollywood is like a big fat man with a snarl on his face and a knife in his hand, and he'll slash your ass to ribbons—unless you're smart. That means you sleep with one eye open. One hand on your bankroll and the other on your gun. No one makes it out here in Tinseltown any other way. Trust me, Shirley Temple would tell you the same thing. I used to hang out with Shirley, actually. Taught me a lot. For example: always walk back to your ride with your keys between your fingers. That way, if you have to fend off an attacker, you can hit him in the throat and rip down through the jugular. Unless, of course, he can help your career. In that case, offer him a ride, and remember: saliva is a natural lubricant. Shirley was full of gems like that. But we're getting off track. My point is, anyone who's climbed to the top of the bone pile lives by the same rules: never trust anyone, and always look out for number one.

Maybe you won't believe half my story. That's all right. I probably wouldn't believe it, either, if it hadn't happened to me. But I was sitting orchestra center for the whole thing and brother, this is exactly how it went down.

Let's get the bio out of the way.

In July of 1917 I get squished out in a shit mining town called Beaver Falls. The medical community may say it's impossible, but I remember life inside my mother's womb. It was toasty and humid, as it tends to be inside a person, and there I was: floating in goo and sucking on this little tube. It was a pretty boring routine—goo, tube, goo, tube—and I just remember thinking, "I have to get out of here. I have to get something going." Next thing I know I'm shooting through a tunnel the size of a walnut, and then it gets windy, and out of nowhere this big hairy lug's got me by the ankles and he's smacking my ass. (He could've done it again, too, if he'd ever bothered to call me.)

My folks were A1.

I mean, sure, they were poor, and they'd never seen a day of school. Dad signed his name with an X, and mom's teeth were messed up, so she laughed with a hand over her mouth, but I rolled straight sevens in the mom and dad department. They worked themselves ragged trying to give me a better life, dad in the mines and mom cleaning houses and playing piano for the local vaudeville theater.

I didn't even know we were poor until the first day of school. That's when I realized we were flat broke. It was the first time I mixed with kids from the fancy part of town, and I showed up in a dress my mom made me for the occasion. She'd used a pretty red checked cloth, and I thought I looked gangbusters. Turns out that red checked cloth was what the grocer used to line the fruit crates. The kids laughed at me. They called me Crate Girl.

I came home deeply depressed. I walked in the door, and there was Mom, all excited to hear about the conquests of the young scholar. Well, I just burst into tears and spilled my guts out. She took it in silently and then went right over to the coffee can and peeled a couple bucks off our precious wad. That was a big deal. We only had seven dollars to our name. Then she grabbed my hand and took me into town and bought me a box of animal crackers for fifteen cents and a brand-new dress for two dollars. Talk about a pick-me-up. When she handed the saleslady the dress and said, "Could you wrap this up?" I almost screamed with joy. It was a chocolate-brown velvet number with a creamy white Peter Pan collar and mother-of-pearl buttons, loaded with class. The next day, when I walked into the schoolhouse, my balls were practically dragging on the floor. No one said dick to me that day.

I often think back to that afternoon, because my mother's tender act of generosity taught me an important life lesson: nothing is more important than cash.

Dad died in the mine explosion of '24 and they planted my mom two weeks later, after a drunk pushed her out of a trolley car and she got trampled by a horse. The funerals were open casket, but I prefer to remember their faces like they were on the last afternoon we spent together, at the Beaver County Carnival. I was sitting on my dad's shoulders, and my mom handed me a big red candy apple. It's a happy memory, with the sunshine kissing my cheeks and a fresh spring breeze flapping my mother's cornflower-blue dress. I miss those fuckers, but what can you do? Life shoves you up against a dumpster and has its way with you, and it's up to you to find your way back to the road and hail a cab.

But here's the upshot, for all my glass-half-full amigos: turns out getting orphaned was great for my career. See, my parents were sweet, gentle people, and if *they* had raised me, with lots of love and hugs and shit, I never would have developed the bottomless hole inside me that you need to succeed in showbiz.

The orphanage I got dumped into was Catholic, and spread out across a big brown lawn on the Jewish side of town. Catholics in Jewtown, go figure. I've never had a problem with Jews, by the way. Why should I? They're a hardworking people. Focused, motivated. What's so bad about that? It's the Italians who belong in cages. Have you ever seen an Italian eat? You won't see a mouth open that wide outside of a cathouse.

But we're getting offtrack again: at the ripe age of seven, I punched in at the Beaver County Home for Little Wanderers. If you've ever had the pleasure of staying at one of the Ritz-Carlton family hotels, then you have a pretty good idea of what Beaver County wasn't like. I walked into that joint a rosy-cheeked ray of sunshine who didn't know a stranger, and I limped out a rusty son of a bitch with a heart of lead.

My first day there, I got nailed for taking an extra apple, and Sister Mary Agnes made me stand on a chair in the corner. That lardass left me there until sundown—and that turned out to be par for the course. Those first years were rough, but every night at lights out, when I slipped into my cot and grabbed my rat stick, I felt *it* inside me. I'd always had "it"—that buzzy feeling somewhere between your belly button and your asshole that tells you you're going to be somebody.

That buzzing was strong.

See, I knew from jump street that I was meant for big things. I just didn't know what kind of things until I was fourteen, when I went on my big trip to Harrisburg. That trip changed everything.

I went to Harrisburg to have an operation. Here's how they found out I needed it: the orphanage doctor was a pervert. He was constantly wrangling the girls into his office for pelvic exams. One day when I was in there, he paused from his normal routine and actually looked at me. He noticed some swelling in my stomach. It was worrisome enough that he talked to the head nun, and she sent me over to the children's hospital, where they opened me up and found a mango-sized tumor snuggled right up against my appendix. Don't worry, I'm fine now, but it was a pretty big deal at the time. That bad boy clocked in at six solid pounds. Sometimes, in fleeting moments of spiritual clarity, I reflect on the fact that if God hadn't made that doctor a serial pedophile, I'd be dead right now.

While I was recovering, I got slathered in special treatment. Literally. I was given a daily rag bath, and every couple of hours a nurse dabbed my lips with a damp sponge to keep them from drying out. The mayor even visited the children's ward one Saturday and gave every patient a balloon! Mine was banana yellow. After the rough treatment at Beaver County, the hospital was a welcome change—and I lapped up that sweet attention like a rottweiler slurping from a busted fire hydrant.

When I was strong enough to get out of bed on my

own, I started shuffling over to the nurses' area and telling jokes I'd learned from the janitors at the orphanage. I liked those janitors. I'd bum cigarettes off them, we'd shoot the breeze. We weren't so different, at the end of the day. They might have been middle-aged Polacks with hair on their hands, and I was just a ten-year-old kid, but we were all doing time. Anyway, I picked up a bunch of great material from those guys. There was the one about the three chugs in an elevator, the midget with the dick made of wood, the farmer and the Jewish cow—the punch line was something about udders, and a mohel shouting, "Thats a-gonna be extra!" The accent was kind of wobbly, but I got the white-caps laughing. And you know how it feels when you get a crowd going. It's the best feeling in the world.

Pretty soon I became the MVP of the ward. Nurses shared their cigarettes with me (I've been a smoker since I was nine— Oh, I should quit? Never heard that before, thanks for the tip). They even wheeled me down the hall to the operating room to tell jokes for the surgeons while they worked. All of a sudden, if I wanted an extra cup of Jell-O, all I had to do was tap a button. My stock had risen faster than Charlie Chaplin's pulse at a Girl Scout cookie drive. And it felt good! Really good. For the first time in my life, I was being recognized for my talent as a performer. And it's important to squirrel those early praise nuts away, so you can gnaw on them in the lean times.

When I got back to the orphanage, the rats had gotten bolder. The rat stick only went so far. Before we went to bed we'd smear our faces in VapoRub; the smell repelled them. During those nights, lying in bed, my face and hands oily and reeking from the ointment, I started planning my escape. And I kept that plan close to the vest. I didn't tell anyone except Bobbi.

Bobbi Capello was the closest thing I had to a friend at Beaver County. (Yeah, she was Italian, but they're not all like that.) After Sister Mary Agnes stuck me on the chair that first day, she was the only kid who was nice to me. She snuck me a handful of gingersnaps. Right away I felt a connection.

Bobbi came from hill people. She was pretty, plump, and quiet, with big, expressive eyes, jet-black hair, and pale, almost glow-in-the-dark skin. Rumor was, her whole family—both parents and five brothers—were murdered in an Indian raid and she hadn't said a word since.

We were born the same year, three days apart. Neat, right? I was July third, and she was the sixth. I called her Squirt.

Anyway, you wouldn't have known it to look at her, because she gave off a strong weirdo vibe, but Bobbi was a goddamn delight. She was an easy laugh, and she wasn't a suck-up, unlike the other goody-two-shoes girls in our class who were always cozying up to the sisters.

Because she was so sweet, Bobbi was also easy to take advantage of. The nuns used to let us pick a treat to enjoy once a week—pretzels or gum or a peppermint stick. Well, I hate to say it, but I scammed Bobbi out of her treat more times than I can count. In the beginning, I'd just make up some dumb game, like, I'd bet her her candy that she couldn't guess the number that I was thinking of. But pretty soon I started flat-out lying. One time I told her I heard on the radio there was a poisoned bag of pretzels going around. I "tested" her bag of pretzels right in front of her until they were gone. Eventually Bobbi just started giving me her treats, because, she said, "You like them more than I do." She was right, and I ate them, but that took the fun out of it.

We also bonded over these little nudie cartoons she used to draw.

Heh. Those cartoons were goddamn hilarious. Fuck. I wish I'd saved one so I could show it to you. They were these caricatures of the nuns, always naked, performing degrading sexual acts, or in the moment right before a violent death. She sent me one when I was in the hospital. Bobbi had drawn a picture of Sister Mary Agnes on the can, squeezing one out while at the same time sucking off Saint Anthony of Padua. The caption? "Ecclesiastes 4:13: As the turd leaveth the ass, so in the mouth cometh the dick." Pretty funny, right?

Hey. Let's check in for a second. How you doing? Just to keep it completely real between us, I don't blame you for a second if you've been skimming through all this childhood stuff. It's hard to pay attention to stories about kids. Oh, you had a red bicycle? You didn't get enough attention from your dad? It always sends me straight to snoozeville. Well, don't worry, now we're leaving kiddieland for the good stuff.

Fast-forward to 1935. It's my eighteenth rotation on this crazy blue carousel, and by this point, Bobbi and I had busted out of the orphanage, hopped on a bus, and booked it west for the bloody, pumping heart of the entertainment industry: Fort Wayne, Indiana. It was as far as we could get on our limited funds. But as soon as we saved up enough cash, we were gonna complete the journey to L.A.

And we wouldn't have to wait long, because Bobbi and I got gigs at Radioplane, a munitions factory that made airplane parts for the war.

Radioplane was easy money. All you had to do was push your tits out for the foreman and spray down the plane sidings with fire retardant. The chemicals didn't smell great, and you weren't allowed to take breaks, and sometimes you coughed up blood, but there was a great camaraderie with the other girls on your line. Plus, the hours were regular, so you got out of work with plenty of time to go home, heat up a can of dinner, then quick-change and make tracks for the Rusty Flamingo.

The Flamingo was this dance hall where if you checked in with Salty by seven, you got on the lineup and the guys paid you a quarter a dance. By the end of the night, Bobbi and I could generally come out with a nice chunk of change. On the weekends they'd have these dance contests, and that was another way to clean up. I was the Rhumba Queen three months running, actually, until a feisty little froggy named Claudette stole my crown. But that's life. You win some, you lose some. You know how it is.

Whenever we came home with a wad, Bobbi and I stuffed it into a coffee can we kept under a floorboard. We were saving up to pay off this gorgeous beaver stole we'd seen at Kaufmann's, and I'll never forget the day we finally brought it home. You've got to have one thing in your wardrobe that's untouchable, and for us it was that stole. You just slipped that furry fucker on and suddenly it was like, anywhere you went, you had reservations. Bobbi and I went halfsies on the cost, but I'll admit I wore it a hell of a lot more than she did. We ended up with a system: I'd get the stole on weekends and weeknights when desired, and if Bobbi wanted it, she'd put in a request and we'd work something out.

I was wearing the stole one night at the Flamingo when I got into it with this Russian chick. She'd been moving in on my regulars, and it was starting to chap my ass, so I went over to her and gently explained that she was out of line. She told me to fuck off, and pretty soon we were in each other's faces.

Bobbi rushed over to smooth things out. That was always her first instinct in a scrap, ever since our days at Beaver County. The Russki wasn't hearing it, though, so eventually Bobbi grabbed my wrist and started pulling me out the door. Just as we were about to disappear, a beer bottle whizzed past my head and smashed on the wall, courtesy of my new comrade.

I marched straight back to the bitch and clocked her in the jaw. She stumbled back, then bent down and slid a knife out of her garter. There were gasps, and everyone around us took about ten steps back. Except Bobbi. She just sighed, then grabbed a barstool and broke it over the Russki's back.

That was Bobbi for you. True fuckin' blue.

By now you're probably thinking: all right, already. When the hell does she get her "big break"? Well, here's your payoff. One day at Radioplane I noticed a mousy-looking guy with a camera looking me up and down. A couple minutes later, the foreman's in my ear saying there's a photographer from the newspaper and he wants to take a couple of pictures of me and Squirt doing our thing—for the war effort, for the boys' morale. I'm not surprised we got singled out. Bobbi'd lost the baby fat in all the right places, and I had one of those faces where when I walked into a room, people clapped.

Now, I don't typically give something for nothing, but at this particular juncture I wasn't in a place to ask the foreman for extra scratch. See, I was on thin ice at Radioplane for being late all the time. I was always sleeping past my alarm, tuckered out from my rhumba exertions at the Flamingo the night before. So I went along, no questions asked: chin up, chin down, more teeth, etc. I don't want to blow my own horn, but the guy asked me to pose alone for the last couple pictures.

Later, on the bus ride home, I asked Bobbi if she minded that the photographer gave me special treatment.

"It's not my fault that fruit has bad taste," she said, reapplying her lipstick in the window and winking at a passing sailor.

That's what I liked about Bobbi. Resilient. She'd just let shit roll right off her, like water off a duck's ass. That's the expression, right? Ah, whatever. I never said I went to Yale.

The very next morning, guess what happens? *The Journal Gazette* ran my mug on page one. There was a big headline across the top that read "WOMEN AND THE WAR EFFORT," and below that, a smaller headline: "POLLY THE PROPELLER GIRL." Right below that was a picture of a girl holding up a propeller, looking adorable as hell.

I was that girl!

I didn't know it that day, but every paper in the country ran that picture. My face was on every breakfast table from Salem to San Jose. Pretty sweet, right? Well hang on to your balls, because the next day I spot another mystery gentleman at Radioplane. He's a good-looking guy in a suit, shorter than the first guy, but suaver. He walks up to me and delivers the line I've been waiting to hear my whole life—and I might have been a little loopy from the chemicals but I swear I actually saw the words stretch out of his mouth and into the air, arcing toward me like a rainbow bridge to Candyland:

"Hey, kid. How'd you like to be in pictures?"

Bobbi helped me pack. Inside, I knew she was probably going through hell, but I was so excited about my fuse being lit that I didn't pay it too much attention. She kept it together right until the end, when she sat on my suitcase to help me latch it. That's when the waterworks started. I just gave her a hug and promised I'd call her the second I unpacked. I meant it, too. That nutty runt had been there for me through thick and thin.

But when you've got stars in your eyes, it's hard to see straight.

Three days later, I sauntered onto the MGM lot in Hollywood like the biggest-dicked lion on the Serengeti. I was a nobody, but I didn't know it yet—and that gave me an X factor that shone straight onto the celluloid. I did that first screen test in a bathing suit, and every crew guy in a ten-foot radius had a hard-on. I'm talking more pitched tents than a Bombay slum.

I was feeling pretty dandy by the time I wrapped and headed over to the commissary for lunch. But the second my feet crossed the threshold, I got cut down to size. Everywhere I looked there were stars, sashaying in and out like they owned the place. There was more wattage in that cafeteria than in all of Times Square. I stared as I ate my chicken salad alone, thankful I hadn't stopped in before my screen test. These were big shots, real VIPs, and I was just a measly glowworm from bumfuck, Pennsyltucky.

As I was stuffing another forkful down the chute and feeling kinda shitty, I spotted her: the legend herself, the lady lion of MGM, the Big Kahuna Mamalooma: Marlene goddamn Dietrich.

I shit you not.

The chicken salad slid off my fork, and my face froze in a lopsided smile. I couldn't believe we were breathing the same air! Marlene had seen me through some rough times, brother. Bobbi and I used to slip out of the orphanage to catch her pictures. She was my favorite star, bar none. Bobbi was more of a Claudette Colbert fan, but I needed the hard stuff, and that was my girl Marlene. Vivacious, charming, like a coupe of pink champagne—but with a messed-up edge, you know? You felt like she could fight or fuck her way out of any situation, and I fell for that—hook, line, and sinker. Plus, if you squinted at her in her profile, she was a dead ringer for my mom.

Well, I forgot all about how I was a know-nothing hay-seed. All of a sudden my legs were moving. I couldn't help it. Owning a slip of paper with her name on it, scrawled by her very own hand, that was too good to pass up. She was sitting at a table with a bunch of dapper-looking suits, and I felt a phantom surge of pride at how they were staring at her, rapt, as she told some story. Then she got to the punch line—she could barely get it out; she was already laughing—and the whole table burst out in howls. I just stood there and laughed along with them. Not my slickest opening, I know, but I was starstruck.

As she was wiping a tear from her eye, she noticed me hovering, and then the rest of the guys swiveled to get a load of me. I dug a pen out of my purse and got right to the point.

I put on my silkiest voice, the one I still use to get out of shoplifting charges. "Excuse me, Miss Dietrich. I'm a great admirer of your work. Could I have your autograph?"

She looked me up and down. "Straight off the bus," she muttered to the guy sitting on her right.

I looked down at my outfit. I was wearing a periwinkle polka-dot dress with a big bow at the collar. I'd seen it in a magazine and sewed it myself. What was wrong with it? I looked at Marlene and then glanced around the commissary. The women were wearing suits, blouses, all in dark colors. Hats. Gloves.

It was just like that first day of school. I was Crate Girl all over again. She scribbled something on the napkin and handed it to me with a sly smile. I turned and walked out of there as Marlene and her boy toys laughed behind me.

I made it outside into the blinding sunshine and opened my hand. The note read:

For when you get a few pennies:
  Saks
  9600 Wilshire Blvd
  Marlene Dietrich

Walking to the bus, I couldn't help but wonder if it would have killed Marlene to be just a tiny bit less of a bitch. But then I thought, Holy fucking shit. *I just met Marlene Dietrich!*

. . .

My screen test landed me a five-line role in a musical, so I had my foot in the door, but that didn't feel like much. It was hard being so close to my dream, yet so far. Like a poor kid in a toy store, or Charlie Chaplin in a toy store. Trust me, I saw him at parties, that man had a problem.

I ended up getting some great intel from a pair of screen-writers. By the way, whenever you want the straight dope, pump the scribes. I've never met a group of people who feel more wronged and underappreciated. While that's an easy recipe for heartache, it also means they don't kid themselves about the way things really work. The writers tipped me off that, if you were a young kitty cat like myself, you either hung around the lot and proved yourself role by role or you caught some fat cat's eye at the Tropicana. Writers. They're the last thing on earth you'd want to fuck, but they're loyal as collies.

The Tropicana was the hottest club in town, like the Rusty Flamingo on steroids. A lot of big mover-and-shaker types hung out there. Dancing in the rhumba contests was a great way to get seen, and of course I wiped the floor with the other girls. It was like one big audition, and I always tried to leave an impression. One time I got dipped back so far I ate a dinner roll right off of Louis B. Mayer's plate! Judging by the wink he gave me, I don't think he minded.

A year into my Hollywood sojourn, I'd had bit roles in six pictures. I was getting noticed at the Trop, but it wasn't translating to any real gigs. I was twenty-five by this point, and girls younger than me were already starring opposite Bogie and Spencer Tracy. Lauren Bacall was only nineteen for fuck's sake, and she had a trailer and everything. So I started sniffing around in earnest for the inside track. There's always an inside track, muchachos. It's just a matter of bringing an expert's eye—as well as a patient, inquisitive spirit—to bear. So I took out my magnifying glass, donned my Sherlock Holmes cap, and set about sleuthing it out.

It's suckjobs. The inside track turned out to be run-of-the-mill suckjobs. I gave one to David O. Selznick in his office and all of a sudden, guess whose name was number two on the call sheet? You're damn right it was mine! Ruby Russell, by the way. Should've gotten that out of the way earlier.

Selznick offered me my pick of several hot scripts. I got it down to two: *Casablanca* and *The Rootin' Tootin' Rebel of Rio*. I thought long and hard about it, and settled on what I thought was the surefire winner.

Like they say, hindsight's 20/20.

Rootin' Tootin' was set to shoot five days after Selznick handed me the script, with Duncan Wylie directing. Wylie had a reputation for doing big dance numbers. We met for coffee, and he told me about the set piece he had in mind—a sensual samba number that would take place in a nightclub in Paris. My character was a Brazilian spy who ends up flying for the RAF on intelligence missions, then crash-lands in France and has to dance her way to freedom. It didn't make a lot of sense to me, either, but the costume designer's sketches for the sparkly crop top and high-low skirt I'd wear in the nightclub dance number were too yummy to pass up. *Rootin' Tootin'* was a gut call, and sometimes your gut is wrong.

The upshot of the whole thing was that my pal Ingrid

Bergman made out like a bandit, since they handed her the *Casablanca* script when I turned it down. You may have heard of that picture. It made a little splash. Even though *Rio* fucked me six ways to Sunday, I'm still glad Bergman ended up with points on the board. That chick was cool. She gave me a tampon one night at the Trop when I started bleeding all over Clark Gable.

Anyway, when I booked *Rio*, I didn't know I'd just made the biggest mistake of my life, so I felt like celebrating. I thought about calling up Bobbi. I'd gotten a postcard from her the week before, saying she just moved to L.A. and to give her a buzz. Part of me missed her like hell. I made it all the way to a pay phone, but once I had the operator on the line I lost my nerve and hung up.

See, she'd written me a bunch of letters since I'd moved out here, and I read the first couple, but then I just started tossing them. Bobbi was a part of the "old" me. She reminded me that I was small-time. It wasn't her fault, but that's the way it was. And anyway, I knew she could handle herself. She'd been through worse than a pal cutting her loose. So that night, I headed to the Trop by myself and whooped it up with a group of homo sailors.

But enough boo-hoo shit.

The very first night on the set of *Rootin' Tootin'*, we're out on this dusty field, shooting the big dogfight scene where my plane gets gunned down. I wasn't actually gonna do any flying—just sit in the plane with scenery screens behind me to make it look like I was in the air. You know, movie magic. So there I am in the cockpit, doing my best fighter pilot act—grabbing the throttle, flicking knobs on the control board, the whole works—when suddenly my elbow accidentally catches this lever marked Turbo.

I hear a muffled boom from inside the plane, then a slow whirring sound that gradually gets faster and faster, and I can see the director and the DP and the crew waving their hands and going crazy, but there's nothing I can do: before I know it, I'm tearing down the runway at ninety miles an hour. I keep flipping switches and pulling levers, trying to turn the damn thing off—but by that point, the engine's revved up and it's rumbling through my guts, and I feel this goofy weightless feeling as the wheels lift off the runway and I'm going up, up, up and now the clouds are streaking past the windows, and my face feels like it's being wiped off my skull, and then there's another loud boom, a blinding flash, and total silent black.

I wake up in hell.

That's where I figured I was, anyway. It was roasting hot, and I felt like I'd been run over by a Panzer. But then my lids fluttered open and I saw I was lying on a beach. I peeled my head off the sand, looked around, and tried to piece together what happened. I didn't see the plane. Didn't see any crew. Just a muscle-bound Chinaman standing over me in a tank top that read SWEAT IS FAT CRYING.

He crouched down and laid a gentle hand on my shoulder.

"Hey, are you okay?"

Groggy, I focused on his face. He had a shaved head, an eyebrow piercing, and pink diamonds in his earlobes. I grabbed his arm.

"Where am I?"

"Bikini Boot Camp with Brad," he said. "I'm Brad."

Boot camp. Huh, I thought, I must've crash-landed at an army base. But the nearest one was all the way in Inglewood. Holy shit—did I fly that far on my own?

"Thanks, soldier," I said, using his arm to steady myself as I got up. "Just point me toward your commanding officer."

Brad cocked his head. He was around my age, hard as a rock and wearing skintight hot pants. Even though I was wobbly on my feet, I released his arm. The last thing I needed was for a shutterbug to catch me canoodling with a flamboyant Oriental. Universal still had me on notice after I got caught whooping it up with that Creole drummer. I needed to keep a low profile.

"Are you in the military, ma'am?" he asked, gesturing to my pilot getup.

I reached into my brassiere, found the five-spot I always kept there, and handed it over.

"You know what? Just call me a cab, honey. I gotta scoot back to the lot." But Brad just stood there, looking at me in a very worried kind of way.

"I think you might have a concussion."

"Sweetie, what's going on?" I heard a new voice say. Then I watched dumbstruck as a smooth, blond man walked up behind Brad and slid both arms around his waist—right where any vice squad could see.

"I found her lying here," Brad said. "I think she needs to go to the hospital."

I winked, nodding to the two of them. "Your secret's safe with me, fellas. All I need's a ride."

But the blond man just touched his fingers to my wrist and checked my pulse. "Miss, what's your name? I'm a nurse."

I couldn't help it. I burst out laughing.

"And I'm the king of Siam."

At that moment a beautiful colored man with a little machine on his arm ran past us wearing nothing but shorts. Then three more people raced by—two more shirtless guys followed by an elderly woman.

What the hell were they running from? Suddenly it hit me: the Japs! The invasion came after all! Just my luck that they'd pounce right when I'm filming my biggest picture yet. For a split second I wondered if this would delay *Rio*'s release date, which would really stink, since I was getting points on the back end and had just leased a Caddy that sure as hell wasn't going to pay for itself. But then I remembered the danger at hand.

"We gotta beat it!" I tried to pull the guys in the direction the others were fleeing. "They'll fillet us like salmon! Let's scram!"

But the little blond stopped me. "Miss, just stay here and relax. We'll call someone to help you." He turned to Brad. "Can you get your phone from the car?"

Brad nodded and started to go. That's when I noticed the back of his tank top. The words there sent a chill down my spine.

BIKINI BOOTCAMP WITH BRAD
JUNE 19–24, 2021

"Hold it!" I shouted after him. He stopped and turned back to me.

I had a couple questions for Brad.

. . .

Twenty minutes later, I'd finally pieced the puzzle together enough to see a clear picture.

It seemed I'd been blasted eighty years into the future. I couldn't get my head around it at first, and neither could Brad, but the little blond nurse thought he had it figured. He was a college man and had a whole theory about how time travel was possible—something about superluminal travel and exotic negative mass—but I didn't care about that mumbo jumbo. I was more interested in the catch-up lesson they gave me on what the world was like now. Because if these fellas were feeding me the straight dope, 2021 was kookier than any sci-fi saga they'd been able to dream up back in my time.

I tried to sum up what I'd learned. "So let me get this straight. Boys can be girls now, girls can be boys, and I'm not allowed to say 'ching-chong'?"

Brad winced. "There's a little more to it than that, but that's a good place to start."

I was starting to get wise. But then the blond one threw me for a new loop.

"You might start to age rapidly," he said, looking concerned. "Like Mel Gibson in *Forever Young*. It's a movie about a pilot in World War II who gets cryogenically frozen and wakes up in the nineties."

Now there was an idea for a picture. I'd been drowning in scripts just the week before, and couldn't help feeling a little peeved that I hadn't run across something as good as that.

"That's a great idea. How'd it do at the box office?"

Brad looked down at his phone computer and tapped around on it. "A hundred twenty-eight million."

"Hot doggie!" I said. A lot might have changed, but one

thing was clear: Tinseltown was still a money machine. And I was wasting time. I needed to get back to the action.

"You said one of you boys has a car nearby?"

"Yeah, my Volt's just off Abbot Kinney."

I smiled. "How about giving a girl a ride to Universal Studios?"

Tucked safely into Brad's buggy on the way to Universal, I asked Blondie to fill me in on what exactly happened in "World War Two." When he finished explaining, I yelped with joy.

"Take that, you Kraut bastards!"

For any of my amigos out there who don't regularly peep the headlines, I've got great news. World War II was this big dustup between the good guys and the Nazis, and *the good guys won*! Which is great because I would've had a hell of a time learning Deutsch. But seriously, Uncle Sam, right? Bet your chips on that lanky bastard every time.

Forty-five minutes later we were driving up Lankershim and I could feel my jitters floating away.

Brad pulled over next to a giant stairway. "This is as close as I can get," he said. "Otherwise we have to go into the parking structure and it's a whole thing."

I thanked them and started up the stairs, the hot California sun beating down on my ragged perm. It wasn't the most glamorous way to enter the lot. It reminded me of my first day in Hollywood, when I got off that dusty choo choo from Fort Wayne, sticky and reeking but full of hope. Back then, I needed to convince this town that I was worth taking a chance on. Now all I needed was for someone to remember who I was.

I crested the hill and my jaw hit the ground.

Universal had really changed. I didn't see any of the bungalows or sound stages that had been there just this morning. The lot I saw was just a big midway, and it looked like they were working on some kind of carnival picture. Thousands of tubby extras were milling around eating ice cream cones and hot dogs.

I scanned the crowd for someone in charge and zeroed in on a tall, good-looking guy in a fedora and a leather jacket. I noticed he also had a bullwhip. That's a little odd, I thought, but I liked the boldness. This was clearly a guy who didn't take any guff. Probably a producer. I made a beeline for him but got cut off by a couple of roly-poly youngsters waving autograph books.

"Indy! Indy!"

The guy turned, grinned, and produced a pen. So he wasn't a producer after all but a fellow star. I waited for him to sign the kids' books, then made my move.

"Hey, pal," I began, sauntering up to him with my friendliest smile. "It's been a little while since I've been on the payroll here. Who's the studio head these days? I have to go see him."

He chuckled, then looked around and said softly, "Good for you for staying in character! You're the new King Kong girl, right? My girlfriend's a sound designer over there. Kong 360's in the amphitheater over by the Minions gate."

I sighed. "Look, I don't have time for all that. Just give me the name of the studio head."

He laughed again, less amused this time.

"Hah, yeah. Anyway, good luck with the new gig."

What game was this guy playing? I grabbed him by the lapels and repeated my request.

His expression changed then. I knew that look. It was the same look I saw on Pa's face the day he realized our mutt Sparky had the sick.

"Okay, ma'am. Take it easy. I'm going to call the studio head, okay?"

I nodded as he leaned down and muttered something into the mic clipped to his collar—something that sounded a lot like "Code orange by the Yogurt Frog." He looked back at me with a reassuring smile. "The studio head is on his way. Just chill here for a second, cool?"

Something didn't smell right. You don't get as far as I have without being able to spot bullshit. A quick glance over his shoulder confirmed my hunch: a pair of Universal security guards was headed straight for us.

I switched into survival mode, my coconut firing on all cylinders. Universal was a bust. What I needed more than anything now was a safe harbor. A place that didn't ask questions, where I could rustle up some cash and a square meal. What I needed was the Tropicana.

I spun on my heels and dived into the river of fatsos, Indy's calls fading behind me. Using my dart-and-weave method—perfected over years of running from over-friendly uncles and, on one particularly unpleasant ferry ride down the Monongahela, Siamese-twin brothers—I found the street. I hiked up my dress and stuck out my thumb. Next stop, the Trop.

When the cherub-faced Mexican who was kind enough to give me a lift dropped me at the corner of Sunset and Vine, I hopped out, shut the door, and leaned back in through the window.

"Josefina's not done with you, Pedro. She just needs to know you're not done with her."

Wiping a tear from his eye, Pedro nodded. "Thank you, Miss Ruby." Then he drove away.

I turned around and tried to make sense of what I was looking at. The Trop was there, all right, or at least the building was. But nothing else was recognizable.

The big neon sign over the porte cochere was gone, and the cracked stucco façade was now painted a smooth baby pink, with slim white letters that spelled THE FOLD.

I walked up the freshly swept cement steps and opened the huge white door. I almost had to squint to see inside. It was maybe the cleanest, brightest place I'd ever been in. And there were dames everywhere: spiffy, uptown-looking broads, front-of-store types, all around my age. I figured they'd turned the Trop into some sort of white-glove orphanage.

I walked down the airy hallway to a gleaming front desk. Deciding to play it cool, I leaned in and spoke in a hushed voice to the girl manning it. "Hey, sister. What is this place?"

She was pretty and pale, with dark, wavy hair and big eyeglasses with clear, chunky frames. She flashed me a friendly smile. "Hi! Ooh, I love your jacket. So, we're a women-focused co-working collective and club."

Huh. Co-working. Did that mean commies? I looked around and tried to make it add up. Hammer-and-sickle types like long wooden tables, soup in tin bowls, but this place was way too ritzy. The girl smiled and went on.

"The Fold is a network of community spaces designed for the professional, civic, social, and economic advancement of women through community."

I kept my yap shut, but I can tell you what I was thinking: that's a lot of words for "cathouse."

"Huh. The Fold," I said. "I like it. Like sisterhood and things."

"It's actually 'the Fold' as in labial fold?"

I had no idea what she was talking about and I didn't feel like sticking around to find out. You practically needed a dictionary to keep up around here. I was just about to head down to the railyard and turn a trick for some hot dog money when another girl breezed by me on her way out.

She called back to the front desk girl. "The audition's in Century City, so I should be back in like an hour."

I swiveled around to get a good look at the speaker. She was a chunky little Yid with big gold hoop earrings like a pirate. Her words were gobbledygook, but I heard "audition" loud and clear.

"Hold on," I said, putting a hand on her elbow. "You're an actress?"

She shrugged. "I mean, technically yes. I'm broke as shit, so at least that part's legit."

I turned back to the gal behind the counter and read her sleek little name tag. "Emma."

"You, too?"

She laughed. "No. I'm actually trying to direct."

The chunkster piled on. "Most of the staff here's in the industry. They're really good about letting you leave for auditions, and the benefits are solid. It's a pretty sweet day job."

You can bet my gears were grinding. I started walking back toward Emma, chin down, eyes bright, lots of teeth. "Any chance you're looking to add one more kitty to this cathouse?"

. . .

Emma introduced me to a few of her fellow employees. There was Marika, a big, pretty colored girl in a black turtleneck and tight overalls, and Suki, a cute Siamese in a mustard-colored muumuu. They were both actresses. Emma, however, explained that she only worked at the Fold part-time, in exchange for free membership. Her main gig was working as an assistant producer on something called a reality show. What she really wanted to do was direct. Then the girls turned the spotlight on me.

"So what's your deal, Ruby?"

I told them the whole story: the broad strokes of my bio and then the fine print about the airplane, the boom, and the woozy wakeup on the beach. The girls listened sympathetically.

"Holy shit," Marika said when I'd finished, bringing me in for a hug. "That's so fucked-up."

Emma took her phone out of her pocket. "Let me see if I can find you."

I gave Emma my info and she tapped a bunch. "Oh my god," she gasped, holding the thing in front of my face. "Is this you?"

It sure was.

I love that picture. It's my first studio still. I'm lying on a divan in a satin robe with feather piping. I felt so pretty that day—lithe and willowy, thanks to the pep pills and shit-shooters the studio doc showered on us like gum-drops. I'd spent the morning throwing up because of the mold problem in my bungalow, so you could see my ribs, and I was wearing my good lipstick—the one made from pig's blood and ground-up lead.

"That's me, all right."

Below the picture someone had written a whole novel about me. It said my name was Ruby Russell and I was an American film star who had disappeared in 1942 in a mysterious plane crash. Neither the wreckage of the plane nor my body were ever found.

I learned a lot about myself on Wikipedia. For starters, I enjoyed a "lively but modest career in early noir" with bit and supporting roles in films like *The Masked Arab* and *Night in the Jungle* (where "Russell's role as a gutsy, tough-talking showgirl remains the only redeeming feature of an otherwise trite and unbearably racist film"). Hey now! This was like getting to go to your own funeral! I wanted to poke around more myself, but right now I needed to know what happened with *Rio*.

"Hey! Look up *Rootin' Tootin' Rebel of Rio*, honey."

I wanted to see if they recast my role. Who knows? We'd shot enough that they might have been able to cut around me.

Emma read from the machine. *"Rootin' Tootin' Rebel of Rio,* 1942, starring Fred MacMurray and—"

"Betty fucking Grable?" By this point, I'd grabbed the little machine and was giving myself an eyeful. I was staring at a promotional poster for the movie, and there was Fred MacMurray—with that medium-talent Grable hanging all over him, wearing *my* sexy samba nightclub outfit! I understood the studio wanting to recast me to finish the pic, but with Grable? They subbed in a Slim Jim for a ribeye!

In general my policy is to support fellow artists, but I was feeling pretty raw at that point. I looked at Betty and shook my head. "They called her 'Million Dollar Legs,' you know," I told the girls. "Ha. Million-dollar legs and a five-cent vagina. Trust me. We shared a dressing room once. I almost fell in."

I waited a beat for them to laugh, and hopefully pile on. But I got crickets. Worse, actually. Their faces were frozen in horror. Or maybe it was just confusion?

"I'm saying her hoo-ha's so loose you couldn't plug it with an apple."

"Ruby, um . . . here at the Fold, we like to create a safe, sex-positive environment?" Suki said gently. "So, while I get that you're disappointed about being replaced in the movie . . . maybe, like, don't make fun of that lady for being sexually active?"

Emma and Marika nodded.

"She was also a huge bitch," I offered helpfully.

"Oh, well then fuck her," Suki chirped.

Suddenly Emma got all excited and clapped her hands together. "Hold on. Oh my god! Did you know my grandma? She was, like, a B-list actress for five minutes. Norma Allen!"

I racked the bowling ball. "Not ringing any bells. What was she in?"

Emma was almost bouncing now. "Her biggest one was *Devil's Dance*? She played a perfume salesgirl who has an affair with Dana Andrews!"

Dana Andrews. Now there was a man. I starred opposite Dana in *Sayonara Key Largo*. He played a private eye and I was the mob boss's girlfriend. Not the world's greatest dancer—he cost me a couple of rhumba contests—but he was great in the sack. You know who does the best impression of Dana Andrews? Anyone who grabs a ten-inch cucumber and holds it in front of their pants.

I'd never heard of Norma Allen, though, and it's always

a downer when you play the name game and come up short. So I shifted the direction of our chat. If I was going to pick up where I left off, I needed to play catchup. What's hot now? Where could I fit in? I tried to get a sense of the scene.

"What's the biggest picture out right now?"

Emma did a little tapping and pulled up a screen with a picture of a screaming machine. *"Lego Hellboy XXVII: Stewards of the Stratosphere."*

I chewed the inside of my cheek. "Is that a musical?"

"It's a superhero movie."

I didn't like the sound of that. "What else is out?"

"Let's see. There's *Transformers: Wrath of the Big 'Un, Cousin of Spiderman, Batman: Crunchtime, Justice League: Equity Cometh . . .*"

"Do any of those star women?"

"Eh," she said, scrolling through her phone. "Well, there's *Thor: Ragnarok: Cathy.*"

More blank stares from me.

Emma read from her phone: "The God of Thunder comes to Earth to take a human bride and meets Cathy, a single workingwoman looking for love in all the wrong chocolate."

It turned out what people wanted to see now were bats and insects fighting to save the world. I didn't blame them. From what I'd seen of it so far, it definitely needed saving.

There was a lull in the conversation. It's always been my instinct to keep a crowd going, so I dusted off one of my trusty crowd-pleasers. "Say. You girls like jokes? What do you call a Puerto Rican midget with a hard-on?"

Ninety minutes later I emerged from something called "emergency sensitivity training" with a porky *African Amer-*

ican named Elise. Turns out Boot-Camp Brad and his boy-friend hadn't told me the half of it. *All* the words were new now. I was like a baby in a crib learning googoo gaga.

Let's see. For starters, they've got all these letter jumbles. Like LGBTQIA. That's more letters than it takes to spell "fruit," but what do I know? Colored people have their own letter string, too; they're BIPOC. Call girls are "sex workers," ladyboys are "trans men," Indians are "Native Americans." What else . . . Oh yeah: you don't say "hobo" anymore, it's "person experiencing homeless-ness." Also, fat is sexy, thin is bad, white women are evil, white men are assholes (some things never change), and I have to stop there because my head's starting to pound.

Nutty, right? You're telling me. But, sis, I was thrilled to get that lesson. I did my best impression of a sponge and soaked everything up. I even asked for a pencil and paper and wrote out as many new vocabulary words as I could scribble. I meant to hit the ground running, and the best way to look like you don't belong is to say the wrong thing.

Now, did all that new lingo make perfect sense to me? I'll be honest with you: hell no. But the general gist seemed to be that, you know, words matter. Especially the words you assign to people who aren't like you. And believe it or not, that concept resonated with me deeply.

Take this bucktoothed gimp I used to know back in Beaver Falls. He sold reefer on the trolley. Bobbi and I ran into him a couple times on the days we managed to escape the orphanage for a few hours. Anyway, I guess Bobbi felt sorry for him, because one day, when we saw him riding alone on the trolley, she said hi to him and asked him his name. I remember cutting in, saying, "People call him Gimpy," and being shocked when Bobbi told me to can it.

It's the only time she ever did that. The kid blushed and mumbled, "It's Howard." After that, Bobbi made a point of calling him Howie whenever we'd see him on the trolley. And I remember thinking, Damn, the poor sap probably never heard any kids call him by his real name. And that's when I was like, Shit, you know? Words.

I always kind of admired Bobbi's soft spot for losers. It was sweet. Personally, I never had the time. If you let yourself feel sorry for every tire-tracked dope you trip over, it'd be a full-time job.

Anyway, after my sensitivity training, I decided to swing past the front desk to thank Emma on my way out.

"So long, doll. And thanks for the road map." I turned and headed for the door. "Keep your nose clean."

"Okay, um, no problem," she said, then called after me: "Hey, Ruby, if you don't have anywhere to stay, you could crash with me for a couple days while you figure stuff out. My roommate basically lives with her boyfriend, so you'd get your own room."

That was a sweet offer, but I wasn't about to take charity. I'd scooted forward a bunch of years, but there must be some old friends who were still kicking. I knew some heavy hitters.

I asked the kid to look up my agent, Merv Allen, on her devil's rectangle.

Emma gasped. *"Merv Allen is your agent?"*

I clapped my hands in delight. "So we do have a friend in common!"

She tapped around on the thing and held up a picture of an orange lizard. "You're talking about this dude?"

He was huge and fat and old and disgusting, but it was Merv, all right. A headline above him screamed, "DIS-

GRACED PRODUCER EVADES JAIL WITH PLEA DEAL."

The kid filled me in on Merv's rap. Apparently, he'd left the agent game behind and become a major player as a studio exec, but then did some bad things and wasn't allowed to leave his house anymore.

"Then I guess we know where to find him," I said.

When we showed up at Merv's place in Bel Air, I couldn't believe how well he'd done for himself.

A Caribbean maid in a pastel-mint uniform showed us into a living room with overstuffed chairs and couches that looked like it went on for miles.

Merv hobbled in, took one look at me and Emma, and turned to the maid. "Give them twenty thousand each if they'll sign the NDA," he said, and began shambling down a glistening marble hallway. He called back to the help. "Hey, Janella. Do we have any more of that egg salad?"

I ran after him.

"Merv! It's *me*. Ruby Russell! It's *Ruby*, Merv! *Remember?* 'The Mouth'?"

Merv looked at me again, hard, and finally the recognition bloomed in his face. Then he fell down and died. At least that's what the medic said later, after he was revived, propped up on pillows in his satin canopy bed.

When Merv regained consciousness half an hour later, he was terrified. Despite his Hebrew faith, he seems to have a pretty strong suspicion that he's going to the hot place. It took me a while to convince him I was real and he wasn't in hell. I went over how I'd gotten here, the kaboom on the plane and the time-traveling and everything.

Finally, after a tranquilizer and a glass of seltzer, he sat back in bed with a cigar and regained some of his old Merviness.

"You look aces, baby," he said, patting my cheek. "You haven't aged a day since '42."

I cut to the chase. "I need work, Merv. I was *right there*, right on the cusp. I gotta break out."

"Yeah, but it's not the same biz," Merv said, munching his stogie. "You're smart, Rube, but there's a lot of catch-up. You gotta be online. You gotta have followers. The studios don't create a persona for you anymore. Audiences are hip now, they don't buy the bullshit. Honestly, honey, I think you're better off finding a new line."

He was playing hardball, but I knew how to hit a homer in that department. I gave him that sexy, pouty baby look that works every damn time. Then I reached for the draw-string of his pajamas.

Emma piped up from her seat on a nearby ottoman. "Whoa whoa, what the *hell*?"

Merv caught my hand tenderly. "She's right, honey. That's not how they do things anymore. And it's no go, anyway. The NBC board voted to have my chorizo removed in '09."

Merv's nurse came into the room then and started screaming at everyone in Jamaican. She said Merv's lawyer said Merv wasn't allowed to talk to anyone ever again and we all had to clear out.

As we drove back to Emma's apartment, it crossed my mind to look up Bobbi, but I squashed that pretty quick. First of all, she was probably dead. And even if she was alive, I knew her feelings were probably gonna be hurt. I had enough on my plate without wading through all that. Besides, she probably wouldn't want to see me, anyway. She'd be an idiot to talk to me after I treated her like I did, and Bobbi was no idiot. Ah, well. What can you do? It looked like I'd be taking Emma up on that charity cot after all.

I looked out the window at the familiar donut shops and the not-so-familiar billboards for freezing your fat, and I thought, You know what? This is fucked. Why does crummy shit always happen to me? I thought about my dad getting buried in that mine, about the horse kicking my mom, about my tumor, about all my bad luck. But then I mentally grabbed myself by the shoulders and gave myself a little shake. What the hell was the matter with me? I was Ruby fucking Russell! Number two on the call list! And, baby, that's one line away from number one.

I'd sucked my way to the almost-top in 1942, and by god, I could do it again.

Emma's apartment was a cute little two-bed in Studio City. On the kitchen table she had a vase filled with dyed purple water and a big tuft of purple carnations. That was a trick Bobbi used to stretch our flower budget. You get a bunch of white carnations, and you can turn them any color. Seeing the flowers made me like Emma even more. It spoke to an enterprising nature that hummed in sympathy with my own. Not that I was looking for friendship, of course. I was looking for one type of relationship only: a no-holes-barred orgy with me, Jackson, Franklin, and Grant.

After giving me a tour, Emma dashed off to some religious thing called SoulCycle, and I decided to make myself useful around the apartment. There wasn't much to do, so I just swept the floor, dusted the shutters, mended a tear in the living room curtains, and washed out the refrigerator. After I'd fixed a loose hinge on her armoire, deboned a chicken and made a dress, I sat out on the fire escape with one of my patented pick-me-up shakes: two raw eggs, a splash of vinegar, a dash of Tabasco, and a handful of hamburger meat. I slurped it down and made a mental note to pay Emma back for the groceries I'd raided. Just as I was starting to feel revived, I heard her keys in the door.

"Ruby?" she called out. Then: "Hey! This place is spotless!"

I climbed back in and washed out my glass. Emma slung her bag onto the kitchen table.

"Super unnecessary, but thanks so much for cleaning," she said, sinking down onto the couch. "I've been meaning to. I was just slammed this past week, editing my Web series."

I nodded like I knew these words.

"It's about these two girlfriends in medical school," she went on.

"Sci-fi, huh? I like it. Bold."

Emma laughed. "I actually used to be premed. It's about all the dumb shit you do in med school."

"How much do you charge per ticket?"

"There aren't tickets. It's just online."

"Where's the line?" I looked around. "I don't even see a sign, honey."

Emma gave me a quick primer on social media while

she grabbed some snacks from the kitchen. She came back and arranged the assortment of bags and boxes on the table in front of us.

I picked up a bag of potato chips and glanced at the back. OUR STORY was printed in big letters on top, and below it: "Every day is a gift. Here at Valley Bounty Snacks, in our family-owned manufacturing facility tucked inside a horseshoe bend in the Rapahoe River, my brothers and I often end our days with a whiskey, staring out at the sunset glinting off the lake. Our grandpa battled Alzheimer's for ten years before he died, and each bag—"

In the space of ten seconds I knew more about the chip man than I did about my own father. I wasn't used to my food having a story. The last time I went to a grocery store, the story was "This is the food. We sell it for money."

As we snacked, Emma opened up and told me more of her "Our Story."

Directing movies had always been her dream. She hated her day job, working as a field producer on some show called *The Bachelor*. *The Bachelor* was a program on television, which is radio you can see. I said a silent prayer for the poor slobs I used to know in radio. Television must have kicked them straight to the breadlines. Anyway, Emma's job was planning the program's "group dates," and she was currently scouting locations for an upcoming bikini-skiing shoot. She didn't like her job, but it paid the bills while she beefed up her directing reel.

Eventually the conversation turned back to what I could do for cabbage. Emma said she'd introduce me to her manager at the Fold, which would really help with clinching a job. She said they'd definitely want to see a résumé and offered to help me put one together. I sat across from her as she opened her computer and pulled up a blank page. She typed my name at the top.

"Okay. What was your last job?"

"The Matchgirl and the Mighty Injun."

Her fingers hovered over the keyboard, and she bit her lip. "How about before that?"

I thought for a minute. *"The Octoroon Rapist!"*

Emma closed her machine and said maybe I didn't need a résumé after all. She said the Fold was looking for something called an "intern coordinator," and they burned through them pretty quickly, so they might take me without asking a lot of questions. I wasn't crystal on what the position entailed, but judging from the way Emma talked about interns, I understood they were some kind of insect or rodent. That didn't worry me. They couldn't be worse than the night rats at Beaver County. One time I woke up to a big one gnawing on my toe, and it wouldn't unclench its teeth, even after I stabbed it to death. I had to pry its dead jaws off with my fingers. So, yeah, I'd be able to handle the interns.

Turns out I didn't end up having to dust off my knife skills, because Emma wrangled me a job as a part-time receptionist at the Fold. About a week in, I finished my shift and came back to the apartment exhausted. I felt like turning in early. So I decided to hit the showers and get squeaky.

I went to the john, and as the water was heating up, Emma knocked on the door and stuck her hand in, offering me this weird neon puff.

"What's that?" I said.

"It's a loofah."

"A foolah?"

"A loofah. It's—"

"Luftwaffe?"

"A *loofah* is a—"

"I'm getting 'Lou Gehrig,' loud and clear."

It turns out a loofah is a shower sponge. It's made from weightless plastic, and Emma bought me one. I took it and turned it over in my hands, mesmerized. It was so new, so clean, so pretty.

"How much do I owe you for this?"

"Don't worry about it," she said, still behind the door. "Sorry, pink's all they had."

I cradled the loofah in my hands and stared at it in silence.

"Oh my god—are you okay?" Emma had cracked the door a few inches and was staring at me.

What the hell was going on? My throat felt tight. Hot water was pouring out of my eyes. And there was this nutty feeling in my chest, like my heart was hooked up to a little monkey in a fez riding a unicycle, and he was pedaling hell for leather, his tassel swooshing back and forth, and each rotation of the wheel squeezing my heart tighter and tighter.

"You're crying," she said.

I wiped the salty stuff away from my eyes. Huh.

As an actress I know all about flipping on the waterworks. A little onion in the eye, you squint like you're trying to read a sign from far away and make your voice go quivery. But I'd never felt it start from inside my body like this. And it didn't add up. It wasn't like I'd never gotten a gift before. On the morning of my mom's funeral, a neighbor lady gave me a hoop. And in the hospital, the mayor gave me that balloon. And Bobbi made me those cartoons. But I guess technically, I'd never gotten a store-bought gift from a friend. I dug the heels of my wrists into my eyeballs and tried to pull myself together.

"Thank you," I mumbled, flicking my eyes up to meet hers for just a second so I didn't spring another leak.

Emma laughed awkwardly. "Well, I guess now I know what to get you for your birthday!"

She left the bathroom and I let the monkey man pedal some more.

That Friday, after work, Emma gave me the heads-up that her friend Chloe was headed over for a night of frosé.

"Boy troubles," Emma said, undoing her bra, snaking it through her sweater, and launching it through the open door onto her bed. "She's alone. And she's scared she'll always be alone, you know? I just want to be there for her."

I nodded gravely. Finally! A friend in trouble was something I knew how to handle. I cracked my neck, rolled up my sleeves, and put a pot of water on to boil. Then I headed to my room to gather some supplies.

A couple minutes later, Chloe buzzed up, and I came out to meet her. She was a small, elfin blonde holding a bottle of wine and some Thai takeout. Emma greeted her with a long hug.

I gave her a sympathetic nod and held up the turkey baster and the Clorox. "Okay, kiddo," I said, in my most comforting voice. "Water's almost ready. This'll only take a minute." They looked at me, confused. "Don't worry, you're doing it the right way. No need to let a doctor take your money. There'll be some puking and a little blood, but in about an hour you can tuck right into that grub."

After they explained to me that Chloe wasn't pregnant, we all sat down on the couch and Chloe started to unload. Here was the kid's dilemma in a nutshell: she had the hots for a friend of hers, and they had great chemistry, but the guy hadn't made a move. Chloe was considering writing the man an email about her feelings.

"Or should I just, like, ask him out on a date?"

I couldn't believe what I was hearing.

Emma listened thoughtfully. "When did he and Sasha break up again?"

"August," Chloe said.

"Hmm." Emma nodded, considering. "It's definitely complicated."

I couldn't take it anymore. "Fake like you got a run in your nylons," I said, topping off Chloe's glass. "Once you know he's looking, bend over. Take his eyeballs on a tour of Hershey Park. If he doesn't go kablammy for you after that, break out the whipped cream, because you've got yourself a slice of the fruitiest."

Emma and Chloe shared a look.

"I warned you," Emma said to Chloe. "She's learning."

Chloe took a gulp of frosé. "Or I'm thinking maybe I could text him and see if he wants to, like, go on a walk? And then I'll just tell him how I feel?"

I tried to reason with her. "You can't just come out and tell a man how you feel. It's why lions die in zoos, honey. They don't like it when you drop the antelope in their lap.

What they want is the chase, the capture, the blood and the glory. A guy wants a fight."

Chloe looked at me suspiciously over her wineglass. "Were you ever in a sorority?"

"Ruby, things are different now," Emma said. Then she turned back to Chloe. "Let me see his ex. I wanna know if he has a type."

Chloe pulled up the guy's Instagram page, and I got a glimpse of him. I couldn't believe my eyes.

"Holy Geronimo—he's a *BIPED*?"

"She means BIPOC," Emma added, apologetically.

I laid a sisterly hand on Chloe's tiny thigh. "Honey, no offense, but a Black will break you in two. Why don't you sit on someone your own size? I'd personally recommend a Chinese."

Chloe's eyes bugged out and Emma slammed the remote against the coffee table. *"Ruby!"* she yelled.

Uh-oh. Looked like another rolled-up-newspaper treatment for yours truly.

"You can't just stereotype entire races!" Emma was really mad this time. Her cheeks were flushed and her eyes were kinda wild. "It's *racist*."

I started to explain that I was only speaking from experience, but then I saw that she had a point. It wasn't as if I'd gotten sticky with *every* son of the Manchu Empire, or every BIBOP fella either, for that matter. Ah well. I wasn't exactly an A student yet, but at least I'd remembered to say "Chinese."

After the dust settled, we all went back to chatting. My ears perked up when Chloe asked Emma what was up with someone named Micah. Given how Emma never brought guys around, I'd just gone ahead and figured she was one of those LGBTQ'ers.

Emma groaned. "Ugh. He won't leave me alone. It's so fucking unprofessional."

"Who's Micah?" I asked.

"Micah Kessler," Chloe said. "As in *Kessler Industries*? He's this trust-fund indie-producer guy. His dad's a real estate billionaire, and Micah throws money at whatever movies he wants to make. And he's super into Emma."

The shriek of joy that erupted from my body was clear as a bell. "Roll back the rugs, sister!" I went to the liquor cabinet and pulled out a bottle of hooch. "We're gonna tear up the floor!"

I was two verses deep into "Tallahassee Tuxedo" before I noticed Emma wasn't joining in. In fact, she looked pretty glum.

"Geez, Ruby," she said, really ticked off now. "I want to *work* with him. Not date him."

I believe I've mentioned our family dog, Sparky. On his birthday we used to give him a pig head from the rendering plant as a special treat. We'd drop it on the floor and he'd rip at the meat so fast it was like he was choking on it. That's what it was like for me as I tried to respond. I couldn't get my mouth around the words fast enough.

"But—but—*exactly*! You know how easy it's going to be to get him to finance your movie now? This is your break!"

She looked at me like she'd just caught me sucking my own dick. "That's not how I want to get a break."

At that moment, Chloe shrieked, "It's on!"

She zapped the TV to a program where a group of men in terry cloth robes sat clustered inside a limousine.

Emma groaned. "Please don't make me watch this."

"Come on, just through the first group date," Chloe begged. "They're naked bungee jumping!"

Emma shuddered.

"Isn't this the show you work on?" I asked.

Emma shook her head no and explained that she worked on *The Bachelor*, and that *The Bachelorette* was a different show, where they flip it, and a lady tries out a stable of bucks.

"It's the most ridiculous, addictive shit ever," Chloe said, perking up for the first time since she'd walked in. "I mean, obviously *The Bachelor*'s king, but this gets you through the off-season. The guys are always sooo basic and boring, so the producers have to do the craziest shit to make it good."

"So, the people are boring, and sometimes they're naked," I said, trying to make sure I was getting it.

"Basically," Chloe said, scooping out a palm full of crackers and eating from it like a feedbag. "And I'm hashtag fucking here for it."

The next morning, as I was rolling out the dough for another lard pie, it occurred to me that maybe Chloe and Emma weren't off the deep end. Maybe I really didn't fit in here. I mean, this was a new world. I might have to play more catchup than I thought. And there was an obvious solution. Why hadn't I thought of it before?

I grabbed the remote, and several hours later managed to turn on the television.

I was gonna take a crash course in Today. The TV would be my teacher.

Taking a pad and pencil from a drawer in the kitchen, I

flipped around until I landed on the only channel devoted to the theatrical arts.

"All right, Bravo," I murmured. "Get me up to speed."

I. LOVE. BRAVO!!!

Finally! Something that made *sense*.

I'd always had a hunch that Emma and her Fold friends weren't telling me the whole story about the way things are now. Don't get me wrong: they're sweet kids, and they mean well. But a little birdie kept chirping in my ear that they didn't know the whole score—and Bravo proved I was right!

What these Bravo cats understand is that it's exhausting keeping up with all those new words and letters, so they don't make you do any of that. In the beautiful world of Bravo, women are women and men are men. There aren't any "Web series" about lady doctors. Instead, there's the kind of hooey people actually want to watch: rich women screaming at each other in evening clothes, conniving, sexy waitresses, million-dollar homes, and plenty of well-dressed gays to make snide remarks and keep it interesting. It's the exact same shit as the matinees Bobbi and I used to sneak out of the orphanage for during the Depression. Suddenly, I didn't feel so out of the loop. In fact, watching Bravo, I felt like I was home again.

I was googling the net worths of the Real Housewives of Orange County later that afternoon when Emma got back from SoulCycle. She seemed annoyed.

"What's up?" I asked.

"Chloe called me crying right as I was going in to class, and I ended up talking her down in the parking lot for forty-five minutes."

I shook my head. "Chloe being messy is a train that always arrives on time." I shrugged. "That's not tea, that's facts."

Emma looked at me quizzically, then glanced at her phone and groaned. "It's Micah. He wants to know if I'll come with him to this outdoor movie thing tonight."

I felt like I had made my feelings on the subject known, so I said nothing and resumed my googlings.

"Come on, Ruby, help me out here. How can I go but make sure it's just as friends?"

I sighed. "When it comes to men, there is no 'just friends.'"

"Yes there is. *I* have guy friends." Her face started getting all red. *"Girls can have guy friends!"*

Oriental cripple by the name of Ito. Sorry, Jap. Wait, that's not it. *Japan-man?* Anyway, even with a peg leg, the guy ran a tidy little grocery on Wilshire across from Merv's old office. I used to go in there a few times a week for some licorice or orange creams. Ito had a gentle and sunny demeanor, always easy with a smile and some kind words. There were actually exactly four words, in total: "Nice day" or "Anything else?" Now, I never got it notarized, but all signs pointed to Ito being male, and I guess you could say we were friends. But that's the closest I've ever come to innocent fellowship with a card-carrying member of the Johnson Club, and that's because there's no such thing as just friends.

I tried to explain this to Emma, but it just made her madder, so eventually we shifted to plotting a course of action. Emma texted Micah that she had plans with me tonight, but that we could both come to the movie—thereby, in her estimation, "giving off a strong friend vibe."

Her phone buzzed again and she clapped.

"He's into it! Great! Thank you so much for doing this!"

I just shrugged and headed for the shower. It was no skin off my back.

Emma called to me.

"He says they're doing an Old Hollywood theme night. We're supposed to dress up. Will that be triggering for you?"

I didn't give it a second thought and called back to her. "No problemo."

As I lathered up, I actually had the nerve to think, Hey—maybe they'll be showing one of my old flicks. I'd learned that several of my movies actually had "cult followings." Emma didn't seem too impressed when I'd mentioned it, but *The Matchgirl and the Mighty Injun* was apparently extremely popular with lesbian bikers over fifty. If I may be so bold, I think it's some of my best work.

Now, if I'd had any idea what the night actually had in store, I'd have run screaming for the canyon. But that's the thing about the future. You just have to step into it blind.

The night turned out to be one of those calm, clear Southern California evenings where the air feels fresh and cleansing, like a bath of holy water. Or maybe it was just the edibles. We each did half a rainbow worm on the ride over to the Hollywood Forever Cemetery. Since parking was a shitshow, Micah ditched his Tesla on Highland and we hoofed it the rest of the way with our blankets, beach chairs, and plastic grocery bags of picnic chow. Emma and I were both in red lips and heels, in keeping with the Old Hollywood theme. A makeup-melting, foot-scrunching march didn't sound like my idea of a party, but we kept our heads down and forged ahead.

I could see why Emma wasn't apeshit for Micah. There was something weaselly and overconfident about the guy. He didn't wear socks, his "old-timey tuxedo shirt" (which he'd paired with salmon shorts) was unbuttoned one button too many, and he had a high-pitched laugh that he deployed constantly, mostly at his own unremarkable comments. Like when he'd finally found a parking spot and announced, "Killin' it, Kessler!" to no one. Emma had looked at me then. I'd responded by holding up my phone, where I'd pulled up the Kessler family's net worth: $110 million.

I hadn't been on Hollywood Boulevard yet in 2021, and my jaw was pretty much on the ground the whole time. Not from the crotchless panties on the mannequins at the lingerie shops, or the thigh-high-booted hookers strutting in the golden twilight. No sir. It was the stars on the Walk of Fame. I couldn't believe how well my friends had done.

Sir Laurence Olivier? Sheesh. Someone got fancy. That's the same guy everyone called "Fat Larry" back when he was a gofer on *The Gondoliers*. Angela Lansbury was another shocker. To be fair, she was famous when I knew her, but only for giving out two-dollar handies behind the Esso on La Brea and Beverly. Jimmy Stewart was the one name who didn't surprise me. That guy blew any producer he could get his mouth on.

We made it to the cemetery gate and Micah flashed our

tickets on his phone. Inside, a crowd was milling along a wide gravel path flanked with palm trees and rows of gravestones. It was a sea of hip sunglasses, with men in geometric-patterned pastel T-shirts, and women in rompers and muumuus and short-shorts. Not an Old Hollywood ensemble in sight. As we rounded a bend, I saw a movie playing on a white stucco wall at the far end of a lawn packed with picnickers. According to the banners hanging from the palm trees, the picture was called *E.T.*

"Ah, shit," Micah said, whipping out his phone. "Sorry, guys. Looks like the Old Hollywood thing is *next* month. Hope that's not a dealbreaker."

That dumbo. I found it pretty annoying, in fact, but Emma just laughed and unclipped the cloche from her hair. "Welp, I'm taking this thing off, then. It's super itchy. But I'm keeping this *on*," she said, wrapping her stole a little tighter around her arms. "I'm always freezing."

"Sure. You're tiny," Micah said, his eyes twinkling.

I was starting to work up a bit of an appetite, so I followed my nose over to a cart manned by a friendly-looking Aztec. He glanced my way.

"Two churro, one dollar."

It was one of the greatest opening lines I'd ever heard. I fished a buck out of my bra and, seconds later, stood enjoying twin sticks of hot, sugary fat. No "Our Story" on the paper, either. Nice.

When I rejoined my compadres, Emma hissed at me. *"Don't leave me alone with him.* You're supposed to be friend-zoning this, remember?"

"Sorry," I muttered, and then piped down as the opening credits rolled.

The plot of *E.T.* is pretty straightforward. It's a tear-

jerker about a little white boy who befriends an elderly
Black man. He's one of those adorable, wrinkly old gentlemen who obviously wouldn't hurt a fly, but—surprise,
surprise—the world doesn't welcome their friendship.
Now I hate to be a wet blanket, but after all my sensitivity
training, I found the depiction of the old man to be problematic in the extreme. For one, they only gave the guy a
single, measly line, and they shoved it in at the end. Something about making a phone call home. You think that
didn't factor into the poor schmuck's salary? The studios
will grind you down any way they can, and nonspeaking
roles net you a pretty skimpy slice of the pie. It burned me
up seeing him get taken advantage of like that—especially
since the longer I watched him, the more I found myself
thinking of a few things I'd like to see him do with those
knobby fingers of his. What can I say? Jungle fever stays in
the blood.

About halfway through the picture I remembered my
duty and looked over at Micah. It wasn't a moment too
soon, because he was staring at Emma in a distinctly hungry way.

"So, Ruby," he said, keeping his eyes on Emma. "You
two are roommates, right? That's a special bond."

I swallowed some more wine and suppressed a churro
burp. "You got it, partner." Then, remembering my Bravo
training: "I feel super lucky, because she's *such* a sweet girl."

"She is," Micah said, glancing at the screen for a moment. Then he turned to me. "So, what's your deal?"

He seemed bored by the question, but I tried to get it up
all the same. "Well, I'm an actress—"

"Heard that." He nodded and produced a few pills from
his pocket. "Wanna do an oxy?"

This caught Emma's attention. "Are those *opioids*?"

Micah laughed, smitten. "You're adorable. Trust me, I promise *E.T.* will be a fuck-ton more enjoyable with these."

Emma laughed tightly. "We're good on the *prescription medications*. Thanks."

Micah shrugged, broke a pill in half, and swallowed it dry. "Suit yourselves."

Personally, I never got the allure of pills. You pop one and, biff bang bing, twenty minutes later you're a puddle on the floor. Where's the fun in that? Don't get me wrong, I'm all for getting wacky, but pills are too quick, too crude. Take this opium den in Chinatown me and my costars used to hit up after a long day of shooting. It was homey. Freshly washed pillows all over the floor and cute little buckets to throw up in. Everyone called the proprietress Mom-Mom. I went there once after a New Year's Eve party and didn't wake up until February. Call me old-fashioned, but there's more to a party than thirty milligrams of space dust.

Micah chased the pill with some vino, and Emma got really interested in the hummus for a few minutes, then tried a new angle.

"Hey. How's *The Architect* coming?"

I'd learned on *Watch What Happens Live,* one of the foundations of my Bravo education, that *The Architect* was a new movie starring a man named Paul Dano. Micah rolled his eyes. "The script's all over the place, but I gave P.T. my notes, so we'll see."

Emma stage-whispered to me, excited, "He means *Paul Thomas Anderson.*"

"Oooh, fancy," I murmured. I had no idea who that was.

"I'd love to work with him someday," Emma said softly.

Micah nodded thoughtfully. Hey, I thought. Maybe the soft touch really is the ticket these days. I silently commended Emma for planting the thought of her career in his mind. He seemed to be actually considering it!

"How about you guys kiss?"

"Excuse me?" Emma said.

Micah mimed signing a form. "You have my affirmative consent to make out with each other."

Emma tried to laugh it off, but I could tell she was nervous. "Um . . . I guess those pills work fast, huh?"

"Wow," Micah said, an edge in his voice. "So, you're actually, like, zero fun."

I thought back to the Kessler fortune. That cool 110 million. Then I leaned in and, before she could pull away, pressed my lips against Emma's.

"*The fuck?*" Emma screeched, jumping back.

"Holy shit," Micah murmured.

"Jesus, Ruby!" Emma exploded. She got up and stalked off. Micah and I sat there in silence for a beat.

"I'm just going to close my eyes and sit with that for a minute," he said, then stretched out on his back, face to the sky.

I got up, brushed a layer of pita dust off my dress, and started to look for Emma. It took me a few minutes, but eventually I found her in a neatly mowed row of gravestones over by a fountain. She was staring down at a headstone, her bare arms folded over her chest, the beaver stole drooping around her elbows.

"What's the big deal, sis? He remembers my name, and you make a splash without having to touch him. It's a win-win. Heck, Joan Crawford had to scissor with Winnie Lightner on Ed Goulding's porch for three hours to get the part in *Grand Hotel*. What just happened to you was a gift."

She looked at me like I was a bug. "I don't want to perform some sex show for Micah. *Don't you have any self-respect?*"

I sighed. Self-respect was a luxury, but the world hadn't opened Emma's eyes wide enough to see that. She was like a princess who'd never traveled beyond the palace walls. When her tooth hurt, she simply picked up the phone and called a doctor instead of walking around until the pain went away or killed you. Emma floated through life in a shimmering bubble of privilege. Of course she couldn't understand what it was like to be me. "I'm just doing what I gotta do."

Emma groaned. "That's really sad. You're better than this!"

I put my hand on her shoulder. "Listen. How you feel is one thousand percent valid, because what I did was shady as hell. But I don't have a family or a fancy college degree to fall back on. So I'm gonna take care of me, and in the meantime, you can check ya ass."

She laughed, but it was hollow. "Listen to yourself. You sound like one of those stupid shows."

It was true that, through careful study, I had absorbed the language and behavior of the Bravo personalities. But Emma was wrong about one thing. They weren't stupid. And I was smart for watching them!

"I'm just looking out for number one, honey. You'd do the same thing if you were in my shoes."

"Would I?" Her eyes narrowed. "You're really selfish, you know that, Ruby?"

I laughed, happy to finally get down into the shit. I got

in her face, clapping in between each word. "And. You. Are. A. Spoiled. Baby. Buttface!"

Emma glared. "You know what? Why don't you find a new place to live? Maybe Micah's got some room on his dick."

Okay, bitch! I had one locked and loaded. "Is your ass jealous of the shit that comes out of your mouth?"

She snorted, real bitter, and turned to go. As she did, the stole slid off one shoulder, and for the first time I noticed its familiar purple satin lining.

My heart stopped, and before I knew what I was doing, I snatched the garment all the way off her shoulders.

She whipped around, furious, as I held the lining up to my face and searched along the seam for the inscription I knew couldn't really be there. But there it was.

R. R.
B. C.

It was the same beaver stole I'd bought with Bobbi.

"Where did you get this?" I demanded.

"It's my grandma's. What do you care?"

I gripped the stole tighter. "This belongs to me and my friend Bobbi."

Emma froze. "That was my grandma's name before she changed it. Norma was her stage name. So you *did* know her!"

And just like that, it all fell into place. The dyed carnations. The at-home feeling I felt with Emma.

Suddenly I was falling ass-backward down memory lane. I thought back to the long, cold nights in Beaver County, Bobbi on the next cot over. Bobbi next to me on the line at Radioplane. Dancing our way through the Flamingo. Bobbi sitting on my suitcase, crying as I moved out of our Fort Wayne shitbox for the big city . . . then following me outside to the cab and forcing me to take the wad from our coffee can. Sixty-three dollars and eighty-four cents. Our whole savings. Telling me she knew I'd pay her back with interest one day, because she was sure I was going to make it. She was sure I was going to be big-time.

Suddenly, all I wanted was to see my old friend.

"Ruby?" Emma asked gently.

"Where is she now? Think we can visit her?" I asked. It came out a lot softer than I meant it to.

Emma pointed behind me. "That's what I was just doing." Then she walked away and left me standing there, the stole wilting in my hand.

I turned to where she had pointed and saw the gravestone.

ROBERTA ALLEN CAPELLO
1917–2004
BELOVED WIFE, MOTHER, GRANDMOTHER, FRIEND

Standing there looking at it, I felt strangely numb. Huh, I thought. She must have done well for herself. Husband, children. Fancy plot. All in all, it looked like Bobbi's life had gone gangbusters. What was there to be sad about?

I took a step closer and tried to think of what I wanted to say. "Hey, Squirt," I started. Then I covered my face with my hands and let the fez monkey do his thing.

. . .

After wiping my eyes down and weaving my way back to our blanket, I saw that Micah had passed out. Emma was gone, and she'd taken her purse. I sat there for a few minutes as the heir to Kessler Corp. snored lightly. I knew I should probably wake him up to finish the deal, but nature was calling, so I got up to find a can.

I try not to whine, because I believe mental illness is a choice and it's contagious, but I was feeling down. The triple whammy of the fight with Emma, the sugar crash from the churros, and Bobbi's being dead wasn't sitting too easy.

On the edge of the cemetery was a long line of plastic outhouses lit up by floodlights. Selecting a vacant hut, I stepped inside and locked the door. Right away I could tell something was wrong. The little bar clicked down crooked when the door closed, and it made an unnatural screechy sound. I tried to open it back up, but it wouldn't budge.

I was trapped in the plastic feces house.

Some nights, right?

I pounded on the door. *"Hello? Hello?* THIS THING WON'T OPEN!"

A few moments passed in silence, and then I heard a man's voice: "Can't you unlock it?"

"That's why we're having this chat, pal. It's stuck!"

I heard him exit his john and try to open mine. No dice. He tried again, a little more forcefully, but nothing doing. There was more tugging, then he gave it a few kicks. "Shit," I heard him mutter. "Okay, hold on—I'm gonna get help."

His footsteps receded. I looked around and thought, Oh well. Might as well take care of business while I'm here. I took a seat and got to work.

A second later the guy was back, right outside. "Hey! They're going to break the door down, okay?"

Then a different man's voice: "Step away from the door!"

I glanced behind me. "I don't exactly have acres to roam here, pal—"

"*Step away from the door!*"

As I scrambled up, I heard several guys grunt, like they were picking up something heavy, and then there was a huge bang on the door.

"Fellas! Handle with care, okay?"

There was more grunting, then another violent bang. This was shaping up to be the roughest entry I'd experienced since Selznick offered to let me "read" for the title role in *The Lady Eve*. Outside, I could hear the guys gearing up for another run. Then a new guy shouted, "Harder this time!" I steadied myself against the back wall.

There was a brief silence, and then it seemed like a bomb went off right in front of my face. As the door busted open, the john tipped back, and I felt this terrifying weightlessness for a split second as it teetered in midair.

You know how your whole life is supposed to flash before your eyes right before you die? Well, that wasn't quite what happened. But just before the john came crashing down and the shit flowed over me, one particular memory came rushing back in Technicolor.

It was a rainy November night a couple months after I'd moved into my bungalow, the ritzy one Universal paid for once I finally made the roster. I was having a drink in the kitchen when I heard a knock at the door. I peeked through the curtains and saw Bobbi standing there holding a slim white box. I closed the curtains and was about to tell Margaretta, my maid, not to answer it, but it was too late. She opened the door and I heard Bobbi's voice.

"Is Ruby in?"

It was a messy scene. I gave Margaretta the "me no home" gesture, and she covered for me, but I knew Bobbi put two and two together. I could hear the hurt in her voice as she thanked the maid and gave her the box she'd brought. There was a card tucked into the ribbon, with her new address in L.A. Some shitbox in Koreatown. As I stood in the living room and watched her climb back into the cab and drive off down the wet street, I forced myself to open the gift. Inside, an envelope with my name on it sat perched atop crisp peach tissue paper, and folded underneath was our beaver stole. I took out the card and saw she'd drawn a cartoon of me, standing victorious on top of big block letters meant to look like the Hollywood sign, only it said "RUBYWOOD." Below that, she'd written in her small, neat handwriting: "Proud of you."

I handed Margaretta the stole and told her to send it back. And evidently she had.

The outhouse smashed backward onto the ground, baptizing me in a river of lukewarm waste. Then a man pulled me out, up onto my feet. I sputtered, wiped the crap out of my face, and blinked my eyes open. A sizable crowd was staring at me in stunned silence.

I coughed, to kind of break the mood. "Anyone have a phone I could borrow?"

No one moved. They just gawked at me, fascinated, disgusted, amazed. The way the white children looked at the little Black fella when he said the thing about calling home in *E.T.* That gave me an idea. I stuck my finger out kind of wobbly and croaked it out:

"*E.T.* Uber home?"

More silence. Sheesh. I hadn't worked a crowd this dead since the summer I did cosmetics at the funeral home in Fort Wayne. By the way, the key to corpse hair? Shellac spray.

The guy with the earring started first. Just a single, loud "Hah!" And then the churro man followed, giggling. Then the whole crowd was laughing. I felt that familiar rush of happy sauce flood through my veins. It didn't even matter that it was just rabble in a graveyard—it felt good to find an audience again.

"Hey, lady!" a man shouted out, holding up his phone.

I turned toward him and, smiling, covered in filth, I posed. It was pure instinct. I didn't give it a second thought.

Since there was no way in hell I was crawling back to Emma, especially seeing as I was covered in feces, I went to the one place I knew I wouldn't be turned away. Mostly because I had an access card.

The Fold's Wellness Room had a shower and a medita-tion hammock. I deep-cleaned myself in the shower, grabbed a Fork the Patriarchy T-shirt from the merch case, curled up in the hammock, and immediately plunged into a deep, dreamless sleep.

Marika woke me the next morning with a piercing shriek.

"You're hot shit, girl!"

It's nice how the girls around the Fold greet each other with ringing affirmations. "Cute shirt!" "Your skin looks amazing!" "Funky visor!" etc. But right then I wasn't in the mood. "I don't really feel like hot shit, but thanks."

"No. You're *Hot Shit Girl!* Look—you went viral!" Marika shoved her phone in my face and explained. "You're a GIF! And BuzzFeed wrote a listicle about you. Look!"

I grabbed the phone and tried to make sense of the neon jumble. There was a picture of me from the night before, right after I got pulled out of the john. Like a tiny two-second movie. My hair and clothes were matted onto my body from the waste, and I was doing this wink-and-coquettish-wave thing that I had to admit was kind of cute. Below the minimovie was a list.

10 REASONS WE ARE ALL HOT SHIT GIRL

10. Because tbh outdoor movies suck, so you might as well get stuck in a porta-potty.
9. Because the world is literally on fire and this girl could give a shit. Shit, get it?
8. Because even when we get raw sewage dumped on us, we still look smoking as hell (OK actually that's one way we're probably NOT all like Hot Shit Girl lol).

Increasingly confused, I skipped ahead to number one.

1. Because sometimes, even when life literally throws shit at you, you just have to smile.

My hand floated up to my forehead. Oh brother. How the hell was I going to retake Hollywood now? I was Feces Woman! I handed Marika her phone and she crouched down next to me.

"Your face is all red," she said, touching the backs of two fingers to my cheek. "Ruby, you're burning up." I started breathing all heavy. "Are you having a panic attack?" She waved her hand in front of my eyes. "Hello?"

I was thinking about the photographer back at Radioplane. A picture had shot me to the top, and now a picture was going to drag me to the bottom. There was a dark symmetry to it that rubbed me the wrong way. What was the lesson here? I grabbed ahold of my brain and gave it a shake: forget about lessons, sister—let's noodle our way out of this.

I concentrated so hard I broke a sweat but I came up with nothing. Then I grabbed Marika by her fashionable jumpsuit.

"How can we fix this?"

"Fix it? Ruby, it's great exposure!" She laughed. "You're a viral freaking GIF!"

Sweet, dumb Marika. I looked at her plump, happy face and patted her hand gently. The fat had seeped into her brain.

I was starving, and the hunger was only making me feel more mixed up. So I forced myself to get up and make tracks to the nearest place that served grub.

The only thing nearby was called Juice Cloud. I'd never actually eaten there, even though I'd noticed it was popular with the Fold ladies. I got on line, thinking I'd get a sandwich with a nice big pickle—but the menu printed on a board above the cash register made no sense. I didn't see any food, just a long handwritten manifesto in chalk that started with "Cut the bullshit."

I opened a refrigerated case on the wall next to me and took out a little package called "Goji Balls." I wanted to ask the girl in front of me what they were, but I was sick of feeling like a lost puppy. Then I remembered the advice

Suki had given me—to engage with my followers. She'd created an Instagram account for me my first week at the Fold, but I had yet to post anything. So I took a picture of the goji balls, wrote "what is this," and posted it to my stories. Within one minute I had twenty-eight hearts, and comments like "lol" and "truth."

I got to the front of the line and leveled with the sweet-faced girl behind the counter. "Can I just get a BLT?"

She nodded, and her eyes stayed on me. "Oh my god. Are you *Hot Shit Girl*?"

I blew some hair out of my face and shrugged.

She leaned in, giddy. "Okay, so I'd love to say 'On the house,' but they're being super strict right now, so all I can give is my employee discount. But you fucking rock."

Somehow she still managed to ring me up to the tune of thirteen dollars. I didn't have the energy to faint or scream, so I just paid and stood waiting by the wall off to the side.

"Beets Light Truth," called the girl, and then she handed me a clear plastic cup of blood. She must have seen my face, because she said, "Beets, lychee, and tahini. Sorry— did you want the hemp boost?"

I grabbed the cup and stumbled out onto the sidewalk, where I chucked it in the nearest trash can. Then I sat down on the curb and waited to die in the desert sun. That's when I heard Marika squealing my name. I looked up to see her pulling some good-looking guy in a nice button-down toward me.

"This is her!" she was telling him. "This is Ruby!"

Ah, well. The gig was up. I didn't mention this before, because it wasn't essential to the story, but ever since I'd started working at the Fold I'd had a little side business selling their free snacks to this Mexican kid for a dollar a pop. I'd pulled down maybe three hundred clams. I was a little disappointed Marika had ratted me out to this plain-clothes cop, but it was her ass if anyone found out about my hustle, so I couldn't blame her.

Marika and the young policeman walked right up to where I was sitting.

"Okay, you got me," I sighed, reaching into my top drawer and pulling out a wad. "That's today's haul. I can get you the rest by the end of the week and we can settle this quietly."

The guy just looked at me and laughed.

"This is Stu Levy," Marika announced. "He's an *agent*. And he saw your GIF!"

Agent? I squinted up at the guy. He was cute, unlined, like a fresh, rich baby.

"You were hilarious," he said, sticking out his hand. I shook it warily and muttered thanks. I recognized the gleam in his eye. He was hungry.

Marika looked at me ecstatically. "Stu's with ICM!"

Levy sat down next to me on the curb. "Have you ever thought about a career in TV?"

My mind whirred. ICM. Was that one of the big dogs? I mean, I wasn't about to sign with just any old agency. No siree. I was Hot Shit Girl!

I ended up signing with ICM Stu, and right away he got me booked on *Kimmel*. That went great, and it gave me a little heat going into the next phase of things, which was general meetings.

I showed up for my ABC general ten minutes early, checked in, and made myself comfortable on one of the low orange couches in their cavernous lobby. Young, attractive men and women in shaggy haircuts and oversized tortoiseshell glasses buzzed by holding cups of coffee. There were big, leafy potted palm trees everywhere, some growing right up to the ceiling. It felt very jungle-meets-spaceship, and I started to get nervous. I had to calm myself down by taking deep, slow breaths and thinking about money.

Soon enough a smiling, gorgeous man was striding over to greet me. I'd never seen an executive this attractive. He was tall and tan, with a million-dollar smile. He walked me back to his office, which was behind a bunch of glass cases filled with awards, and offered me a beverage. I selected a French seltzer, *pamplemousse*-flavored. About two minutes ago I'd been covered in shit in a boneyard. Life, right?

"I saw you on *Kimmel*. Super funny," he said, and flashed me that grin again. Was this guy a Parker House roll? Because I was about to butter him up. And then put him inside me.

"You're young to be the head of a studio," I purred, crossing my legs invitingly toward him.

He found this funny. "Haha, uh, no. I'm Abidemi's assistant."

"Abi-whatti?"

Just then his cleaning lady walked into the room. She was a middle-aged Black gal in a beautiful red blazer. It was a very dignified uniform. I'm telling you, this building. Class out the waz.

"Sorry I'm late, guys," she said, real confident for a maid.

"No problem, sis, but this room's been done," I said,

nodding to the door. "You might want to check out the can. There's a situation in stall number two." I winked. "Pun intended."

As far as I know, heart disease does not run in my family. But my ticker came pretty close to exploding when I finally got wise that this cleaning lady was the head of Universal Studios. I wrapped my head around that info during a brief exchange that went something like this:

Yours Truly: "Hold on. What?"

Abidemi: "I'm the head of the studio."

Me: "You're ahead to sue Dio? Who's Dio?"

Abidemi: "I'm the head of Universal Studios."

My eyes bugged out of my head as David excused himself to get Abidemi's latte, leaving us alone. We sat in silence for a moment as I scrambled to catch up. I was in awe of this woman. I knew from Bravo that race relations hadn't come all that far in eighty years, so this chick must have really busted her hump to wind up in the captain's chair.

I tried to play it cool.

"Love that *E.T.* flick," I said. "I've been saying it for years: it's about time a Black carried a picture."

She stared at me with a quizzical look on her face. I definitely was off my game. I tried a different tack.

"It's good to be queen, huh? You picked one hell of a stud." I gestured to the door, where David had just walked out.

She cracked open her pastel can of bubbles. "Hah. Thanks. We love David."

Hey now. I was getting warmer. But there was still the question of how to seal the deal. I had never done the slappy with a broad. How would that work?

Finally I just blurted it out.

"So do I do it to you, or . . . ?"

Abidemi cocked her head. "Do what to me?"

Okay, now she's being coy. Coy I can work with.

"Well, I don't exactly have a menu, honey, but for an opportunity like this? Let's just say the buffet's open. King crab, lobster, whatever you want."

She still didn't seem to be following. Was there someone even higher up that I had to finesse? I decided to lay it all out there.

"Whose ham do I have to glaze to get something in writing?"

Abidemi stared at me for a second, and then burst out laughing. When she recovered, she looked at me thoughtfully. "Would you be open to unscripted?"

"Sister, I'll put a cowbell around my neck and let you milk me if it'll get me on the payroll."

Abidemi smiled. "Then I have something in mind for you."

Over mimosas at the Polo Lounge, ICM Stu and I decided to accept ABC's offer to be a contestant on the eighty-ninth season of *The Bachelor*. For me, it was a no-brainer. I'm great at contests. As a four-time Rusty Flamingo Rhumba Queen, I know a thing or two about greasing up judges and winning over a crowd.

I could see my path to the top. If I just hung in 'til the third rose, that would give me enough time to break out as a fan favorite, which in turn could land me a few appearances on *Good Morning America*, a couple of club promotions, and at least one influencer partnership with a major brand. If I got six figures in media impact per post,

I could level up to my own brand—a fashion line, fragrance, or vodka. I could even get cast as the next Bachelorette, or better yet, get my own reality show. If I did that for a couple of seasons, it wasn't crazy to start thinking about my own network.

Only one tiny thing wedged itself between me and my happy dance. You may recall Emma, my former roommate. I never thought of her, actually, but I did remember that she was a field producer on *The Bachelor,* and I worried she could make it a bumpy ride for me if she wanted to. But I shook it off. I had to focus.

According to the packing list from ABC, *Bachelor* contestants provided their own wardrobe and makeup and were instructed to pack "for any weather." Stu gave me a couple of tips on what to include, starting with a parka and blotting paper. Apparently they keep the A/C cranked, but when the cameras are rolling, they turn it off for sound and you boil. He also told me to pack as many oranges as I could fit in my bag. I forgot to ask why, but Stu knew his shit, so I did as I was told.

There's so much you can't control on a shoot: how long the day goes, when the director takes his penis out, what they serve for lunch, when the producer takes his penis out. But the one thing you *can* control is your own preparation. So on the Uber ride over to the house, I reread the Bachelor's bio a few times. I wanted to study his psychology so I could come up with a game plan.

Packer Tracy, 26, is named after the Green Bay Packers, which turned out to be a great fit for this life-long athlete and virgin. Packer was an All-American football player before an injury forced him to retire from the sport he loved. Now he's a physical therapist and amateur pilot who enjoys playing Call of Duty, not having sex, and spending time with his pocket beagles, Rampage and Hellion. They're small, so he can take them flying! Packer is looking for a teammate to join him in the cockpit and fly through the goalposts of everlasting love, and he's confident he's going to find her on *The Bachelor*. If you've had sex once, you've had more sex than this man.

This was going to be a piece of cake. The guy was a sweet football virgin. I can wrap a man like that around my pinkie finger faster than you can say snap, crackle, pop.

Next, to get a sense of the competition, I read through the other contestants' bios, starting with Kaylee C.

Kaylee C.
25
Dental Hygienist
Tampa, Florida

Kaylee C. is a Florida girl through and through. When she's not helping clients achieve their perfect smile, she's playing volleyball on the beach, rollerblading down Bayshore Boulevard, or boating with her besties! Kaylee has a hairless cat named Belle (named after her favorite Disney princess) and they do literally everything together, from binging Netflix on the couch to tanning on the lawn with a good au-

diobook and a big bottle of water. Kaylee and Belle
are definitely partners in crime, but they'd be willing to bring on a Prince Charming—and they're
hoping it's Packer!

-Kaylee's best friend is her mother. They talk every
   day.
-Kaylee's biggest fear is being trapped on top of a
   Ferris wheel.
-Kaylee believes that in some cases, capital punish-
   ment is not only warranted but righteous.

Kaylee didn't strike me as a threat. The kitty's a dead
giveaway. Girls who are goofy for their pets never get in
the way.
I scrolled down.

Kayleigh S.
23
Dental Hygienist
Pensacola, Florida

This Florida girl loves to stay active—whether it's
hiking, teaching yoga, or line dancing. If she's not
out hitting the trails with her golden retriever,
Sunny, you can find Kayleigh teaching yoga to se-
niors or cutting a rug as Pensacola's self-proclaimed
"two-step queen." Her weakness is junk food. Her
ideal Sunday breakfast is Waffle House hash
browns—in bed! Kayleigh's looking for a partner for
the dance floor of life—and feels like Packer might
have all the right moves!

-Kayleigh is Lee Harvey Oswald's great-niece.
-After Kayleigh works out, she rewards herself with
  a home-baked protein bar.
-Kayleigh does not look away when she gets her
  blood drawn.

Hmm. Kayleigh S. was obviously a contender. I'd have to keep my eye on her.

It occurred to me that I didn't remember writing a bio myself. Wait a second. Was that what that phone call with the producer was about? I scrolled down 'til I got to my name:

Ruby R.
25
Actress
Los Angeles

Ruby R. is a down-to-earth girl who loves the nightlife! If she's not making it *caliente* on the dance floor, she's out hitting the local watering holes alone, because, in Ruby's words, "All I need in this crazy M&M store is me, myself, and I." Ruby's favorite color is green, and her favorite sweet treat is a blueberry pie! Ruby was an up-and-coming film star in 1942 when she accidentally flew into the future and achieved viral fame as Hot Shit Girl. As Ruby put it, "I've used men—for pleasure, for money, hell, sometimes just for a cigarette and a warm bed. But I've never been in love. Maybe it'll happen, maybe not. Either way, you can bet your chips on Ruby Red. Because I know I'll get mine."

In retrospect, it might have been a little too unfiltered. But you know what I say about regrets? They get in the way of my beauty sleep.

When I checked into the mansion, I found out I'd be bunking with Kaeli P. in Room L. Dragging my bag up the spiral staircase, I caught a glimpse of Emma in the living room below, checking in another girl. She glanced at me and looked away. Ah, well. What can you do? My MO was to leave her to her business while I looked after mine.

I opened the door to my room to find Kaeli P. doing bicycle crunches on the floor, a blur of tan legs and straight-ironed blond hair. She bounced up to greet me.

"Hey, roomie!" she said, her arms outstretched to bring me in for a hug. We embraced, and I noticed that her torso was rock-hard. She took in my plain white blouse. "Ooh, cute shirt!"

I was familiar with this ritual and ready to complete it. I scanned her person. "I like how your body is hard," I said.

She shrugged adorably. "Thank you, Pilates!" she said, picking up a glass bottle of murky green liquid from a bedside table. "I used to do gymnastics, but I broke my pelvis." She made a frowny face and then took a sip.

As we unpacked, unzipping our sparkly formal gowns out of garment bags and hanging them carefully in the closets, arranging our shower caddies (I made sure to hide my loofah behind my shampoo, in case she got any bright ideas), Kaeli turned to me with wide, shining eyes. "I can't believe I got picked for this. Isn't it *insane*? I mean,

Ruby—we might meet our husband tonight!" She squealed like a taut, happy piglet.

Kaeli P. was not going to be a problem.

The first night in the house, everyone assembled on the patio for orientation. The girls were all swarming around a big glass coffee table piled high with boxes of Domino's. I counted thirty of us altogether: Kayleigh B., Kaylee C., K-Li W., Kaelie T., Kayli B., twenty-three more Kayleighs, me, Veronica, and Ombeku. Most of the Kayleighs were dental hygienists from Tampa. Ombeku was a medical sales rep from Orlando, and Veronica was a professional influencer from Beverly Hills.

I knew these women were my competition, but my first impulse is always to try and be friendly. So as we settled into the sectional around the firepit, I warmed them up with a joke. "What do you call a Black chick with a knife?"

I shot a look over toward the producers and saw Emma had her face in her hands. I waited a beat for the rhythm of it, then hit 'em with the punch.

"Head of Surgery at the Johns Hopkins School of Medicine."

Emma exhaled, and I got a couple of confused looks and nervous titters. I've been updating my jokebox, and clearly it still needed some work. At any rate, it broke the ice. The chuckles loosened people up, and we all got chatty.

The executive producer, a deeply tanned, reptilian gentleman named Steve, came out to go over the ground rules. His teeth were square, and so white they were purple; his face was orange-brown. Even though he never stopped grinning, behind his eyes there was incredible pain. He stood in a wide V and clapped his hands together.

"Okay, so to answer the most popular question: the mics are always on. Always."

Steve paced the length of the living room like a warden patrolling a cellblock, making eye contact with each contestant. "Yep, in the bathroom, too. When you shower, shave, and shit. Rest assured, we'd never use any of that on the show. But if you talk in the bathroom, that audio's fair game.

"You're here to find love," he continued. "And so is Packer."

I glanced around and saw that the Kayleighs were listening intently. I looked down the line until I got to the only other brunette. Who was she, again? I pulled out my phone and scrolled down the bios 'til I saw her picture. Oh yeah: Veronica, the Beverly Hills chick.

Steve went on. "Packer's a great guy, and I think you're all going to enjoy your time with him, whether it's a week, a month, or—for one of you lucky ladies—a lifetime."

Steve noticed my phone and cracked his neck.

"That reminds me. Let's get electronics out of the way now. Kevin's going to come around with pouches. Seal in every device you have—phones, laptops, iPads. If it glows, it goes. We'll keep them safe for you and return them when you leave the mansion." He smiled, sweeping his eyes once more over the group. "Whenever that is."

A PA buzzed around handing us plastic bags while Steve placed a highball glass under the spigot of a box of rosé. After filling the glass, he lifted it up in our direction. "To love," he said, then drained it and disappeared down a hallway.

. . .

Because of my viral shit GIF, the producers thought it would be funny if, instead of stepping out of the limo, I greeted Packer by stepping out of a nearby porta-potty. I had reservations—just little things like logistics and my dignity—but I quickly realized it would make good TV, so I went with it.

When Steve cued me and I stepped out of the john, I knew right away I'd made the right call. It got a big reaction from Packer. He tipped his head back and laughed, and then he mimicked the little wave I did in that GIF. I strolled up next to him as gracefully as I could in my six-inch platform stilettos, my floor-length sequined lavender gown shimmering all the way, and made sure to show the camera my good side.

It was easy to see why they'd picked Packer. He was a big, pretty fella with the easy nature of a puppy. Sleepy eyes, boyish good looks. We made a cute couple. I leaned into his ear, squeezed his elbow, and apologized if my entrance offended his delicate sensibilities. He laughed and pulled me in for a hug, then whispered in my ear, so soft I knew the mic wasn't going to pick it up, "That virgin shit's just for the show." Pulling away, I stared at him, then heard a producer screaming to clear out for the next Kayleigh. I hustled back to the mansion.

After three hundred sit-ups and a few minutes of gratitude meditation, Kaeli P. was out like a light, curled illegally around a space heater. I'd come to win, but it didn't feel sporting to let her catch fire, so I unplugged the machine and threw a couple of towels over her for warmth. Then I slipped into bed.

Just as I was drifting off, I heard a soft knock on the door.

I padded over and opened it a crack, and there was Emma, looking a little ragged after the long day. She was still in her producer's gear: headset, walkie-talkie, and clipboard.

I stepped out into the hallway and shut the door behind me. Frankly, I was nervous. I leaned on my Bravo training. "There is no need for drama in this club."

But she just answered me with a kind smile. "You were great tonight," she said. "I feel like you're gonna be a fan favorite."

I shifted my weight to one hip and waited for her to say ". . . said no one ever." But she just stood there awkwardly and kept talking.

"I'm sorry about that night," she said. "I feel like crap for yelling at you. And then you got stuck in that porta-potty—"

I waved her off, but her apology made me feel really good. It reminded me of Bobbi, who also always came crawling back, eager to smooth shit down. All of a sudden I was in a generous mood.

"Look, I was out of line, too," I lied. "Let's just put that mess behind us and start fresh."

Emma smiled. "Thank god. This would suck so hard if we couldn't talk." She leaned in conspiratorially. "What do you think so far?"

"A couple of these Kayleighs might be spurs in my long johns, but I'm not too worried."

Emma smiled. "Right. Well, just find me if you ever want to talk."

"Thanks," I said. "Guess I'll turn in and get my nine. There's some stiff competition from the other girls, looks-wise."

"Sounds good," Emma said. "Proud of you." Then she walked off down the hall.

The next morning was our first big group date. As I blew my hair out in front of the mirror, I felt the same jitters I always get on the first day of shooting. I took a moment to process my emotions and reflect on my journey, as well as the respect I had for my craft. Then I slipped on my two-piece with the holes cut out of the ass and headed down-stairs for olive oil bikini wrestling. As I walked down the spiral staircase, my nipples rock-hard from the A/C, I re-minded myself: eyes on the prize, sister. You are not here to make friends.

I made a friend!

I officially met Veronica during yard time, the thirty-minute daily window when we were allowed outside the mansion for exercise. By this point I'd made a mental note to tell ICM Stu that going forward, I'd only do gigs where I could order what I wanted for lunch and sleep in my own hotel room. The *Bachelor* mansion was as bad as Beaver County, if you don't count the lice, rats, beatings, night terrors, and molestation. And I don't, because none of that stuff was worse than the bikini wax the producers made me get on the first day. They held me down and ripped my girly hairs out from every which place—and I mean *every which place*. I'm talking about my asshole. A place I reserve for no one but me, myself, and anyone who can help me professionally.

Anyway, one of the rules was no smoking within fifty feet of the mansion, but as soon as we got outside, Veronica pulled out a pack of Ginny Slims and tipped it toward me. We lit up and speed-walked away from the house like it was a tramp begging for loose change. My guard was up, because this was a competition, after all, and Veronica seemed like a pretty serious contender. But her opening line was so endearing.

"Can you believe those fucking morons?"

She nodded back toward the mansion. Alarmed, I jerked a thumb at her mic and made a neck-cutting gesture. Veronica laughed, then leaned over and pinched my mic with her thumb and forefinger, twisting it until it clicked.

"You haven't figured out how to turn these off yet? Guess I overestimated you," she said, winking. I was falling in love with this woman!

We stopped at a waist-high stone wall outside another millionaire's home, and Veronica used it to steady herself while she did leg lifts, calf raises, and squats. I remembered from her bio that she was an "influencer." I joined in with my calisthenics, mostly toe touches and knee lifts.

It was time to toss out a friendly offering to help the conversation flow.

"Hey. Did you know Packer's virgin act's just for show?" I asked.

She smirked. "How'd you find that out?"

I kicked my toes up and gave them a tap. "Told me himself. At the grand entrance."

Veronica exhaled a smooth lungful of smoke. "I'm not surprised. Most of what they print in those bios is bullshit."

I thought back to how painfully accurate my bio was. I hoped she hadn't read it.

"Like yours," she said. "I loved that stuff they put in there. The time-traveling backstory? It's a great gimmick. Like, Ooh, maybe that bitch is the wild card. Every season needs a Victoria C., you know?" She nodded at me slowly. "Respect."

I didn't know who Victoria C. was, but I was starting to get a feel for Veronica—and I was hashtag fucking here for it. Then she did something that made my jaw drop: she took out her phone.

"How the hell did you manage to hang on to that thing?" I asked, gawking. "They practically did a cavity search on me the other night."

She flashed a sly smile. "I had it buried behind the pool house before we got here. Dug it up the first night."

Wow!

We smoked in silence for a minute.

"So, what's your story?" I asked.

She told me. She was a worker bee like myself. Broken family. Hustling since she was a kid—modeling, mostly, but that really takes it out of you. I could tell she'd started out poor from her can-do attitude. You just don't see that kind of get-up-and-go from silver spooners. Recently she'd started a line of something called "body-positive shape-wear," and she wanted to use The Bachelor to promote it.

"You can't buy advertising this good," she said. "Getting to know me, falling in love with me, the way I model my own product, there's no ad campaign that could even approach this."

As far as I could tell from Veronica's description, shape-wear was just girdles that eighty-sixed the snaps. She

showed me a few pictures of her wearing the beige gar-
ments on her Instagram. I wasn't that impressed. You can
call it something fancy, but it's still just a tube you shove
your fat into.

"What about you?" Veronica asked. "Looking for true
love?"

"With that meatball? Hard pass," I said. "Packer's just a
way to get from point A to point B."

Her green eyes flashed. "Tell me more."

It was so refreshing to talk to someone who got it that I
didn't hold back. I told her all about my plan to leverage
the show for bigger gigs. I even brought her in on my pie-
in-the-sky idea for my own network. Emma was good for
a friendly jib-jab, but with Veronica it was different. This
was a broad who was actually playing on my level. I'll be
honest: I enjoyed the hell out of that chat with Veronica.
So much so that I barely noticed it when she nudged her
phone a couple inches closer to me.

My gut told me this was the start of something beautiful. But, like I said, sometimes your gut can be wrong.

I'd figured that shacking up in a mansion for six weeks
would be pretty low impact. But just like that time in San
Simeon when I thought I couldn't get pregnant from doing
it in the pool, I was wrong.

After three weeks in the *Bachelor* mansion, I could see it
was just as much of a cage as Beaver County. It wasn't just
the no privacy thing. They only fed us twice a day, and it
was almost always pizza, or if you were lucky, In-N-Out.
After three weeks without vitamin C, some of the girls
were showing early signs of the sailor's disease. Their

gums darkened and swelled, and their hair started falling out in patches. On top of that, there was the rat problem. All the pizza crusts and wayward fries attracted those suckers like a magnet. Oh, and I almost forgot: There were only two bathrooms for us all to share. You read that right. About an hour after the dinner bell, those stalls saw more action than a bookie on payday.

But even with all that, my main challenge was how ragged they ran you with all the group dates. The dates were nuts. By day twenty-six I'd jumped out of a helicopter over the Grand Canyon, hang glided off the Empire State Building, ridden a bronco bareback while naked, and played something called "zombie paintball," where they made us run through a deserted town shooting actors who staggered around in gory makeup. My loofah was caked with dirt and blood. If I didn't know Emma was sincere that night she extended the olive branch, I'd think she was trying to kill me.

But I hung in there. Halfway through the season, it was down to me, seven Kayleighs, and Veronica. Packer had sent four of the Kayleighs and Ombeku home through the usual rose-related channels, but we lost Kaeylii B. to the scurvy. I'd heard she was recovering at Cedars-Sinai, but was missing several key teeth.

I was sitting on my bed one afternoon, practicing holding my breath for the upcoming Jell-O-diving group date, when Kaeli P. burst in. "If I give you some intel, is that worth half an orange?"

I really owed it to ICM Stu. Given the lack of adequate nutrition in the mansion, my bag of oranges had proved to be more valuable than gold.

I looked at Kaeli P. doubtfully. "Is it any good?"

She nodded.

"What's the dirt?"

She bounced onto her bed and leaned in toward me. "Packer's going to ask you on the first out-of-town one-on-one!"

This was definitely worth half an orange. Advance knowledge of a date allowed me time for a blowout and colored-contact-lens change. I tossed an orange over to Kaeli.

"Here, kid. Take the whole thing."

She fell on it with a growl as I headed to the bathroom to plug in my straightening iron.

My out-of-town date with Packer was pretty straightforward. We flew down to San Diego, BASE jumped nude off the Pinnacle Marina Tower, and then helicoptered over to Coronado Island for a romantic picnic on the beach.

I learned early on that you only have to do two things to get on a man's good side: laugh at his jokes and act like you're interested in what he's saying. You don't actually have to pay attention to the content, just enough of the last sentence to ask something that keeps him going. And if you ever space out, you always have the reset option of squeezing his biceps and going, "Ooh!"

It turned out that, besides the virginity fib, which Packer said the producers threw in because it tested well, everything else about his bio was spot-on. He'd gotten his pilot's license after being forced to quit football because of a bum knee, and flying was pretty much all he wanted to do. When he asked me about myself, I gave him the broad strokes about being an orphan and an actress and how I got blasted into the future and everything. "Man," he said, shaking his head. "You're really funny."

The producers told us to continue our chat in the surf.

As water lapped at our ankles and the sunset cast the beach in a warm, pinkish glow, Packer took my hand. "You know what, Ruby? You're super chill."

I smiled and gave his biceps a playful squeeze. What did I tell you? Piece of cake.

When you're winning, you want to stay winning. So that night, back at the mansion, I threw my coat on over my pj's, snuck over to Packer's room and knocked softly on the door.

"It's open," he called out.

I slipped in and found him sitting up in his enormous California king bed, slouched against the headboard, a controller in his hands and a box of In-N-Out beside him. He paused the game and looked over at me.

"Hey."

"Hi there," I said, strolling over to the bed and perching myself on the corner. "What are you watching?"

I should have remembered from his contestant bio. Packer was obsessed with this video game called Call of Duty, where you use grenades and submachine guns to fight the Nazis.

"I turn my brain off and shoot people in the face," he said, smiling. "It's the best."

I had to admit, it sounded pretty good. "Can I play?"

A sly smile turned up the corner of his mouth. "Fuck

yeah, motherfucker." He smiled and handed me the controller. I took a thumb and pointer finger and jiggled it delicately.

"Here, like this," he said, and put his hand over mine to show me how to hold it.

He leaned in closer, and I could feel the kiss coming. I began to melt my lids closed, ready to close the deal. The last thing I remember thinking was, Hoo-wee, that was easy.

Then all hell broke loose.

There was a screech right above us, followed by a shower of plaster dust. A second later, a fat gray rat fell from the ceiling, bounced off the bed, and plopped down onto the floor.

Packer shrieked and jumped about three feet in the air. If I could have given myself a second to think, I would have remembered to act normal. Scared. Girly. But instinct took over. I snatched a pen from the bedside table and squared off with the little fucker.

He reared his head and hissed at me. I jabbed at him with the pen, but no sale. Then he darted into the can and started climbing up the side of the shitter, hell-bent on a water exit. I followed, waited until he was perched right on the rim, then lunged, shishkabobbing him hard with the pen.

As the vermin twitched in agony, I heard breathing behind me. I turned to find Packer standing in the doorway. We locked eyes.

"Whoa," Packer exhaled. "Intense."

I tossed pen and rat into the wastebasket and washed my hands. Packer made his way back to the bed and sat down slowly. He was staring at the wall. I took a seat beside him, worried I'd killed the mood.

"Fuck, Ruby," Packer finally said, turning to me with awe in his eyes. "You fucking rule."

I started going to Packer's room more often after that. We'd shoot the breeze, play a couple hours of CoD. I didn't fall for CoD hook, line, and sinker, but I have to admit it's strangely soothing. You just hop on, choose your map, and then it's nonstop run-and-gun action—with a level of gameplay that still lets you turn your brain off. Like he said: relaxing.

We also fucked constantly. It was pretty crazy. Get a load of this: the first time we did it, Packer put his mouth on my down-there. Freaky, right? Now, I've never actually looked at my belowdecks, cuz I'm not a pervert and I don't swing that way—no offense to my lesbo readers—but from what I understand, it looks like a plate of roast beef. Well, let's just say Packer raided the fridge. And after a while I got the goofiest feeling. It's hard to describe, but the best I can do is: it was kind of like being on a roller coaster, where you have those butterflies flapping around inside you all the way to the top, and then a crazy, giddy release as you suddenly whoosh down.

Messed up, right?

A week later, I was painting my toenails out by the firepit when Steve ambled over.

"Frozen margs in the kitchen, Rube," he said, taking a slurp of his. I smiled but otherwise ignored him. "PS," he went on, looking around to make sure we were out of earshot. "You might want to start putting in a little more QT with the other girls. I heard through the grapevine that they're grumbling about your 'special relationship' with Packer." He gave me a meaningful look.

I held his gaze and tried to play it cool, but inside I was rattled. I'd thought I'd been pretty discreet with the whole having-sex-with-Packer thing. "Thanks for the tip," I said, capping the nail polish.

I knew this could spell serious trouble for yours truly, because I distinctly recalled a clause in my contract saying after-hours visits were a no go. So I spent the next couple days trying to get on the girls' good sides by asking them questions about their lives, being a good listener, all that bullshit. The crisis seemed to pass, and I congratulated myself on putting out a fire.

Little did I know, the real inferno was still ahead.

The next morning, as we sat in the living room in our parkas gnawing on day-old pizza crusts, a ripple of excitement worked its way through the remaining contestants. Steve and Packer were due downstairs any minute to tell us where we'd be going for the Exotic Group Date.

The Exotic Group Date is a *Bachelor* mainstay, and the network had a reputation for really splashing out on them. Past seasons they had gone skiing on the Matterhorn, gambling in Monte Carlo, and exploring temples in Java. The extent of my jet-setting was a bus trip to Lake Erie with my parents when I was a kid, where I saw an otter and had a snow cone. So I was understandably jazzed to hear where we'd be going.

Packer and Steve entered, and I scanned their expressions for clues. This was my chance to hike the Alps, see the cherry blossoms in Kyoto, raft down the Nile!

Packer cleared his throat. "We're gonna swim with some pigs!"

Blank stares from us. Packer backed it up a little.

"We're going to the beautiful Bahamas, and we're gonna swim with these pigs that live there. It's gonna be sick!"

I looked beyond the camera to Emma. What the hell? She just raised her eyebrows in a "what can you do" expression. The Kayleighs looked uneasy.

The director, an enormous Italian lug named Dante, called, "Cut!" from the kitchen, where producers were watching a bay of monitors. He whispered something to Emma and she bounced over to us, real smiley.

"So, we'll take that again, and this time, let's see a little energy. Clap, get excited. It's the Exotic Group Date! And as a bon voyage treat, we're gonna order in tonight. You know what that means. P—"

Kaelee T. rose to her feet. "If you say pizza, I will shit in your mouth."

There was a moment of silence as her threat sank in. Emma reracked.

"Orrrr how about changing it up? Let's order in sushi. How does Sugarfish sound?"

Kaelee T. set her shoulders back in defiance. "A dozen limes, a sack of quinoa, and a pound of turkey bacon per man."

Steve got up and stood next to Emma. "What if we threw in some margs?" He gulped audibly. "Lotta lime juice in margs."

Kaelee stood firm. "Those are our terms."

Steve saw the way the wind was blowing and turned to Emma, sweating. "Handle that, okay?"

She nodded and disappeared.

Steve clapped his hands and tried to clear the air. "Cool. We're gonna get this take again. And this time, let's see some energy!"

We reset, and Dante cued Packer to repeat his line.

"Bahama Pigs!" Packer exclaimed.

"Woot, woot!" Kaeli P. raised the roof limply, her face frozen in a dead-eyed smile.

Twenty-four hours later we'd flown to the Exumas, a chain of islands in the Bahamas famous for its sugar-sand beaches, azure waters, and pigs. After checking in and dumping our shit at the Marriott, we pulled on our trusty bikinis and loaded into a van bound for Pig Island, where we filed onto a yacht and sat obediently as Packer gave us instructions.

"We're gonna feed 'em, too," Packer was saying. "I have hot dogs. All-beef dogs. When you're done feeding them, go like this." Packer crisscrossed his arms over his chest and looked around at the group to make sure they were taking in this important step.

As Packer yakked, I stared out into the sparkling aquamarine waters, where about a dozen pigs swam lazily alongside the boat, their snouts raised toward us, gasping and smacking their lips. The animals did not look well. They were hairier than I'd expected, and only three were pink. The rest were a dull black. Even through their coloring, I could see they were burned and flaking from the relentless Bahamian sun, and their genitals were engorged—probably from being submerged unnaturally in the water.

K-Li raised her hand. "Why are the pigs here?"

Packer kicked that one over to Steve, who sat sipping a Jack and Coke in the cockpit. "The pigs were brought to the island to create a food source in preparation for Y2K," he said flatly. He took another sip and added, "If you're chased by one of the hogs, try not to scream. Just show them your open palm. They will respect your space."

"And if that doesn't work, tell 'em you've got gonorrhea," I said, climbing down the swimming platform. "Worked on Louis B. Mayer."

Packer laughed, pretty hard. "Ruby," he said, shaking his head affectionately. "Freaking cutup."

Emma cued the stragglers to make their way into the water, and Packer started playing a game with the Kayleighs where he'd see how far he could throw them. They were giggling like crazy. Veronica was sunning herself on the yacht, somehow exempt from the pig swimming. I watched as Packer threw Kaeli P. really far, and one of the larger hogs made a beeline for her. It chased her all the way to the beach, where she stumbled out of the water and stooped down to grab some hot dogs that had washed ashore. Frantic, she chucked one at its face. It gobbled it in midair and continued its charge. She took the other hot dog and, using her wits this time, whipped it over the animal's head, back out into the water. It turned around and swam after it, and she crumpled sobbing on the sand.

I doggy-paddled over to Emma, who was fishing pig turds out of the water with a bucket. I offered to take over so she could rest. She handed me the bucket and fixed me with a skeptical look.

"What's up with you and Tootsie Roll?"

"Huh?" I dipped the bucket into a small wave carrying several clumps of swine waste.

"Veronica," Emma said. "Her family owns Tootsie Roll. She's, like, an heiress."

"You're kidding." I paused for a second to look over at Veronica. Her doll's face was tilted up toward the sun, back arched, chest stuck out. I guess she never actually told me she was poor. I'd just assumed. Well, good for her. In a way, that made her even more impressive. She was out here working hard even though she didn't have to.

I caught her eye and she shot me a smile. I winked.

"Well, there's no story. She's a cool cat, that's all."

Emma rolled her eyes. "Trust me, she's a killer. I could tell in the preinterview. Heads up."

I guess Emma didn't like me having another friend. I wasn't surprised. It's like that with ladies. Kitties like to scratch.

"Roger that," I said, and continued scooping.

Everything came crashing down the night we got back from Pig Island. I was doing one of Kaeli P.'s HIIT exercise videos in our room when Steve knocked on the door.

"Ruby, you're wanted downstairs." He didn't sound happy.

I came down to the patio and immediately saw that the vibe was heavy. The field was now down to me, Kaeli P., Kaylee T., and Veronica, and all three were sitting in silence with Steve on the beige couch wrapped around the gas fireplace. Packer stood nearby wearing a pained expression, like in Call of Duty when Corporal Ronald "Red"

Daniels sees his buddy Sergeant Pierson get blown up mid mission.

"Jesus, who died?" I said, plopping down on the edge of the couch.

Steve looked at Packer. "Okay, buddy. It's now or never."

Packer took a deep breath. "When I started this, from day one, I said my greatest fear was that I would fall for someone, and they'd be fake. My biggest fear was getting blindsided."

He took a phone from his pocket. I recognized the leopard case: Veronica's.

"Today I learned that one of you may not be here for the right reasons," Packer said, laying the phone on the glass coffee table. Then he pressed Play.

"That meatball? Hard pass," I heard my voice say from the phone. And then I went on, spilling the beans about my plan to "leapfrog over this jock-tard to a spot on *Bachelor in Paradise*," then "cash that in for my own hosting gig" and, you know, all that other shit I've been talking about.

Packer turned to me, real tears in his eyes. "Ruby, tell me this is some kind of joke."

You could've heard a pin drop in that outdoor firepit area. Everyone was staring at me—the Kayleighs, Emma, Steve, and the rest of the producers. Even Dante, who never showed his cards and only ever looked at the action through his little monitor, was just sitting over there by the grill, looking straight at me, his brow furrowed in worry. But I barely noticed any of them. Because I was staring daggers at Veronica. My "friend."

"You double-crossing Tootsie fuck," I spat. My eyes welled up with the salty stuff. "I thought we were pals!"

Veronica used two manicured fingers to sweep her perfectly waved hair off her face. "This hurts me, too, Ruby. But I just felt that Packer should know the truth. Because I think my future husband deserves someone who sincerely wants to be here." She angled her face toward the light, her eyes misted with tears. Even as I watched her twist the knife, I had to admire the professionalism.

"Oh, do you, Veronica?"

Out of the corner of my eye, I saw Dante subtly cue cameras three and four to start rolling on close-ups. Say what you want about the old calzone, he earned his check.

"I'll rip those extensions out and shove them up your waxed ass!" I screamed. Then I lunged. I didn't get far, though, because Steve sprang between us and held me back. For a doughy guy, he knew how to move his weight around.

I huffed some hair out of my face, mentally kicking myself for not seeing through Veronica's dime store buddy act. Then I caught sight of Packer, who was looking at me with a stricken expression.

"I may be a stupid meatball, but I never lied to you."

It was sad to see the big guy look so fragile. I put my hand on his knee. "Packer—"

He shook me off. "I'm here to meet my forever."

"Your 'forever'?" This was all getting to be too much. "Look, Packer, you're a sweet kid. I like you. What else do you want me to say? That I'm falling in love with you?" I gestured around to the mansion, the crew, the contestants. "Don't be a sucker. This whole thing is just an ad for Crest Whitestrips!"

Packer looked at me with his sad, sweet face, and I realized I'd made a big mistake. I wanted to apologize, but I remembered my guiding credo: never complain, never explain. So I let the lump in my throat slide down into my tummy and looked at him helplessly.

And then I ran the hell out of there.

I was packing up a few minutes later when I heard a knock on the door. It was Emma, summoning me for an emergency rose ceremony.

Of course. They weren't going to just let me slink away. I'd have to be exposed, humiliated on national TV. That was part of the deal.

Walking downstairs, I considered how I should play it. Should I cry? Would that be kind of cute? What I really wanted to do was roll a fucking Panzer over Veronica's ass. Now *that* was an idea. What if we got into a good old-fashioned catfight? ABC would tease the shit out of it. The episode would be the highest rated of the season. And it would almost certainly clinch me a spot on *Bachelor in Paradise*. I smiled, thinking of the GIFs. If I swung gracefully and connected . . . I could get an endorsement deal with Rumble. Or Equinox! Maybe even my own line of kickboxing athleisure. I knew I'd look good taking the swing, too. I used to box at the orphanage. The nuns set up a ring in the basement. It's a rotten world.

When I got to the bottom of the spiral staircase, I saw Packer and Steve standing across from the line of remaining contestants. Steve was holding a tray of roses. Predictably, the producers had left me a spot in the front row, right next to Veronica. I held down the urge to knee her in the gut as I walked past her and took my place. She smirked, smugness radiating off her like stink off a hobo. Sorry—like stink off a person experiencing homelessness.

Just like I figured, Packer chucked roses at all the Kayleighs, leaving me and Veronica dead last. He took a deep breath as he picked up the final rose, and then he looked up at us. I tried to meet his eyes, but the monkey man was starting to dust off his fez hat, so I just stared at my shoes.

Finally, Packer spoke.

"Veronica," he said.

No surprises there. Veronica beamed and started strutting toward him.

"I think you should leave," Packer continued.

The Kayleighs all gasped and my head snapped up. Huh? Veronica stopped midstride, teetering on her stilettos.

"Excuse me?" she said, steel creeping into her voice.

"What you did to Ruby wasn't cool," Packer said simply. "She trusted you. And you were a shitty friend to her."

Veronica made a strangled, gurgling sound as Packer walked right past her and handed me the final rose.

"Ruby," he said, pulling me toward him, "I thought about what you said. I know that when you told Veronica all that stuff, you hadn't really gotten to know me. But I feel like a lot's changed since then."

I just stood there gawking at him. Was I really getting off this easy?

"You're no bull, Ruby. That's what I like about you. I've been saving a special date for the right woman, and I know you're going to love it just as much as I am."

I heard Veronica mutter "Fuck this" and stalk off, her heels clacking angrily across the marble floor. That's when I started to come around. I dropped into performance mode and decided to milk the moment for all it was worth. "Oh, Packer," I cooed. "I'd go anywhere with you."

He laughed. "That's awesome. Cuz this one's kind of

extreme. I'm gonna take you flying in a real fighter jet! The same one from Call of Duty!"

Fuck me.

I snuggled into his chest, but only to hide. I knew I couldn't have been that lucky.

The plan was to do two loops around the *Bachelor* mansion. My stomach lurched the second our SUV pulled onto the runway and I saw the plane.

It wasn't the same two-seater Mustang we used to shoot *Rootin' Tootin' Rebel of Rio*, but it was close. Too close for comfort.

We walked up beside it and Packer smoothed his hand over the olive-green fuselage. "Sleekest fighter of the war," he said proudly, moving on to the cockpit window. "Plexiglass bubble canopy, wing-mounted machine guns. And then down below the wing you had your rocket launchers. This puppy's fucking *sick*."

I scanned the cluster of producers, found Emma, then pointed to the plane and mouthed, "I am being triggered right now."

She jogged over and put a hand on my arm. "You'll be back on the ground in ten minutes. Trust me, this thing's been through a billion inspections." She squeezed my arm. "I promise."

I bit my lip and took my place with Packer next to the plane. Dante called, "Action," and Packer helped me climb into my seat, then slid giddily into his.

My heart was pounding as the bubble canopy closed over our heads. Seconds later, I heard Dante's muffled call of "All clear," then Packer flicked some switches and the plane started to tear off down the runway. As we zoomed past the crew, I squinted out the window and saw Emma standing in front, two thumbs up, bouncing up and down encouragingly. She looked so sweet standing there. So un-selfishly supportive. So much like her grandmother. God-dammit. There goes the mascara. Down, fez monkey!

As we took off, Packer gave a whoop of joy. "Feel that engine, Ruby!"

"Yeehaw . . ." I whimpered, trying to give the camera something. This had to be a one-take shoot.

We climbed steadily to fifteen thousand feet, and I man-aged to catch my breath some. When you weren't fearing for your life, it was actually pretty beautiful up there. I leaned forward and shouted above the engine, "Hey. I can see why you like this!"

Packer grinned. "Check this out." He took hold of the lever and yanked it up. It broke off cleanly in his hand. We both stared at it.

The nose of the plane wobbled, then dipped, and we started into a dive.

"NO-NO-NO-NO-NO-NO!" Packer stammered. "WHAT THE FUCKING FUCK?"

"DO SOMETHING!" I shrieked.

He jerked the throttle. "I DON'T KNOW WHAT ELSE TO DO!"

The sides of the plane were rattling so hard it felt like they were going to rip off. Then, out of nowhere, Packer blurted, "I LOVE YOU, RUBY!"

Oh Jesus. This was the cherry on top.

"AND I . . . THINK YOU'RE A GREAT KID," I offered. Even if we were both about to eat it, it didn't feel right to lie.

"SHIT! WAIT!" Packer screamed.

"WHAT??"

"THERE'S AN EJECTOR SWITCH UNDER YOUR SEAT! ON THE COUNT OF THREE, PUSH IT IN, THEN PULL THE RIP CORD ON YOUR VEST AS SOON AS YOU'RE OUT OF THE PLANE. GOT IT?"

I nodded like a maniac.

"ALL RIGHT!" Packer shouted. "ONE!"

My hand groped wildly under the seat. I could feel a bunch of knobs and edges, but nothing that was obviously a switch.

"TWO!" Packer yelled.

"I CAN'T FIND IT!!!"

Packer reached back and fumbled under my seat. "I'LL PULL IT FOR YOU! READY?"

"YES!"

Packer yanked his arm, and suddenly the canopy flew back overhead. The next instant he shot up through the hole, and I listened to his scream fade away above me. Then I was alone in the plane.

I knew I should try to meet death with a brave face. But I was ticked off. Royally ticked, actually. I was mad at the producers for sticking me in this tube. Mad at Packer for idiotically insisting on this in the first place. But mostly I was mad at myself, because now I'd never get the chance to fix all the stuff I knew I'd messed up. I felt the familiar sensation of my insides getting all light and skippy and my face being wiped off my skull, and I knew in my bones that it was over. I had reached the end of the line.

. . .

I wake up in hell.

"*Ruby!*"

Satan's booming baritone rumbles through my bones. He whips my face with his scaly tail. My eternal punishment has begun.

"Get her some water!"

Huh. That doesn't sound like Satan.

Someone slaps my cheek and my eyes flutter open. A pair of big, blurry faces hover over mine.

"Who's the president, honey?"

I cough, and it feels like I might have cracked a rib. "In my heart, Elizabeth Warren."

The bobbing faces turn to each other, confused. My vision starts to focus, and I recognize the cleft chin, the wire-rimmed spectacles. It's Duncan Wylie—the director of *Rootin' Tootin' Rebel of Rio*!

"Duncan!"

His face lights up. "Ruby! There's my girl!"

I look at him queasily. This has to be some kind of hallucination. But then why does it feel so real? I need to ask a few questions of my own. "What's her name?" I ask Duncan, pointing to the makeup artist hovering over my face, a lovely woman named Ruth Lebowitz who suffers from dwarfism.

He looks at me like I'm nutty. "The Yid midget? Who gives a shit?"

By god, I'm home!

I scramble out of the cockpit, grab Duncan by the lapels, and plant a wet one right on his lips. "It's 'little person,' Duncan!"

He pulls away and motions to the crew. "Get a medic over here. Something's loose."

I spot my driver in the back of the crowd and whistle at him.

"Jackie, get the car!"

"What? Where the hell do you think you're going!" Duncan barks. "If you walk off my set—" And he screams a bunch more stuff at me, much of it sexist, and a lot of it racist against Italians, I suppose because of my own Italian heritage. I'm Italian, by the way. Ruby née Rinaldi. Yeah, I know. What can I say? I'm fucked up.

I make it into the back seat and give Jackie the address. As we pull away, Duncan bangs on the trunk. But I don't even turn around to look.

I've got bigger fish to fry.

We pull up to the address in Koreatown a little after midnight, and I tell my driver to wait.

As I get out of the car, I'm running through what I'm going to say in my head. The Fold girls were so good at greeting each other. Hey, cute shirt! Your skin looks amazing! Funky visor! My heart starts beating like crazy as I make tracks up the sidewalk.

I'm a backstabbing piece of shit skank. I'm a stupid selfish bitch.

I'm standing just outside Bobbi's door now, panting. My hair's all over the place, and I know I must look nuts. Why would she even want to see me? She's gonna slam that door right in my face, I know it.

Love that top! Have you been working out? You are so fucking gorgeous!

Can you ever forgive me? I'm sorry. I'm sorry. I'm sorry.

And then I lean on the bell and wait to see if she'll let me in.

Acknowledgments

As Ruby might say, everyone needs a fixer in this junk-yard, and I'm lucky to work with the best in the business. Thanks to my book agent, Dan Greenberg, for his encouragement and support.

I'm also extremely lucky to have a stupendous editor in Ben Greenberg. His early enthusiasm, along with Andy Ward's and the late Susan Kamil's, was a huge gust of wind in my sails, and still is. Thanks also to Random House's excellent Avideh Bashirrad, Kaelie Subberwal, and Vincent La Scala, whose names might sound fake, but whose impact on this book was very real. And for the wonderful cover, my hat is off to Mando Marie, Lucas Heinrich, and Robbin Schiff.

A huge thanks to Emma Allen and Susan Morrison for letting me occasionally defile *The New Yorker*, and for giving me the confidence to think that I could write a book.

Dad, I want to thank you for showing me *Pet Sematary*

when I was four. That ended up being way more important than the MFA.

The following people gave me incisive feedback and in one case, an amniotic sac: Charney Spyra, Marsha "Mo" Regenstein, Jeremy Mindich, Jay Katsir, Ali Jaffe, Jennie Kassannoff, Ariel Dumas, Seth Reiss, Django Gold, Mike Pielocik, David Busis, Melissa Orton, and Adam Resnick, whose hilarious book, *Will Not Attend*, is a constant inspiration.

I said earlier that I had the best agent in the business. Well, let me tell you who my *real* best agent is: the incredible Ayala Cohen. Ayala has believed in my writing from the jump, and her right-on-the-money notes always make my work better. I hope Dan Greenberg didn't read this far.

Thank you to Stephen Colbert and Tom Purcell for hiring me. I learned so much from you guys. Although I'm still scratching my head over why "The Secret History of the Women's Club" never made it to prime time.

To Tina Fey and Robert Carlock: your belief in some early pages was a tremendous shot in the arm. Am I still pinching myself that I get to work with you guys? Yes. Should I stop now and never reveal the true depth of my admiration so it doesn't get weird? Yes.

I also want to give a massive thanks to Eric Gurian, who consistently and generously championed my work.

For their support and encouragement of this book and me generally, I am eternally squeezing Joyce Offerman, Bari Weiss, Sophie Pickens, Lena Makaroun, Amy Smith, Benjy Shaw, Lauren Robertson, Gavi Goldstein, Ella Guckman, Shalhevet Roth, Jocelyn Richard, David and Allie Droz, Alex and Caroline Moffat, Jordan Roth, Tina Romero, Jillian Burfete, Eva Wolchover, Will Tracy, Mike Brumm,

Melody Watson, Bridger Winegar, Jimmy Smagula, Suzy Weiss, the Whittingtons, the Dhalermans, the Szygendas, all the Rosoves, and my sisters, Jackie and Gigi.

I'm honored to be a part of The Humorous Literary Readings community, and grateful that James Folta, Luke Burns, and the late, great Brian Agler have given me a warm home here in NYC.

Most of all, I want to thank my husband, Thomas Whittington. He is my first and most important reader, and without his inspired edits, additions, and tireless cheerleading, this book would be nonexistent or very bad.

PHOTO: MACKENZIE STROH

JEN SPYRA is a former staff writer for *The Late Show with Stephen Colbert* and *The Onion,* and a frequent contributor to *The New Yorker.* She lives in New York City with her husband. *Big Time* is her first book.

jenspyra.com
Twitter: @jenspyra

ABOUT THE TYPE

This book is set in Iowan Old Style. Designed by noted sign painter John Downer in 1991 and modeled after the types cut by Nicolas Jenson and Francesco Griffo in fifteenth-century Italy, it is a very readable typeface—sturdy-looking, open, and unfussy.